The Beast in the City,

By Charlie Revelle-Smith

Text copyright © 2017 Charlie Revelle-Smith

All Rights Reserved

For Derek,
Without you, or Bristol, this wouldn't have been possible.

"T'is a fearful thing, to love what death can touch."
                                        Judah Halevi, (1073-1141)

"To live in the hearts we leave behind is to live forever."
                                        Carl Sagan, (1934-1996)

"You only live once, but if you do it right, once is enough."
                                        Mae West, (1893-1980)

1.

It was a beautiful spring morning when the bodies were found.

The first was a young man, face down on the grass where daffodils swayed gently all around heavy with pollen and joy for the new season. The soil beneath him was stained black with blood, flecks of it splashed all about the dew-laden grass. The Groundskeeper was the first to find him upon his arrival at work that morning. The old man tutted to himself. So like the young of today - a student, no doubt filled with booze and God only knew what else; either too lost or too inebriated to find his way home, had scaled the wall and succumbed to his intoxication.

"Wake up, son," the man urged as he prodded gently at the body with the toe of his shoe. "Sunday mornin' services'll be startin' soon."

He crouched over the corpse and shook its arm. The coldness shocked him, as did the pliability of the limb. "Come on now," said the man, hiding his nerves as best as he could beneath a voice that was nonetheless on the brink of panic, "this in't time to be playin' silly buggers."

It was only when he was certain that something was wrong that he saw the blood. Smatterings of it caked the grass and the stone corner of the church in angry, frenzied streaks. The open scissors that rested between his crimson fingers were drenched in the stuff. A fear gripped the man in an instant, as if an invisible hand had broken through his ribcage and clutched his heart.

"Help me!" he screamed, with a voice deep and hoarse with fear, "get help quick. I've found a body!"

2.

Franklin watched the third hand of his watch tick past the twelve mark and listened to the mighty bells of Bristol Cathedral peal to signal the hour. He chewed his lip nervously and listened to the galloping thud of his pulse in his ears.

Internet dating had been so simple until now. The anonymity of that strange space known as "online" was enough to make him believe that he had become lost to shame - here was a space where he was allowed to brag, to be smart, even funny. He took pride in seeing his inbox steadily fill as interested women reached out across the void to make contact and he responded with confidence and wit.

Yet here he was, about to phone the only woman who had shown any real interest in his profile, and all of that bravado had evaporated. Had it even been real to begin with? In that moment, he felt as if he had travelled back in time to when he was a teenager; trembling before Lindsay Engels, stumbling and fumbling over his words in a futile attempt to ask her out. He felt like a fifteen year old boy who had suddenly found himself in the body of a man on the brink of forty - why did this never get any easier?

He called up the name from the address book in his phone, though there was really no need to; he had spent so long checking and rechecking that the digits had been recorded accurately that he was certain he had memorised them by heart. Submitting to his fate, he gulped a mouthful of water from his bottle and pressed "call."

It seemed to take forever to begin ringing and somehow even longer for her to answer, as if she were cruelly aware of the torturous anticipation she was causing. He paced anxiously about the square in front of the aquarium before seating himself next to the giant rhinoceros beetle sculpture.

There was a click on the phone. For a brief moment, Frank hoped that he was about to be sent to voicemail, but instead he heard a voice, a warm summery voice that immediately put him at ease.

"Well, hello handsome!" she beamed and Frank permitted himself a smile.

"Good morning, Emma. How are you this fine morning."

The woman giggled gently. "I'm well thank you... tiny bit hung over but you know what Sunday mornings are like, right?"

"Right," Frank responded, although it wasn't strictly true. It had been so long since he last remembered getting full-blown drunk that the memories of hung over Sundays on the sofa with ice cream and the Eastenders omnibus made him feel slightly nostalgic.

"You've been very punctual." said Emma, "I like that; a lot of men think they can call you any old time, that's if they even remember to call at all."

Franklin was momentarily taken aback - so there were other men from the website; enough of them for characteristics of behaviour to be established, for trends to be identified - or perhaps that itself was a cunning ploy, leading him to imagine that he had competition where there was none; like an estate agent who lets a potential buyer think that a property is in high demand. Franklin forced himself to push his cynicism aside. "Well, I thought I would try and make a good impression, I do try to be punctual."

"Right, right," the woman conceded. "I suppose that with your work and all, punctuality is pretty important."

"Of course," Franklin felt his mouth begin to dry, so he took another swig of his water. This was the inevitable moment of which he had been most anxious - the job questions.

"Tell me more about your work. It sounds fascinating. Party planner, right?"

"Well... No, not quite, I think I described myself as an events organiser."

"Oh, well that still sounds interesting to me. What kind of events? Are we talking red carpet stuff? VIP area secrets?"

"Emma, I don't want this to begin on a lie, so I'm just going to spill it all out. I am an event planner but I left it vague on my profile for a reason."

"Okay..." the tone of her voice suggested that she was barely trying to hide her disappointment - or her suspicion.

"I'm a funeral director."

"Excuse me... a what?"

"I arrange funerals. Prepare bodies, meet with relatives and..."

"You're an undertaker?"

"Well, we don't really use that term anymore, it sounds a bit too... Hammer Horror."

The silence went on for so long that Franklin became certain that she had hung up. "An undertaker?" was her feeble response.

"Yes. I'm sorry if I led you on, it's just... I tried putting it on my profile but nobody would even contact me so I thought that maybe if I held something back - not to be dishonest, just to... put a better sheen on things."

"I see. Well, thank you for telling me - and it makes no difference to me I promise. It's just that... my dog really needs a walk and she's waited long enough. I should really take her out."

"Could I call you back sometime? Perhaps we could arrange something online. Or we could meet up for drinks, tonight maybe?"

He heard the woman sigh as if all of her spirit were leaving her. "I don't think that is appropriate do you? You should have told me."

A click on the line signalled that Emma had gone. Franklin stared numbly at his phone before replacing it in the pocket of his suit jacket. He felt stupid and embarrassed but most of all he felt dreadful about himself and his deceitful dating profile. He had, of course, run into this problem many times before with potential matches online but Emma had seemed different. She was clever and made smart jokes about politics and current affairs; she would post sexy, flirtatious messages to him while he was at work and send him photographs where he could see just a little too much thigh, or in tops that were just a little too tight.

He couldn't blame her though. A man who spent most of his days working with the dead was surely not much of a catch for any woman and at least she was better than the suitors who had been a touch too excited by his job - the women who thought an undertaker seemed dark and brooding; adult women who spent their time reading books for teenagers about sexy vampires and the girls who fall in love with them and had concluded that a funeral director was as close as they could reasonably come to an undead human. Those were the women he avoided at all costs for they were the ones to remind him more than any others, that whatever else he did with his life, his very existence would forever be defined solely in terms of his work. He was the creepy man who touched corpses all day long and lived by himself in the only house in the street that the trick-or-treaters didn't come to visit at Halloween; his wasn't the kind of make-believe spookiness that the kids were in search of.

Franklin began pondering what his evening looked like now. In the excitement of arranging a date for tonight, he had already planned locations and what he would wear. He was expecting a few drinks, some warm conversation and then maybe a little over-the-clothes fumbling about at his flat. Alas it was not to be, and instead, all the man had to look forward to were the remains of the takeaway pizza he hadn't finished the night before, a lone bottle of moderately strong cider and five back-to-back episodes of Neighbours that had been stacking themselves up on his Tivo. He sighed miserably to himself, consulted his watch and decided to return back across the bridge to the south of the river, where a dead forty-something man was waiting on a table for his attention.

Not far from him, but out of sight of the stag beetle sculpture and the aquarium, the Harbour Master's boat pulled alongside something floating just below the level of the water. Beneath the surface, police divers swam through the murky gloom like black seals, their flippers occasionally breaking its smooth surface.

Franklin usually prided himself on his skills of observation. Very little seemed to pass him by unnoticed, but that morning he was too lost in his own thoughts to pay close attention to much at all. He was vaguely aware that the walls of the harbour side were gathering a sizable number of people - goggle-eyed spectators to some kerfuffle that was happening at the docks. Boat races were infrequent in Bristol but they did happen around this time of the year, so he easily discounted the commotion as something of very little interest as he returned to his place of work.

However, for the onlookers around the Bristol harbour side there was about to be a nasty surprise. The sirens had alerted them, as had the sight of wetsuit clad figures diving into the grimy water while the Harbour Master bobbed alongside an unidentifiable form that rested beneath the surface.

He had first been informed that something was amiss in the docks about half an hour before. One of the ferryboats, narrow sixteen-footers that carried workers and tourists about the waterfront, had supposedly collided with something at the breakwater. There had been some alarm when one of the passengers claimed to have seen a human foot strike the vessel, followed by even more distress when the propeller juddered into something below the boat.

For hundreds of years, the harbour at Bristol had been blocked at both ends. No longer was it at the mercy of the perilous, legendary rise and fall of the tides that washed into the Avon. Traffic into the city waters had been controlled by a series of locks that kept both the water in and out and stopped most of the boating irritants, such as logs and even dead animals from entering, but there was always the chance of a body.

Bristol was a drinking city, a student city, and far too often young drinkers had ventured too close to surprisingly cold, dark waters of the harbour side. It wasn't especially deep, nor did it flow or hide secret currents but it had claimed countless lives in the centuries since it had been created. The Harbour Master had dealt with this sort of thing before, as had the expert divers, but that did not make this job any easier, or less heartbreaking.

"Clear the docks!" the Harbour Master was calling as the little police boat drew closer to him. "You can't let them see this. You can't bring her up until the people are gone."

The two young policemen looked at the Harbour Master and then down at the body in the water. It was a woman. Floating face down and gone forever.

3.

The grounds of Gallow & Sons Funeral Home were kept to a standard of impeccable neatness and Franklin himself did most of the work keeping the small garden that led to the entrance in a constant state of studied perfection.

The lawn was forever kept at two inches in length and stripped of clover and daisies upon their first appearance. Flowerbeds lined the walkway and the flowers within were rotated with the seasons - even in the depths of winter, Franklin attempted to bring some colour to the grounds - a little brightness to illuminate the dour proceedings of the day and each plant was meticulously cared for, with the scholarly attention only experience could bring. Spring was when a little haphazard gardening was to be permitted. At the borders of the lawn where it met the brick wall that shielded the funeral home from its neighbours, a few bright daffodils were allowed their annual chance to bloom. There was simply no flower, thought Franklin, that carried with it such joy and hope for the future. If any flower could be seen to truly symbolise the recovery from grief, surely the humble daffodil, breaking through the frosts of winter to wave bright and proud, somehow surviving the ravages of the season and promising that the worst was over and gone, was it.

Franklin had left his keys when he went for his walk so he pressed the doorbell to signal to Meredy that he had returned. The tune it played instantly birthed a fury within the man - the Funeral March, played in a chirpy, electronic note.

"Who is responsible for this?" Franklin snapped upon the appearance of his receptionist. "Is this supposed to be someone's idea of a joke?"

"Guess who?" Meredy replied coolly as she sipped on a cup of herbal tea. The woman was short and boisterously built yet kindly of face and always wore her slightly prematurely greying hair in a loose bun at the back of her head.

Franklin rolled his eyes. "Where is he?"

"Picking up a body - he got a call from the old people's home while you were out."

"I'm going to kill him, I know I've said it before but this time I mean it."

"Don't make promises to me you can't keep," Meredy said with a wink.

Franklin shook his head angrily as he stepped over the threshold of the funeral parlour and into a pristine reception room. The walls were lined with watercolour paintings of flowers and landscapes - no people; Franklin had learned from his father that all it took was a figure in a painting to resemble someone who had been lost to trigger a wave of lamentation. Nor was there a shred of religious iconography. This funeral home was intended for believers of all stripes, and of course, those of none.

"Tell Peterman that I don't care how long he has worked here or how well he knows my father, either that doorbell goes or he does."

"With pleasure," said Meredy as she took her seat behind the antique desk where she was halfway through a crossword puzzle in a celebrity gossip magazine. "So…" she ventured. "How did it go? The phone call."

Franklin sighed and slumped into the deep sofa opposite her. "About as well as I have come to expect."

"That bad then?"

"Same old stuff. Not too keen on settling down with Mr Death."

Meredy said no more until Franklin asked, "Were there any messages for me while I was out?"

"A couple. One from Mrs Pascoe - you're directing her husband's funeral on Saturday. She had a couple of song changes after you told her she couldn't use the Beach Boys one."

"I didn't tell her, it's the law. Anyway, "God Only Knows" is a desperately tragic sentiment for a funeral, don't you think?"

"It was their wedding dance song, apparently. I think it meant a lot to them."

Franklin shook his head sadly; everything about this funeral was affecting him terribly. All funerals played on his mind in awful ways and there was certainly a vast difference between an ancient woman slipping into death in her sleep and a toddler who had been hit by a car, but something about this service was affecting him more than most.

"It's such an unfair rule," Franklin bemoaned. "Banning songs with even a mention of anything religious in a secular ceremony. So like religion to try to control how everyone else is supposed to think or feel. Even a funeral isn't personal enough for their sticky-beaking."

"Careful now," Meredy said as she flashed the silver cross she wore about her neck, discretely hidden from sight of the clients. "We aren't all like that."

"No, but a bloody big percentage of you are." Franklin rose from the sofa before adding, "anything else?"

"One of the interviewees called to cancel, says he's not up to the job."

"So, I only have one interview today?"

Meredy nodded.

"Well, every cloud..." with that, Franklin excused himself from the reception and returned to the job at hand.

The corpse of Mr Pascoe was housed in what had become known as "The Death Chamber" by the staff of Gallow & Sons. It was here that the bodies were kept, on steel collapsible beds and draped in navy blue plastic sheets. Compared to the studied warmth of the reception, this space could not feel colder. Its walls were bereft of decoration and painted a stark white. An entire wall was a collapsible concertina of metal that opened onto a garage, which housed the hearses. There were no windows - to save the bereaved from an unfortunate sight if they had chosen to walk the grounds. Steel and white abounded in the room, as did the ever-constant stench of death, which even the most industrial strength chemicals could do nothing to mask.

The man on the bed was of no fair age to die. What little information Franklin had about him was that he was once named Gavin Pascoe and had died at forty-two of a heart attack. There had been no history of such problems in his family and his death had struck completely out of the blue. His devastated family were still in too much shock to even begin comprehending their loss.

Franklin pulled back the sheet that covered the body and stared solemnly upon it. The man's skin was grey and formless. Without life to support the muscles, even the tiniest ones drooped and flopped around the face, while blood without a heart to keep it moving simply pooled at the lower extremities of the body, running from veins and arteries and washing the whole body free of colour.

Franklin did not like to dwell upon the lives of the bodies that passed his way but he could not help but wonder what this poor man's final day would have been like. Awaking just as normal, eating breakfast, kissing his wife and children goodbye - completely oblivious that the sand timer in his body, the one that had turned over the moment he was born, was almost completely empty. Franklin thought about that timer a lot, imagining that somewhere on a vast celestial plane stood the sand timers for everyone; day by day, hour by hour the sand pouring away with none of us having any idea how much was in our own to begin with.

Looking at the man, Franklin began to understand something about why this service was troubling him so; why it had kept him awake at night, why he had been reluctant to speak to this man's wife and hear the details of what had happened on his final day. Franklin was mere weeks away from turning forty - and he knew that for many, many people, forty years of sand tumbling by was half the sand they were given to begin with. Half of a life was gone and for some people, some unfortunate people who he from time to time found upon a bed in the Death Chamber, forty years was all the sand they got.

There was a gentle knock upon the door. Franklin called to Meredy that she could return to the reception. In the ten years that she had worked here, Meredy had yet to see a single corpse that was not shrouded under plastic and Franklin was not about to let that change. He liked his receptionist; she was flighty and gossipy and sometimes she and he enjoyed a bout of gentle flirtation together; he wanted to keep her around for as long as he could.

Meredy was not in the reception room; she was instead in the corridor waiting for him.

"Your interviewee is here," she whispered.

"What?" Franklin consulted his watch, "She's half an hour early."

Meredy just shrugged her shoulders. "I think she's eager...and young."

"Crap. Another death tourist then. Let me guess, dressed in black, pale skin, white foundation."

Meredy smirked. "Not quite."

"Very well, then. Let's see what we've got."

4.

The young woman who stood in the reception was not at all what he had imagined - and he immediately cursed himself for his assumptions.

She was dressed sensibly with a black skirt, cream blouse and shoes that were impeccably polished. Her hair was held in place with little metal slides that helped create a no doubt complicated yet un-showy style. She had dark brown skin and an unblemished complexion. She really did seem very young.

"Good morning," Franklin began.

"Good morning, Mr Gallow, I am here about the position for undertaker's assistant."

"Funeral director," Franklin corrected her, though he immediately worried this had made him seem bossy or domineering. He had spent much of his student years studying sociology and had read many research papers upon the issues of young people, people of colour and women and the trials they encounter through the job-seeking process to know that he did not want to come across as one of the bad guys, unaware how their own unconscious prejudices were biasing one applicant over another. "Come this way please."

Franklin guided the young woman from the reception through to his squat little office. He immediately saw her looking somewhat nervous at her surroundings.

"Don't worry, there aren't any bodies around here, I promise you. We don't throw people straight into the deep end right away!"

She smiled slightly. "I'm not scared, I promise you. I've seen plenty of bodies before."

That sounded ominous to him. How could someone so young witness multiple bodies in her short life? Franklin briefly thought of war-torn African countries and the unspeakable atrocities that had happened there; countries he could not place on a map but had attempted to learn more about once another cycle of violence began. The man pulled himself away from such thoughts and reminded himself that this woman spoke with a distinct twang of accent that placed her nowhere in the world but Bristol.

Franklin sat at one side of the desk while the woman sat at the other. He retrieved the folder of interview notes and found her CV.

"So... Rowan Kaplan, is that right?"

"Yes it is."

"Excellent, so you are... twenty-five years old?" he had not intended for the question to sound like an accusation, but it had nonetheless.

"No, I'm nineteen. Your advertisement online asked for people aged twenty-five and over, so I said I was nineteen. Do you know it is illegal to ask for someone's age in a job placement advertisement unless it is directly applicable to the position available, for instance tobacco or alcohol sales?"

"I did not." Franklin felt his shame appear on his face.

"Furthermore, I was utterly shocked to hear that door chime. Is that considered acceptable for a funeral home?"

"It wasn't my idea... we have this idiot director here who..."

"...Well, you should change it at once."

"Yes, you are right... I'm sorry about that." Suddenly Franklin was hearing himself. Why was he apologising to this teenager who had lied about her age and was now telling him how to run his business?

"Good. At least we have that straight."

Franklin nodded obediently.

"So," Rowan urged. "Do you have some questions for me?"

Franklin thought for a moment. "I do. I don't mean to sound rude but already I have a feeling that this will not work out. You are very, very young and you seem to be quite... spirited. This job does things to your mind, it affects you in ways that you can't even imagine - you should at least allow yourself a few years of fun before you have to start thinking about death as a long shadow hanging over you. I used to feel immortal when I was your age and that was..."

"...It is also illegal to not allow somebody to sit through a full interview based on their age."

"Crap."

Rowan's eyes widened.

18

"Sorry... Well, it says on your CV that you left college with no qualifications and since then you have had a lot of work experience, but nowhere for much longer than a month, is that enough to dismiss you for?"

Rowan shrugged her shoulders. "I suppose it is, but I did very well at school, everything just went a little off the boil in the past couple of years. Family stuff."

Franklin nodded slowly. He would take the woman at her word, as the last thing he wanted was an interviewee bursting into tears over her parent's divorce or the death of her pet dog. "Well, as you might expect, there has not been a huge amount of attention as far as this position is concerned; people reasonably assume that it would be a bit much for them. Do you mind me asking what attracted you to this particular line of work."

Rowan chewed her bottom lip and contemplated the question. "I suppose... I want to make a difference, to at least try to do things right. I am not afraid of death, but I do feel it everywhere - as if it is always there waiting for me and my final day."

Franklin tutted aloud. "That is a very honest answer but one that suggests to me that perhaps you are not right for this job. Working among the dead changes people - it changes the way you think and how you experience life. If you are someone who already lives with death on their mind, I can't imagine it would do you much good."

"Or perhaps it would help me understand what death actually means."

Franklin could not deny her that. One thing his work was guaranteed to do was to demystify death, to make it something mundane and humdrum.

"How do you imagine working in a funeral home would actually be? What do you imagine it would entail?"

Rowan did not need to think about her answer, evidently she had done her research; "Unlike American funeral homes, the vast majority of corpses in the UK are not embalmed - in fact, embalming usually only happens if a body has to be sent overseas. Most people are cremated in this country and few funerals have viewings of the body anymore, but I think it is proper - and what most families would want - to dress the corpse smartly and prepare him or her for the ceremony. If there is to be a viewing, discreet makeup will need to be used to bring the appearance of life back to the dead. Aside from that, I would expect to be meeting grieving relations and taking copious notes. Making arrangements and even doing upkeep of the building, grounds and vehicles."

Franklin was momentarily dumbfounded. Yes, that was precisely what would be expected of her. Nevertheless, she went on:

"Of course, every funeral is different, so specialised skills may come in to play. Driving a hearse is apparently notoriously difficult and some services may require a procession to be led by horses. I am very experienced with horsemanship - I used to do dressage for Bristol under-tens."

"That's always very useful to know, but if you did start working here, it would be a long time before your duties involved something as central as that. There will be other difficulties. Grief puts extraordinary demands upon people so you may find relatives to be extremely uncooperative, that is not to even begin on the psychological impacts. All of us here find ways and means to unwind at the end of the day. For me, it is ice cream and cartoons; my iPod is filled with the cheeriest, crappiest pop music the past fifty years has created."

Rowan nodded in agreement. "I already have my coping mechanisms."

There it was again, another allusion to some darkness in the past - a scar running on her insides. Franklin did not want to dig at the matter but made a mental note to treat this woman with caution in the future. His mind already having been made up.

"This may be deeply irresponsible of me but I am going to offer you a trial run here. Two weeks should be enough, and after that, we will see if either of us can stand any more of each other."

Rowan beamed. "Thank you, Mr Gallow. I was certain I had blown the interview right from the start with that comment about the door chimes."

"And the constant reminders that I was breaking the law," added Franklin. "But to be honest I had nobody else even in consideration for the job - you were the only one to make it to an interview."

Rowan looked a little deflated but did not appear to suffer any lasting effects when she said: "I promise I shall not make you regret this decision."

"Very good. Can you begin tomorrow morning? We have a funeral on Saturday - there's just a quickie viewing but I might be able to start teaching you the ropes. As long as you dress smart and grey, you should be doing fine. We try not to have too much colour around here."

Rowan agreed and after some discussion over pay, she let herself out of the office. Franklin sat back in his chair and rested his hands behind his head. He knew rationally that this was a wild and possibly foolhardy decision that had been made almost on a whim, but he could not help but smile to himself. The girl seemed smart and fearless and he was going to relish the idea of finally having an assistant to work with. There was, of course, just one more thing that Franklin couldn't help but acknowledge with a smirk. Peterman is going to HATE her!

5.

Franklin Gallow could never truly escape the funeral home, for it was a home in more ways than one. He had lived in the flat above the parlour all of his life and had only left briefly for his time at university in London and for the handful of years that had followed.

His parents had both moved now and lived in Bath and his inheritance of the house had been as much a necessity as it was an obligation (in very much the same way his job had been.)

He no longer slept in the bedroom that he had grown up in and had instead moved into the larger one his mother and father once shared. It was strange how even after all of these years that space did not feel completely his, as if some small bond would forever tie this room to them.

Franklin finished the last of yesterday's pizza and followed it up with a bowl of Angel Delight, both of which he ate as episodes of Neighbours played on the TV in front of where he sat upon the sofa. Felicity, Franklin's ancient and constantly ailing cat was fast asleep in a tight doughnut of fur beside him, she wheezed as she purred and occasionally broke her stupor in order to heave up a ball of fur or to nuzzle against her owner for attention.

Franklin had adopted her from one of the "strangers." The strangers were the most tragic of all cases - the funerals he arranged where there was no family and no friends who would be in attendance. These tragic loners lived lives of such invisibility that oftentimes weeks passed before anybody even found their bodies. Their services were always brief and with minimal ceremony but Franklin cared for these corpses as he would any other person; cleaning the bodies, dressing them in the finest clothing that could be found among their meagre possessions. There would always be a witness to these events - a member of the council, usually one of a handful of people who rotated the duty amongst themselves would be in attendance and Franklin would sit alongside him or her in solemn silence whilst the hasty funeral was conducted.

As sad as these services were, and as heartbreaking as it was to imagine that anybody could exist in the world and be utterly alone, it was this duty that usually left him with the greatest sense of pride in his work. In the United Kingdom, absolutely nobody would ever have a funeral without somebody there to mark that person's life.

Franklin tried not to dwell upon the old woman who had once owned Felicity, for the cat had partly feasted upon her previous owner, as her body was not immediately found and had therefore developed a taste for human flesh in all likelihood. A man-eating domestic cat had not been what he had in mind when shopping for a pet, but the cat had seemed so small and so frightened that Franklin's usually stoic heart had found itself turning into mush at the sight of it.

Almost all of the Strangers had at least one pet but this little cat was not to be yet another who was sent to a rescue centre in the feeble hope that someone might adopt her. Franklin had almost immediately regretted such an act of kindness when, within days, the tiny cat had clawed her way through all of the furnishings in the house - cushions, pillows, bedspreads, even the bathroom mat and had then elected to develop every kind of illness conceivable in the feline world. Constantly ill and seemingly forever on the brink of death, Felicity had cost countless thousands of pounds in veterinary bills so that she had essentially become uninsurable, yet Franklin, for reasons not even fully known to himself, always retrieved his beloved pet from the vet with a smile on his face and a heart filled with love for this ludicrous creature who had cost him more than what many people earn in a year.

Before retiring to bed, Franklin checked his work schedule for the following morning. He was not on call-out that evening (a cyclical duty, he alternated days with Peterman, meaning that anytime throughout the night, he could be called upon to retrieve a body) but he did not feel much inclined to make anything more of this evening. Consulting his email a new message caught his eye in his inbox, as if it were flashing neon colours at him from his laptop screen.

"Verity Duke has approved your friend request." The message was an automated one from Facebook. He had barely recalled sending the request in the first place and it had felt like such a trifling, inconsequential thing at the time, but the joy of receiving this message was tempered by the uneasy panic that quickly followed.

He had joined Facebook in a somewhat futile attempt to force himself into the 21st century. Much like his interest in online dating, his curiosity concerning social media was piqued when he heard just how many people had come to rely upon it for work and even the most basic human interactions. The man had quickly found it a strange, bewildering and even hostile place. The handful of "friends" he had acquired were all from his school and university days and at first it had been a kind of mean entertainment to see how fat people had become and how quickly they had aged but soon he learned that the friends he had made as a child were all now married, mostly with children of their own and had now started bemoaning things about political correctness going mad or immigration, posting quotes from right wing journalists and grumpy Tory politicians that grated on the idealistic morals to which Franklin liked to cleave. Then there was the meanness - people sharing videos of young women singing into their camera phones who were mocked across the internet for their lack of talent, or their looks, or their race, videos of fat children running into things or falling over each other or images of some young Hollywood starlet or pop princess looking drug addled or desperate, with vicious text scrawled angrily all over them. It had not been a place that Franklin had either understood or enjoyed.

But here was Verity Duke; Franklin's first and so far only true love, allowing him access to her private corner in the world of social media. Once there, Franklin found pictures of her drinking pints of beer, just as she always had, and laughing with friends. Age had weathered her beautifully; her dusty blonde hair had a little trace of grey and her eyes a smattering of lines around them but all they did was enhance the earthy sexiness she had carried so perfectly.

He would send her a message, thought Franklin. Not tonight but sometime soon. It would be light and witty and would keep all of the funeral talk to a minimum. It was then that his laptop gave off a cheerful ring and a little red box appeared at the top of the screen. This had not occurred before, so Franklin hovered the mouse cursor cautiously over the strange new shape and waited to see what happened.

"Verity Duke has sent you a message," it read.

6.

Franklin had not responded to the simple message at once and had instead spent much of the night lying awake in bed, reliving old memories from his student years - all the while hoping that maybe Verity Duke was remembering fondly those times they had spent together; maybe even at that very moment.

Nevertheless, Franklin was awake at the first sign of dawn and like every working day he began it with the laborious task of personal presentation. This was no simple affair of ironing a shirt and having a shave; Franklin took such pride in his appearance that a great deal of every morning would be consumed with fastidious hair sculpting, nose hair trimming and nail clipping. Sheer black socks would be held aloft with fastenings that met around his calf muscles and were then hidden from view behind the immaculately starched hems of his meticulously creased suit trousers.

Shirts would vary only slightly in colour, and even then only tones of grey and white. Their style was always identical, six buttons down the front, absolutely no pockets and always holes for sets of monogrammed double-panel cufflinks that would be exposed at the ends of his suit jacket for those with the most expert eye in search of some semblance of glitter behind his colourless exterior.

On any other man, this remarkable devotion to self-grooming could easily be regarded as evidence of extraordinary vanity, but to Franklin, this was simply what made sense. He was a professional in a line of work which required an enormous amount of trust and exactitude. For him to appear slovenly or only half put-together would have been unimaginable; the appearance of neatness was to inspire confidence and to let his grieving clients know subconsciously that they were in good and trustworthy hands - that their dearly departed loved ones would be taken care of on their final journey.

Franklin gave his hair and teeth one final glance in the mirror. Both were up to standard, though his teeth had been brightened a little too intensely at his last dental appointment.

Professionalism was one thing but showy glamour was to be avoided at all costs. The last thing a stricken client needed at times of emotional devastation was a grinning narcissist with sickening white brilliance beaming insincerely at them. Coffee would soon put pay to that.

From one aspect of the building, Gallow & Sons Funeral Home would have looked identical to any of the other detached houses along the verdant street and Franklin had always been glad of this. His ordinary front door led from a small garden to an innocuous hallway with a staircase at the end. There was no access to the funeral quarters from this side of the house and thus Franklin could not help but imagine that this part of the building was the realm of the living - a regular home with a regular man who ate cereal for dinner in his underwear, whilst the back of the building was where death had taken hold, where corpses waited in freezers overnight and life was stoppered under tears and the ever present smell of bleach. It was a strange way to live but in so many ways, it was all Franklin Gallow had ever known.

It was in this realm of the living that Franklin ate his muesli in his cramped kitchenette and pondered anxiously over the upcoming events of the day. There was to be no meetings with bereaved relatives, but Rowan Kaplan was to begin her first shift that morning and the unease with which he found the company of the living was causing him some worry. Fears of awkward silences and uncomfortably forced conversations were making the man feel ill at ease to the extent that he found himself reminding his worried mind that it been he who had elected to take on an assistant - for the first time in his life he was going to be working alongside somebody else, surely that was not something to fear?

Putting aside this worry, Franklin dropped two forkfuls of meat into Felicity's bowl as she emerged from beneath the bed, her occasional nightly hiding place, and began to softly purr as she ate. She had a cat flap in the front of the house but had long since given up using it. The outside world was a huge expanse of infections, noisy cars and the ever-present threat of attacks from foxes, against which age and health had left her with no protection whatsoever. Franklin was always glad of her company but the old and weary cat was beginning to come to symbolise something else - a living (barely) breathing emblem of mortality; the ever constant fear of an untimely death in the very space he needed to escape from such gloomy thoughts.

The doorbell signalled that Meredy had arrived for her shift and the mournful groan of the Funeral March sent both Felicity scrambling for fearful cover and Franklin's teeth on edge. Why hadn't Peterman changed it?

In the doorway of the reception to the funeral home, Meredy echoed such sentiments.

"I thought you told him to fix it?" she chastised.

"I did. He said he has," Franklin said defensively.

Taking her seat behind her desk, Meredy switched on her computer and began scrolling through emails. "Surely you have to fire him over this," she eventually muttered.

"You know how much I would love to, but my father would never let it happen."

Meredy shook her head as she stared at the screen. "Your father doesn't work here anymore."

That was true and that his father's name was still above the door seemed too futile a case to argue. The fact was that Peterman was an old friend of Gallow Senior and as such, virtually unsinkable.

"I suppose he's not here again this morning." Meredy went on.

"Not yet. Sleeping off another one, I should imagine."

"Well, at least the new girl is starting this morning."

"New woman, Meredy."

Meredy offered Franklin a theatrical roll of her eyes before returning to the screen whereupon she added, "It will be nice to have a touch of new blood around here. I'm sure she'll provide some much needed colour."

The doorbell had made Franklin more irritable than he had imagined. "What is that supposed to mean?" he snapped.

"I mean that she is nineteen and probably hasn't had all of her dreams crushed by life yet," she hissed in response. Clearly she was not in the mood for any of Franklin's nonsense. "If you mean am I referring to her colour, then I was doing no such thing - although if it were any of my business I am glad. We're a rather pale lot around here and it's hardly representing much diversity; we're starting to look like Bath."

The word "Bath" was said more of a whisper than anything else. Like many Bristolians who could trace their roots back through many generations, Meredy took immense pleasure in berating Bristol's nearest city. The rivalry was as old as the places themselves. Bath, while many magnitudes smaller than her sister city was a markedly classier affair with Roman architecture and stately, grand houses of such breathtaking beauty the entire city had been awarded World Heritage status. If the two cities really were sisters as the residents of both were so often reminded, Bath was the studious debutante who married grand and wore elegant gowns to functions in high society, whilst Bristol was the sister who attended hen parties in a PVC nurse's uniform and tripped over her high heels after drinking too much. Bristol was louche and graceless; Bath was stuffy and conservative - at least, that is what each of the sisters would be saying about the other behind her back.

"Well," Franklin concluded. "That is good to know, but I don't want anybody treating Rowan any differently just because... well, just because."

"It's not me you need to be telling this too."

"I know. Bloody Peterman!"

With that, the doorbell resumed another blast of the Funeral March and Franklin threw his hands to the air in despair. "I'm gonna throttle him!"

Rowan was waiting on the doorstep, trying hard to mask her disgust at the sound the chime had made.

"We're getting it changed, I promise," was Franklin's first response.

"Good morning, Mr Gallow," she ventured.

"Good morning, Rowan. I'm Franklin and I believe you have met Meredy already?"

Rowan nodded politely. There was a trace of nervousness about her that Franklin found reassuring. Perhaps this day would be straightforward and easy. The woman was dressed very similarly to the day before, with a cream blouse that aged her to such a degree, Franklin was certain that it was no accident. Her hair was again pulled up in slides to the side of her head but this morning they were deep purple butterflies.

After pleasantries were exchanged and coffees offered and declined, Franklin suggested; "Come with me and we will get started." He only noticed the very subtle widening of her eyes because he had been looking for signs of fear. "Don't worry, it's going to be a very straightforward day. Mr Pascoe's funeral isn't until Saturday so we have ages to get everything arranged."

Rowan nodded nervously as she was led from the reception room.

"Now here's the preparation room, although people call it the Death Room, as it is where the corpses are kept. There are two in here today, I'm taking care of Gavin Pascoe and the other funeral director, Mr Peterman is caring for an elderly woman who is getting cremated on Wednesday."

Rowan stared at the blank, white door. "Are we starting here?"

"I thought that this would be the biggest shock for you. If you can handle the bodies, then it really is all downhill from there."

"Okay, I understand."

"There's nothing to be afraid of, I promise you."

"Thank you, and I'm fine - it's all just a little overwhelming."

The young woman seemed quieter, so less sure of herself than she was just the morning before. Franklin wondered how troubled a night's sleep she may have suffered the night before when the reality of what she had put herself forward for had finally settled in. "I'll be right here," he said as he unlocked the door with a hurriedly entered code on a number pad that was built into the frame. He pushed it open and Rowan delicately stepped over the threshold into the bright white room, like a fawn taking her first steps into the sunlight.

"Is that where you keep them?" she asked, pointing to a large steel box, almost as tall as her that took up most of the far wall.

"Yes it is. It is called the locker. It can hold up to four bodies at a time. It preserves them for a while and prevents any visible signs of decay... along with the smells." Franklin used a key on the bottom hatch of the locker and watched Rowan carefully as he rolled the steel bed out from inside. Once the narrow stretcher was in the centre of the room, he rose the bed from knee height to waist height so that the plastic sheet covered corpse was easily accessible. Its form was obscured but no doubt human, it seemed impossibly small, as dead bodies always did as if it were unfathomable for an entire person to take up so little room beneath a simple plastic covering.

"Now Rowan, I know it may seem strange, even cruel to throw you in at the deep end so soon after you have arrived, but I am doing this only because this is your last chance to turn away and go. Gavin Pascoe was not an old man, he was forty-two and to look at the body of someone so young; it could haunt your memories for years, maybe even forever. The reason we are doing this is because I want you to know that you have a way out and do not have to do this just because you have already resigned yourself to it. There is no shame in fearing death and..."

"...I'm not afraid of him. How else am I supposed to confront death other than to confront the dead?"

It was a strange answer and one that caused him more than a little anxiety. He had never even thought of the state of this young woman's mental health until this point. However, who was he to know her mind better than she?

"Very well," he said and in one quick motion, he whipped the sheet from the body, like a magician. There was no reason to force Rowan to suffer the nervous anticipation any longer.

She did not gasp as he had expected, instead she surveyed the man, dressed in the suit Franklin had spent over an hour getting him into last night with nothing but interest in her eyes.

"He looks so dead." was her blunt response.

"Well, he is. Most people say how peaceful they look."

"But he doesn't though. Someone asleep looks peaceful; he doesn't look like that at all. He doesn't even look like a person, not really anyway. He just looks empty - gone. How did he die?"

"Heart attack,"

"At forty-two? Do they think it was related to drugs?"

Franklin shrugged his shoulders. "No idea. They never tell us any of the details. I hope it was though..."

Rowan looked puzzled. "You hope it was?"

"He's my age, Rowan. You'll understand it when you get to my age too. It's not nice to think that death can happen just out of the blue, you like to imagine that something could be done to avoid it."

Rowan sighed. "So what are we going to do with him?"

"I am going to make him look less dead. He has a viewing at the funeral, that's when they..."

"...I know what that is."

"Well, if he's going on show, he has to look his best - that's when we use a little razzle-dazzle."

"Makeup?"

"Yes indeed."

"Can I help?"

Franklin nodded and Rowan offered a wan little smile.

"It is so strange," she suggested. "That so few of us have viewings at our funerals. In the olden days, did you know that families would care for a body together. They would dedicate a room to the corpse and spend the days before the service washing and preparing them, saying prayers over them. Nowadays we keep so much of death hidden away. Maybe that is why we are all so afraid of it because most of us never get to experience anything of it until we have to die ourselves. It isn't a very healthy attitude towards death at all is it? To pretend it won't happen."

"Interesting," Franklin replied. "Although, I've never been one to think it makes much of a difference if we have come to terms with death during our lifetime. It makes absolutely no odds in the end. Death comes for us all eventually whether we are ready for it or not."

Rowan seemed to be thinking this over for a moment. "That's a very gloomy way of thinking," she said. "I think I am going to like it here."

Franklin thought so too; there was something about this strange young woman that he found intriguing. "Are you ready to get started?"

"Yes I am," she said.

32

7.

Side by side, the two bodies lay.

The initial police investigation had been straightforward; a yielding of easy results. Families had been informed and puzzle pieces assembled. Two separate tragedies united only by happening to have occurred on the same night.

One, a young man named Henrik Neilson who had been found among the grass lawn of St Mary Redcliffe Church - a magnificent old beast of a building that bore gargoyles and grotesques all about its steeple and rose higher into the Bristol sky than any other church, like a dagger of defiance against the savagery of mankind.

The man had been twenty. All of the hallmarks, from his age to his sex were suggesting yet another classic case of suicide. "That name sounds Swedish," the police officer remarked as he filled out the appropriate form to authorise an autopsy, "I've heard they kill themselves there more than any other country."

The dead man had been an aspiring poet, a dreamer who had recently broken up with his long-term girlfriend, seemingly out of the blue and apparently at her request. The chosen location of his suicide was no coincidence either; the grounds of St Mary Redcliffe sat within sight of all that remained of Thomas Chatterton's home. The house, now just a facade, that had offices bolted onto the back of it to stay in accordance with city planning measures, had once been the home of one of the nation's great tragic poets. A shy, emotionally unstable youth; Chatterton wrote with a voice that spoke of devotion and desire and yet in his short life his work received none of the acclaim he had needed as validation. By the time he took his own life the boy was only seventeen.

Henrik's choice, a pair of scissors seemed somewhat at odds with the poet's drug overdose but it was a clear case of self-immolation, of that the police were certain, the only purpose for an autopsy was to fulfil a legal obligation and determine if there were any drugs or toxic substances in his system.

Less than a mile away they had found a second body, who according to an early examination, may well have died within an hour of Henrik Neilson. She was a forty-eight year old woman named Donna Hawley, a single mother of an adult child who had already garnered a pair of alcohol related police warnings in her five years of living in the city; once for drunk and disorderly behaviour outside a nightclub and another for attempting to start her car while intoxicated.

Her flat in Southville had revealed a telltale story of woe that had begun with the consumption of a bottle of wine and more than a few helpings of vodka before she headed out for a walk. Police officer Martin Maybridge reported that a neighbour had informed him that these late night jaunts were very common. For whatever reason, her walk across the city involved a stroll by the harbour side, this proved to be her fatal mistake.

Her body was found the next morning, shortly after that of Henrik's. A pair of terrible tragedies that surely could have been avoided had either one been offered the kind of help they needed to avenge the mental demons that were tormenting them. That was the conclusion Martin Maybridge put forward - two deaths of people who had never met before; with not a shadow of a reason to link them together.

8.

It had been less than two hours since Rowan had begun her first shift at the funeral home and already Franklin was impressed.

It wasn't just how fearless she had shown herself, confronted by a body the young woman had barely let out a gasp, it was more that she had demonstrated a real aptitude in handling a corpse.

Franklin had begun the presentation of Gavin Pascoe by trailing a plastic smock about his chest.

"He is wearing the same suit and tie he was married in," Rowan added wistfully as she looked over the photograph the man's wife had provided Franklin as a guide to how he looked in life.

"We see that quite a lot. Although I find it best not to dwell too much on it, you can be overwhelmed by tragedy if you let that happen - you have to keep it at bay as best you can."

"I'll be fine, I promise you. I am not the overwhelmed type."

Franklin smiled at her but she could not make out his smile from behind the paper surgical mask he wore. "Well, at least one of us is then." She might have smiled in response but Franklin could not tell for the same reason.

"Most people when painting a body, dress them afterwards, to save the clothing from marks or stains," Franklin explained. "I however, would rather do it first. The top layer of makeup takes quite a while to set and it is not always clear when it is completely dry. Too often I have seen directors smudge their work by dressing them too early. I find it easier to cover cuffs and collars than it is to repaint a face."

Rowan watched with fascination as Franklin glued the dead man's lips and eyelids shut and then began applying a dull, greyish-blue paint to his face with a narrow airbrush, no wider or longer than a pencil that was attached to a paint canister affixed to the man's utility belt. Navy blue overalls covered both Franklin and Rowan from ankle to neck.

"This is the base colour," Franklin informed her. "Regardless of skin tone, we always begin with this blue. It's like a primer when you paint a room and it allows you a blank canvas on which to begin."

"If I died, would you use the same colour on my skin?"

Franklin raised a quizzical eyebrow. "It is not healthy to think of your mortality like that, but if you are asking would I use it on someone with your skin tone, then the answer is yes. Everybody starts out stone blue. There are more modern paints that people use that can paint colour directly onto skin but I learnt my trade with this stuff and I may have got stuck in my ways. Of course, it has caused problems in the past - not with me, but I heard of a funeral director over in Weston who was working with a few bodies at once - he painted a black woman white for her funeral. Needless to say, her family were not happy."

Rowan's eyes widened as she gasped before she threw her hand to her mask covered mouth. "She had a white face at her own funeral?"

Franklin nodded and the woman began to giggle before pulling herself short, as if ashamed. "Sorry, that was inappropriate."

"Not really. Just because this place is solemn and respectful, it does not mean we can't laugh from time to time. It really is what keeps us sane - a little gentle gallows humour to keep the darkness at bay."

"Like the door chimes?"

"No, nothing at all like the door chimes. That is unacceptable."

Rowan seemed sated with this response and returned to looking at the photograph. "He was very handsome on his wedding day."

Franklin looked up, "Yes he was. She was quite the bride too."

"It was a spring wedding," Rowan said, though Franklin did not understand how she knew this.

After the first coat was given sufficient time to dry and all of Gavin Pascoe was turned a pigeon shade of blue, Franklin removed one of his latex gloves and pressed it against the cheek of the dead man's face. "We are ready for some colour."

Again with the airbrush, Franklin worked steadily across the face of the corpse, masking the blue beneath a layer of pinkish yellow. It took Rowan a while to notice that he turned his head often while using the airbrush and looked away from the corpse; it took her even longer to work out why. So steady and skilled was his hand, Franklin was not prepared to even breathe upon the man, lest his breath disrupt the flow of makeup.

"He is starting to look like a human being again." Rowan said.

Franklin nodded his agreement. "I rather like this part, for a moment it can be almost like bringing life back to him, even if it is just for a little while."

Rowan was startled to see that the final stages of the man's makeup were not so different to the routine she used herself. Blusher on the cheeks was applied with a kabuki brush, his lips were defined with a very ordinary looking lipstick, while a whisper of mascara to his closed eyelashes and brows brought an illusion of health back to them; even his fingernails were painted with a transparent varnish to hide the withering of death.

Finally, Franklin placed the dead man's hands to either of his sides before declaring, "And that is how we dress a corpse for a viewing."

Rowan almost felt compelled to offer a smattering of applause but thought better of it at the last moment. "I am very impressed. But I thought you were supposed to put the hands to the chest, crossed over, palms down and all."

"We don't really do that anymore. Dracula movies kind of put paid to that, we find it looks more natural to have them look as if they are just sleeping. I hope this hasn't been too much for you. At any point during the day, or this week, just say and I'll ease you into things slower." Franklin made this statement earnestly but already he thought he knew this young woman enough to know that such a thing would not be necessary.

A musical rat-a-tat-tat drummed upon the door and Franklin rolled his eyes at Rowan and removed his facemask.

"If you can't handle Mr Peterman, however, then there is very little I can do. I'm afraid we are stuck with him."

"Is that him?"

No answer was necessary as a deep voice with a thick, south Bristol accent boomed, "Gallow, it's Peterman. Meredy said you want to see me." Then without invitation the huge bald man who filled almost the entirety of the frame, appeared behind the opening door. He was a tower of a man in a crumpled suit and with a ruddy complexion. He looked ancient, so old that even the corpse of poor Gavin Pascoe seemed better preserved.

"Ah, I see. The new girl has started. Meredy didn't say she was so young."

Rowan felt her flesh crawl as the wheezing mountain of a man inspected her from top to bottom.

"Peterman, can we speak in our office?"

"But wait, you haven't introduced me to..."

Without a word, Franklin stepped forward and Rowan was surprised to see that this ogre of a creature backed out of the room at the approach of a tiny irritable looking man with a wiry frame.

Upon leaving, Franklin closed the door behind him.

"Gallow, who knew you were such a dark horse? It is one thing to like them young but a touch of jungle fever too?"

Franklin's hands formed fists. "Don't be so disgusting. She is young enough to be my daughter, Peterman - she's young enough to be your granddaughter and as for the rest of what you're implying, I'm not even going to respond."

Peterman did not react either, save for a wide grin spreading slyly across his face.

"I suppose you know why I wanted to talk to you." Franklin continued as he led the way towards his office. "That doorbell has to change."

"What? It's a joke! Just a little banter, nothing more!"

"Do you even listen to yourself? Banter? That doesn't even make sense! We're a funeral home, Peterman. We don't do jokes here; we look after dead people and arrange their funerals."

"When was the last time anybody came to the door anyway? Don't they arrange it all over the phone nowadays?"

"They come here all the time, Peterman. Do you know how I know this? Because I live upstairs and I'm the one who has to wake to find a grieving mother sobbing on the doorstep because she wants to hold her dead son one last time - do you ever think of things like that? Do you ever even think of anything but yourself?"

Peterman huffed and folded his arms across his barrel chest. "Fine, I'll change it. It's just a little button on the side."

"That's not the point and you know it. How long have you been working here for? How can you treat this job with such contempt and show up here every day - late, and stinking of last night's booze and still expect me to have any respect for you at all, or imagine that you still have any respect for us, or this place, or for the families of the people we are looking after. Retire! Please!"

"That's not up to you, Gallow, I think Gallow Senior has final say on all of those matters and..."

Franklin found himself storming out of his own office, feeling as petulant and enraged as a teenager on a hormonal rampage. He slammed the door behind him and threw his hands to his face. The gentle tap that fell on his shoulder felt like a static shock; it was Meredy.

"No luck then, I suppose?" she offered wanly. Franklin just shook his head. "There's a call for you, should I say you're busy?"

"No, I'll take it."

"It's your brother, he's calling from the police station."

"In that case, I will ignore it."

Meredy sighed to herself. "Very well. He was talking about a pair of bodies being released in a couple of day's time. He was wondering if you wanted to take them on."

"I don't think it's up to us to decide. Whatever the families think is most appropriate."

"He says they both want you."

"Well. We have the space, what do we have?"

Meredy consulted the note she had taken over the phone. "A twenty year old suicide and a forty-nine year old drowning."

"Perfect..." Franklin huffed. "Trust my brother to always give us the terrible ones. Why can't we just have a straightforward centenarian who died peacefully for once?"

"We do - Peterman gets them all. He has one right now. There is a reason why the emotionally devastating ones always go to you."

"Because I'm the mug who takes on everyone else's dirty work?"

"No, because you're the very best, and we all know that you'll get it right." With that Meredy offered a wink and returned to the reception.

Once back inside the death chamber, Franklin found Rowan seated in one of the two wire-framed chairs that formed the entirety of the furnishings in the room. She looked concerned so he quickly offered: "I'm sorry if you heard any of that, Peterman is an idiot but..."

"...I didn't hear anything, I promise."

"Oh. Okay."

"It's not that. While you were gone, I looked at the photograph and thought of something - I hope it isn't too much."

Franklin followed her gaze to the corpse. Its arms had been moved from either side to its chest, where one rested upon the other. In the crook between the thumbs a single daffodil lay.

"I'm sorry if I went too far. I saw them outside and thought I'd grab one."

"I don't understand. Why?"

Rowan passed him the photograph and once again he inspected the beautifully posed image of the youthful bride and groom. "I don't understand."

"It was a spring wedding. Look at the bouquet."

In the arms of the bride rested an abundance of vibrant yellow daffodils. In the groom's lapel another shone.

"You said she couldn't have her wedding song, so I thought maybe she could hold a memory of that day with him instead - and that he could even be cremated with it, so that his ashes and it were..."

"...Please stop. I understand it," and before he knew how to stop it, he felt a teardrop run down his cheek. "It is beautiful and I never would have thought of it."

"I'm sorry Mr Gallow, I didn't know it would make you cry."

"It's nothing," he smiled. "Just finding myself getting a little emotional at my age. At his age."

Franklin wiped the tear from his face and pulled the plastic sheet back over the corpse of Gavin Pascoe. He was certain of two things at that time; firstly, that Rowan had proved herself worthy of Gallow & Sons Funeral Home within the space of a few hours and secondly, that as he was about to turn almost the same age as his latest corpse, he really wasn't happy about having to die, whether it was tomorrow or a hundred years from now.

It was so sad and it was so unfair.

9.

It was the morning of Gavin Pascoe's funeral, the first Saturday of May and the weather was beautiful. An unseasonal heat wave brought people out from under their wintry attire and into shorts and sandals, blinking into the sunlight of the first truly warm weekend of the year after an atrocious season of wind and rain. Ordinarily, this vibrant weather could feel like acid on sunburn set against the solemnity of a funeral, but Franklin could not help but think of that daffodil between Gavin Pascoe's thumbs and imagine it to somehow spell good fortune.

Franklin began his day the same way he did every funeral morning; with a visit to "Herman's Barbershop" - a swanky and refined establishment in Clifton Village, renowned across the city for Herbert Herman's unbeatably close shave.

"Good morning Mr Gallow," the barber began, as Franklin sat back in the reclining chair, which Mr Herman then raised to a suitable height. "The usual, I presume?"

"Of course, midday funeral today."

"See, that is why I like you, Mr Gallow. So many people have forgotten the fine art of sophistication. Long gone are the days of refinery; everyone seems to have grown so slovenly in their ways."

Franklin smiled and Mr Herman draped a white sheet over his shoulders and neck. He liked Mr Herman very much; he seemed to have fallen out of a different century and awoke one day to find the whole world had become a maddening place he could no longer understand.

The usual meant a close wet shave with an old-fashioned cutthroat razor, followed by a neatening of Franklin's already very well-kept hair. Mr Herman had taken to using a little electric clipper to deal with Franklin's nose and ear hair which had suddenly appeared in the past few months as if to taunt him about his upcoming fortieth birthday.

Once the matter was completed and wet, warm towels were peeled away from his face the old barber held up a round mirror and showed off his handiwork to the funeral director. "Terrific as always, Mr Herman." Franklin was not lying; each of his reddish-blonde hairs had been waxed into mathematical precision, his face was fresh and without a hair upon it, even his eyebrows had been trimmed around the edges. Franklin had always found himself passably handsome - certainly not dashing but good looking in a wholesome kind of way but Mr Herman's attention did seem to bring something out in him that would otherwise have stayed hidden, a shadow of golden days of Hollywood, an air of debonair finesse.

Franklin thanked Mr Herman and made his way south of the river by car - a tiny Smart car that was selected solely for the fact that it was the complete opposite of the hearse he so often had to drive about the city.

Back at Gallow and Sons, Franklin was greeted by Rowan who was dressed from head to toe in black, with a matching top hat, she was watching four of the funeral workers slide Gavin Pascoe and his coffin into the back of the waiting hearse. She looked anxious.

"Don't worry," Franklin reassured her. "We won't be there for the service, just a quick meet and greet at the door. These guys will be carrying the coffin in, so you need not be involved at all. I just wanted you to understand what we're all about - everything we do is leading up to this."

Rowan nodded but did not seem any more comforted. "Who are all these new people? I haven't seen them before."

"The day workers. They come to assist with the services."

The casket now rested in the back of the vehicle. Like so many families did nowadays, the Pascoe's had opted for an environmentally sound wicker coffin, which Franklin had originally liked until he discovered how many pallbearers found such a contraption disturbing. An old fashioned coffin of dense wood hid the weight of its contents, a wicker version did no such thing and so it was more apparent that the weight of the box was the body of a human being.

Once flowers were arranged about the hearse and a simple fisherman's hat placed on a cushion on the coffin, Franklin and Rowan drove from the funeral home to where they were expected at noon, in Redland towards the north of the city, in a quiet residential street favoured by families and those wishing to start one.

They arrived five minutes early so Franklin parked in an adjoining street for the remainder of the time; for it was almost as great a crime to arrive early as it was late.

"How are you bearing up?' Franklin asked kindly.

"I'm just nervous, that's all."

"It's very straightforward, the service is likely to be over and done with in twenty minutes."

"I know. It's just that…" Rowan turned to look at the casket that rested in the vast cavern at the back of the hearse. "It sounds stupid but I'm going to miss him."

Franklin chuckled gently. "You never forget your first one; and you should never let yourself get used to it. I know you said you have seen corpses before but it's a different thing when you are working with some poor person who…"

"I've never seen a body. Not really anyway."

Franklin was taken aback. "You lied in your interview?"

"I'm sorry, I didn't lie, not completely. There's a mummy in Bristol Museum and it still technically counts as a body, doesn't it?"

"Rowan. That mummy died thousands of years ago - Gavin Pascoe died a little over a week ago; that's a big difference. I thought you said you had seen lots of bodies before?"

"I go to the museum a lot. I'm sorry, Franklin."

Franklin sighed to himself and shook his head. "You shouldn't have done that."

"I know."

Franklin consulted his watch and started the hearse. "Whatever you do, don't mention it to anyone else at work - and don't tell me any more lies."

"So, I'm not fired?"

"Not unless you want to be and are looking for a way out. Who hasn't bent the truth a little in an interview? Honestly though, if you want an escape, you can leave anytime you want."

Rowan was shaking her head. "Absolutely not."

"Good," Franklin smiled at her. "I think I might need you even more than I thought I did."

They were at the door of the house in Redland precisely as the digital clock on the dashboard ticked over to noon.

"Wish me luck," Franklin said and Rowan did. He placed his top hat upon his head and let himself out of the car. Rowan watched as he stepped through the front gate and past the leafy front garden with hanging baskets that bore nothing but fresh shoots. He tapped gingerly upon the door, which, opened immediately.

Mrs Pascoe was the first to appear. Rowan recognised her as the youthful bride with the bouquet of daffodils in the photograph. Soon she was flanked by two boys, both teenagers, sobbing inconsolably and clutching onto either of her arms. Her face, a mask of pure stoic dignity as she stared blankly towards the hearse. Her eyes seemed empty, if she allowed herself even a moment of thought, her mask would shatter and she too would be weeping with her sons.

A line of mourners followed her . One, a man who could easily be Gavin's brother stopped to swig from a hip flask before entering a car on the passenger side.

Soon, the procession was on the move with the hearse at the front, followed by car after car of mourners. Rowan was surprised, and softly charmed to see that some of the residents of Gavin Pascoe's street had stepped out onto the pavement to bow their heads as the vehicle passed. Even on Whiteladies Road, people, mostly elderly ones and almost certainly complete strangers, stopped to silently watch the hearse drift by.

The crematorium was at the far side of the Downs, a vast, flat and grassy park at the top of the city that was intersected by roads. On this sunny Saturday afternoon, it was filled with picnickers who stopped to stare as the procession of vehicles passed in and out of view. Rowan and Franklin sat in complete silence until they reached their location.

The crematorium was an understated building, not unlike a church in its vaulted design but bereft of any of the religious imagery she had come to associate with such an establishment. Already waiting were some of the funeral workers, who bowed their heads respectfully as the hearse arrived.

"Now," Franklin said. "All you have to do is wait by the entrance and stay quiet. The men will take the coffin in and put it out on display. We won't be going inside."

Rowan nodded but did not say a word in response.

The procession of cars found their spaces across an empty car park and four of the workers opened the back of the hearse and heaved the wicker casket out and onto their shoulders. Rowan and Franklin followed stiffly behind.

Two huge doors were opened and Rowan briefly glimpsed the inside of the crematorium; a wide, bright space with a huge window at the back that overlooked the Downs and the majestic Clifton Suspension Bridge. The room was decorated with funereal purple tulips in enormous vases on plinths, whilst rows of pews lined the aisle leading to a small lectern and the stand on which the coffin would be sat and from where a curtain would be drawn around it as it glided off to the furnace hidden somewhere about this property.

The casket led the way, guided by the four workers and followed closely behind by Mrs Pascoe who was now physically trembling under the weight of grief. As she drifted by, pale as a ghost, Rowan almost felt compelled to touch the woman, to comfort her somehow but she knew she couldn't and nevertheless, her two sons, now sobbing to the point of exhaustion clung to her so intensely, that there would never have even been a chance to behave so foolishly.

Soon, all of the mourners were flooding into the building, all in various states of distress, softly, from inside the room, music began to play which Rowan could not quite place at first until a familiar voice struck through the noise. It was the Spice Girls singing "Goodbye, My Friend" and the sound of it was enough to send Mrs Pascoe over the edge into fits of unceasing, loud grief. Like an explosion it erupted from her, an agonised wail of pain as real as if she had been stabbed through the heart. With that, the doors were quietly pulled closed and the music and the sobbing were no more.

Rowan released the air from her lungs, only now realising that she had not taken a breath in quite some time. "Is it always like that?" she asked Franklin.

"Sometimes, quite often. Especially with the young ones," he replied, his voice narrow and soft.

"Goodbye Gavin Pascoe," she whispered to the door and then turned to Franklin, who seemed a little red of eye. "The Spice Girls was a nice touch - simple and sweet. It sounds as if Gavin was a pretty straightforward kind of man, I think I would have liked him."

Franklin just nodded. "I need to get something from the car. Can you wait here please?'

Rowan confirmed she could and watched as the man; hunched over and weary, walked across the car park to the hearse where he took his seat behind the wheel. She did not want to pry but could not help but follow him with her eyes. Was he like this with every funeral? She thought about Gavin's age and began to wonder how much it may have affected the man but before she could ponder the toll his job must take upon him, Rowan saw he was not just crying, but weeping uncontrollably into his hands. That evening he returned to the crematorium to retrieve the ashes of what had once been Gavin Pascoe.

10.

Every night following a funeral, Franklin treated himself to an Indian takeaway and a bottle of medium strength cider. This small appeasement, coupled with an animated film on DVD was usually sufficient to clear away the last of the grief of the day. Tonight was different though.

He had never broken down at a funeral before and was not sure even now what had been the cause, but something had been triggered in him; a deep and unsettling sense of foreboding that he had been aware of for quite some time, hidden just below the surface - a sense of mortality, of a gathering darkness as forty approached like a slow moving yet unstoppable train. The awareness that were he to die, he would die alone.

Franklin was very aware that turning another family's tragedy into a personal problem was the kind of self indulgence he usually avoided at all costs but something felt restless within him; usually soon after he had kicked off his shoes, showered and dressed in his pyjamas for a night in front of the television, the strains of the day melted away. This evening they would not let him free.

There had been no responses to his dating profile in several days but Franklin was not surprised. He had changed his bio so that it clearly stated just what he did for a living and this had been sufficient to turn away almost all potential partners on sight. They were still visiting his profile; Franklin had been proud of finding a handsome picture of himself to adorn his site and had set parameters of age for those interested between thirty and fifty which he thought were both broad and generous, considering that ideally he wanted someone as close to his own age as possible. The women would come and soon they would leave and Franklin could not blame them for it at all.

His online life on Facebook had, however, taken a turn for the better. Verity Duke, his adoring love throughout his three years at university had welcomed Franklin back into her life with open arms; or at least, had continued a rally of messages back and forth between the pair of them over the past few days.

Her first message had been cheerful and welcoming: "I couldn't believe it when I saw your name. Good to hear from you again. I've been looking for you for years! I always wondered whatever became of you!"

Franklin had agonised over his response. Initially staring at it for over an hour, torturing himself with how best to reply to what was no more than a simple greeting. It had been two days until he had found a suitable response. "Good to hear from you again. How have you been?" Franklin had convinced himself that he had left his response too late; the iron had gone cold and he had missed his only opportunity to reconnect with his one and only love, but she responded within an hour with. "Good thanks. You?"

So began their back-and-forth, nervously Franklin edged forward pressing her for ever more personal information which she gladly provided. Through these conversations and a close examination of the photographs on her Facebook page, he was able to assess that she was unmarried but had a son, that she lived in Cheltenham (not far away at all, Franklin was quick to note) and that she too had a cat, who seemed to be in much better health than Felicity had ever been.

"How is turning forty treating you?" she had asked. "It's not that bad, I promise you. I had been so worried last year but it was nothing at all."

Back in their university days, Verity had been a whole year older than Franklin but in the same English class. She had taken a year off, working at a trendy, underground music magazine that reported on the kind of music that made Franklin feel nervous and queasy. She had been the older, wiser woman who knew things about the world and had radical opinions about sex and revolution. She came from a wealthy family with whom she had travelled the world and had brought back with her a taste for exotic food, unfathomable writers and foreign languages. She had been perfect in every way and then one day, she was gone from his life, never to return.

Franklin had found himself being honest about his work and how, try as he might to escape it, he had been pulled back into the family business out of duty rather than choice. She had been sympathetic and understanding but even when she said: "I'm sure you did what was right and you should be proud of that." Franklin could not help but feel an overwhelming sense of disappointment from her. He, a charming young man with a smart mind, swallowed up by death and grief as his business. The apple that wanted to fall far from the tree but just couldn't make it far enough.

It was this evening though that Verity's message had sent Franklin into a seizure of anxiety that sat even worse than it ordinarily would on his troubled mind.

"You should give me a call sometime." it had read.

Franklin blinked at the words on the screen and read them again. It felt like a trap, like bait to lure him in so that one day when they spoke over the phone, she could tell the full story of how her life had no doubt been - endless parties at rich people's homes, casual lovers from all around the world, flirtations with lesbianism and Marxism while all he had to offer since his university days was that he immediately returned to Bristol to work for his father in a job from which he could never escape.

Franklin's response was a cautious: "That would be nice. We should arrange something sometime." After it had sent, he spent so long staring at the message, still on his screen that the film he was watching had ended and returned to the DVD menu.

A little red indicator in the top left of the monitor beeped and Franklin nervously moved the mouse pointer to see her response but it was different this time. It wasn't a new message but another friend request; his second in a week.

"Rowan Kaplan has sent you a friend request." it notified him and Franklin smiled to himself, touched that his assistant would think to do such a thing. He agreed with their becoming friends and immediately began trawling through the young woman's profile for some indication of why and how Rowan came to be the way she was.

There were not many photographs on her page, nor did she appear to have many friends - almost as few as Franklin.

51

Her profile picture was of his assistant sitting outside in what looked like a pub garden at night, next to an edgily cool looking black woman with threads of red woven into her huge, frizzy hair. Despite Rowan clearly looking underage, they were both drinking elaborate looking cocktails and grinning and slightly wincing into the flash of the camera. A sister was Franklin's guess as the two were close enough in age and bore a striking enough similarity in appearance.

Aside from that, her profile was bereft of information, save for her birth date - 1994, which Franklin found particularly jarring as a reminder that his assistant was younger than the film Jurassic Park, and made him feel immensely old and irresponsible for taking on such a youthful protégé. There seemed to be no comments from friends, no embarrassing images of her on drunken nights or irritating invitations from acquaintances to discover which Disney princess she was by taking a simple quiz. There was nothing there at all.

On the other side of the city in the poor-but-proud, yet suddenly quite arty-and-cool district of Stokes Croft, in a small room lit only by the glow of an iPad screen, Rowan Kaplan nodded her agreement at Franklin's acceptance of her request. She clicked on his name and scrolled through the photographs he had uploaded of himself. Picture after picture appeared of her kindly looking boss with his neat, red hair and always immaculately pressed shirts. He seemed to travel a lot for every photograph showed him in some interesting Taverna or Parisian cafe. Always smiling, always with that telltale missing arm that suggested he had taken the image himself because there was nobody else there to do so.

Downstairs, her parents were arguing again. That was all they had done for the last year. Rowan passed through the house unnoticed, helping herself to microwave food and eating it in silence in her room with hardly a glance in her direction from either of them as she came and went. She could not bring herself to resent them for all of their rows, day and night the endless cycle of recrimination and accusation, that if one of them had just sat down to talk to her, or if one had kept an eye on her that evening, or if they hadn't said that thing to her, then none of it would have happened.

They screamed because they had to. Because the space she had once made, the vibrant, silly, joyous space that had filled every room with a noisy bluster had been filled by a void, an absence in every corner of the house; a nothingness so massive it felt strong enough to bring the walls of the house in upon itself. They screamed because they thought if they screamed loud enough, their voices would somehow fill that void and that silence her death had left behind. It was as if passion and volume were enough to pretend that she had never died and would one day return.

In the early days it had been so much worse. The weeks and months that followed Ruby's death had been a constant reminder of what had been lost - her socks were still in the wash basket in the bathroom, strands of her ridiculous red weave were still in the plughole. Every day another taunt that she was gone and would never return, now, even those reminders were gone, with nothing to replace them but an ever present emptiness to remind them that none of them would ever truly be happy again.

A message came through on her iPad. It was from Franklin.

"Thank you for the friend request, and thank you for today. You were excellent and a real help."

"No problem," she responded. "It was very interesting. How is Gavin doing?"

"He's in his urn in my office. Nice oak barrel-style one. Will be passing him on to his family on Monday. Two more bodies coming in on the same day. Hope you're up for double the work. I've heard one is young, that can be upsetting."

"I'll be fine. See you Tuesday morning. Thank you for trusting me today. Have a good night."

"You too. Sleep well."

Rowan removed the plate of crumbs from her bed that had once been four Findus crispy pancakes with ketchup and placed it on the floor before shutting down her iPad and crawling beneath the covers.

Downstairs she could hear that her parents were no longer screaming at one another and were now weeping hysterically together. Rowan turned over in her bed and put her headphones on. She listened to a podcast on science; she understood a little of it, but not enough to distract her from sleep and the soothing voices of the two men lulled her into a blissful slumber, whereupon she dreamed of Tuesday and returning to the funeral home - where she could not only escape this house, but see death close up; to understand it and then maybe live inside it forever.

11.

When Rowan arrived promptly at the reception of Gallow & Sons on Tuesday morning, she was surprised to find Franklin standing in the doorway waiting for her.

"Good morning," she began but Franklin did not seem in the mood for pleasantries.

"I can't let you in, Rowan. The two bodies we have are just… horrible. You haven't been working here long enough to see violent death. It's too early."

Rowan would stand for none of it. "I hope this is nothing to do with my age. I don't want to be treated any differently just because I am young. I can handle it, I promise you. Plus, I'm going to have to deal with it eventually."

"It's not that you're so young, it is that he is so young."

Rowan simply shrugged her shoulders. "I'm sure he looks terrible, but I'm not a little girl."

Franklin gazed over her shoulder, as if pondering the acceptability of this response. "Very well," he finally concurred. "But I have warned you."

Making their way through the reception and after she offered a good morning to Meredy, Franklin and Rowan stood outside the death chamber. Franklin was about to enter the four-digit code but Rowan intercepted him and keyed in the numbers herself. 1. 7. 7. 6.

Franklin was momentarily shocked. "I never taught you the code, did I?'

"I'm very observant," she replied with a grin. "And it's a very easy number to remember. That was the year the War of Independence began."

Franklin nodded. "My dad set it. He is utterly obsessed with America to an embarrassing degree."

"I actually guessed that," Rowan replied.

Franklin raised an eyebrow. "How so?"

"There are plenty of Frank's running around England but not too many Franklin's - I assumed that you had to be named after Ben Franklin, one of the founding fathers of the USA."

55

He seemed impressed. "You really are observant; are you sure you shouldn't be in education still?"

Rowan did not respond and instead stepped into the death chamber. Franklin produced the two corpses from the freezer and set their stretchers side by side. They were each covered in the same navy blue sheets. "Are you sure about this."

Rowan took a deep breath. "Let's get it over with."

Franklin slid the sheet off the first corpse with merciful speed. The body was encased in a paper apron but appeared to otherwise be nude. The young man's mouth and eyes were wide open, exposing brilliant white teeth embedded in shockingly blue gums. Rowan, who had been fearful of seeing blood, was relieved to discover that there was none. The body seemed intact; his dark hair was still parted at the side and gelled in place, a tattoo on his upper shoulder was of a flag, the inverted colours of the St George's flag of England which Rowan vaguely recalled as being that of Denmark. The only sign that this body could not be living was the vast, deep and angry slashes across either wrist that were cut with such intensity, milky white bone had been exposed through the flesh around the gaping wound.

"How could someone cut themselves so deep?" Rowan asked, aghast.

Franklin simply shrugged his shoulders. "Who knows what drives anyone to do that to themselves."

"No, I mean literally. If you slashed either wrist that deep, how could you then hold a knife with that hand and slash the other one? Don't you cut through all tendons and nerves in the wrist if you go that far in?"

"It is quite disturbing how much you know about slashing wrists, Rowan."

"It's just anatomy isn't it?"

Franklin thought about her question for a while. "Well, the police are convinced that it was suicide. They have reason to believe that things in his life were somewhat tragic - not to mention… he was Danish, you know what it is like in those Scandinavian countries; Sweden has more suicides than anywhere else in the world."

Rowan turned to face him. "Actually that is not true at all. Why does everyone think that?"

"Oh, well. Good for Sweden." Franklin cleared his throat and then shuffled over to the next corpse. "Now, I warn you, she is looking horrible." Rowan said nothing and instead just watched as Franklin removed the sheet.

Franklin had not been lying. The woman, who appeared to be middle aged looked terrible. Her hair that seemed as if it had once been a mousey shade of blonde was still wet and thick with blood and had formed little ice particles while resting in the freezer. All about her body, huge, unskilled stitches held together pieces of flesh that had ruptured along jagged rips and tears.

"The police mortician stitched her up," Franklin offered, perhaps in defence of the bungled effort that had been put into their repairs. "They do that sometimes after performing an autopsy, it helps to keep the body... together if it has to be moved."

"You said she fell into the harbour. What happened to make her so slashed up?"

"At least one propeller hit her from one of the ferry boats, maybe there were others."

"It is just terrible, just horrid."

Franklin was already covering her up with the sheet again. "I'm sorry, I knew it was the wrong thing to do."

"No, no. I needed to see it, it's just that... it takes a little getting used to."

" Would you like a few minutes to go for a walk?"

Rowan nodded. "Could you come too? I think I want some company."

Franklin was touched by her request. "I haven't anything to do for the next couple of hours. I'm meeting her poor family later, I could probably use a little air too. Have you had breakfast yet?"

Rowan shook her head slowly, not taking her eyes off the sheet-covered corpse. "I'm not really a breakfast person."

Franklin smiled softly. "I know somewhere that will change your mind... Come with me, we're heading north of the river."

To Franklin, north of the river meant anywhere in the city that wasn't the under privileged and slightly dog-eared district of Bedminster where he lived and worked. It was the sprawling, busy city centre, the majestic Clifton with its splendid Georgian mansions and vast residences that went on and on as far as the eye could see until the city became countryside. The river in question was the Avon, a murky, silty and occasionally rapid stretch of water that rose and fell enormous distances depending on if it was flowing into or away from Bristol. It was here, as they passed over the pedestrian bridge that took them north that the pair began their walk.

Rowan studied the water rushing far beneath her feet through the slats of the bridge as the pair walked side by side in the pedestrian lane, while bicycles whizzed past in the other. "Have you heard of the Bristol crocodile?"

Franklin nodded. For the past few months, residents of the city had begun reporting sightings of a huge crocodile in the waters of the river. "It's people seeing logs, it must be. All of that rain brought down old trees into the river."

"Perhaps," said Rowan, "But you don't think that woman could have…"

Franklin burst into laughter. He thought for a moment about the possibility of a tremendous and fearful beast in the water, allowing just the idea to take root in his mind; eventually he shook it away. "No.. no, of course not!"

Rowan allowed herself a small giggle and the pair proceeded in silence until Franklin said; "Thank you for adding me on Facebook. It was very thoughtful of you."

"You're welcome."

"I'm only just starting out on there. Don't really have many friends yet. The whole Internet thing kind of passed me by somewhat and I'm only just catching up."

"Be careful," she warned. "It can swallow you whole unless you're careful."

Franklin was feeling bold. There was something about Rowan that put him very much at ease; she had a relaxed and unpretentious way about her; he ventured something he thought he would never confess to anyone outside of his cyber life. "I've been using the internet for other things too."

Rowan scrunched her face up. "Oh no, I don't need to hear about your porn habits."

Franklin laughed again. "No, no, no! I meant online dating - got myself set up with a profile and everything."

"Wow. This is actually considerably sadder than porn." It was now Rowan's turn to laugh, which she did without a hint of meanness or condescension. "Only joking. I think it's a great idea if you're looking to find someone."

"Well, I would agree but it has been less than successful so far."

"I'm sure the right person is out there for you. How long have you been looking for... him?"

Franklin tried not to look as flabbergasted as he felt. "Him? I'm looking for a woman. Why did you say him?"

Rowan's just laughed. "I'm sorry, I just thought what with all the neatness and the hair - and how good you were with the makeup and flowers the other day that you might be gay..."

"...No, very straight thank you very much; and all of those reasons you gave are reductionist stereotypes. Heterosexual men are allowed to take pride in their appearance too!"

Rowan looked almost pained with embarrassment. Her dark skin was flushing with a deep red. "I'm really sorry."

Franklin chuckled. "Well, it's an honest mistake and I would be a fool if I was truly offended." he suddenly stopped in his tracks, Rowan followed his gaze far away into the distance, along the harbour side wall. "I don't think it's a good idea to walk this way. Forget about the Brunel Buttery for breakfast. I believe up ahead is where they think that woman fell into the harbour."

"I'm okay, I'll be fine."

Franklin's eyes narrowed as he tried to read her face. "OK then. We must go - breakfast awaits."

The harbour side wall led them past the museum of Bristol history and under a trio of unfathomably tall industrial cranes that had once served the ships coming into the city in its heyday. Now fixed in place and unmoving for decades, they marked the skyline like vast robotic dinosaurs.

"What was she doing here in the middle of the night?" Rowan asked.

"She went out for a walk after drinking; apparently she was very drunk indeed. The police say she had been drinking at her home in Southville well into the night. I guess she wanted to sober up a bit."

"How do they know she fell in around here? Couldn't the water have carried her farther afield."

"Cameras," Franklin said, as he pointed to one of the poles that lined much of the harbour atop of which was a CCTV camera. "Apparently they caught her walking this way sometime after midnight, but I don't think they actually caught her falling in"

"Why would she come this way? That's quite a walk if you're that drunk"

"No idea. Perhaps she thought she would walk off the worst of the next day's hangover. I remember doing that back in my university days, an hour or two of walking can shave off a few percentage points of pain the following morning."
Rowan smiled at the thought of the very proper Franklin Gallow stumbling away from a university campus in the middle of the night to save himself from the inevitable headache. "Still, it does seem like an odd thing to do. I have always favoured the head-down-the-toilet technique myself."

They both fell silent as they passed what could only be a memorial left to the dead woman. Bunches of wilting flowers were tied around a lamppost while a single photograph, printed on paper that was flushed blank by the exposure of the sun, showed a toothy, happy woman with a glass of white wine in her hand. The paper flapped limply in the gentle morning breeze. A tall, heavyset and grey haired man was inspecting the hasty memorial with all the dispassion of a stranger; morbidly peeking at another's misfortune.

"Do you think this is where she fell in?" Rowan asked.

"I think so. At least, it is probably the best guess according to the police."

Rowan examined one of the camera poles quietly. "It is rather strange that the CCTV cameras did not catch her falling into the water, don't you think?"

Franklin followed her gaze but could not grasp what had caught her attention. "Not really. They say we are under enormous amounts of surveillance in this country, but I am certain that there are still plenty of places where we are hidden from view."

"Not here though. Look." Rowan traced the line of the surveillance cameras with her finger. "You could probably be caught by each of the cameras in turn as you came along the harbour side; except for this spot, where there isn't one."

Rowan was correct. Where there should have stood a supporting pole for a CCTV camera, instead there was one of the old metal cranes.

"Well..." Franklin pondered, "I suppose it is rather coincidental but like I say, there must be thousands of places across the city where someone falls out of sight of a camera. What of it?"

"Oh nothing really. I'm just saying that if I had wanted to murder somebody along the harbour side, here is the exact place I would choose to do it."

Franklin rolled his eyes. "You cannot think like that, Rowan, it will make you lose your mind in no time. This job is stressful enough as it is without inventing flights of fancy like murder."

Rowan nodded but did not seem to be taking what he had said in. "It's just strange, that's all."

The pair continued on to the Brunel Buttery, a small cafe in a wooden shed. Two toasted cheese sandwiches and coffee on a bench by the water and Franklin and Rowan were ready to go back.

As they walked Franklin could not help but count the cameras along the harbour side. The spot by Donna's memorial really was the only place she would not have been seen.

12.

Later that morning Franklin left Rowan in his office to work at his computer. He needed a list of times and dates for crematoriums across the city so that he could get to work arranging when both of the upcoming ceremonies could be held.

Rowan had said that she was skilled in using computers and Franklin had no reason to doubt her. Aside from the fact that she had already proven herself to be astute and reliable she was also young, and Franklin was of the belief that all people younger than him were experts on a computer, they were brought up with it.

He had an appointment with the nearest family member of Donna Hawley. She had three children but it had been decided that the eldest of them, her son Evan and his wife Lucy, were to be handed full control of the arrangements. The sensitive and heart wrenching minutiae of funeral planning with those torn asunder by grief was the part of his job that Franklin found the most distressing.

He made his journey further south of the river to Knowle West, an impoverished district that had become riddled with the social blight of poverty and its accompanying issues of drug and alcohol dependency - but had managed to do so far enough from the central city itself as to not prove a problem to the average Bristolian. Franklin found himself yet again pondering Rowan's odd assertion on the unlikely location of Donna Hawley's demise.

Surely it could only be a coincidence, he eventually concluded. Donna seemed an unlikely candidate for foul play, such an elaborate and well thought out plan in the one spot it would go unrecorded on CCTV. Besides, Franklin reminded himself, why go to so much trouble doing away with somebody who his own brother had reported from the autopsy results had likely not many years of life left in her, considering the state of her liver.

Upon arrival at the flats, Franklin parked his Smart car behind another that was waiting in the bay outside the housing block. The bulky man sitting behind the wheel was full faced and grey haired. The pair locked eyes and Franklin immediately felt uneasy – something to do with drugs, he assumed, on spotting that though the car was unmarked, the man was wearing a full police uniform. Trying his best not to let snobbery of the perceived troubles of the area get the better of him, he approached the entrance to the building. Franklin read through the list of dwellings by the door until he saw the name of "Farmer" on the third floor. He pressed the adjoining button and was immediately buzzed in.

The lobby of the tower was bare and grey, with exposed breezeblock walls and a lift to his left and a set of grubby stairs to his right. He contemplated taking the lift but it gave off such an overpowering stench of urine that he elected on the echoing staircase instead.

Evan Farmer, Donna Hawley's eldest child was already waiting for him in the doorway when he made it to the landing.

"I don't blame you," Evan grumbled. "That lift is a bloody disgrace."

"Well," Franklin ventured, not wanting to insult the man's home. "I can always use a bit of exercise."

Evan Farmer was a tall, round-faced and handsome man, who was dressed in expensive looking trainers, jeans and tee shirt. Franklin guessed his age to be somewhere in the early thirties. The man led the way into his flat, which was humble in size but felt more cramped than it perhaps should have. Baby clothes and toys were littered about the space, while an overflowing ashtray had begun spilling its contents over a small coffee table that was covered in magazines that seemed to concern themselves with the dual interests of cars and women who wore very little clothing.

Evan used a games console remote to pause the game he was playing, then cleared a space on a sofa for Franklin to sit. Evan seated himself across the far side of the coffee table and lit up a cigarette. Franklin always tried his best to keep his judgements discretely to himself but Evan seemed to sense his displeasure at seeing the man smoke next to a pile of baby clothing.

"I don't do it when the baby's around." Evan said quickly.

"It is absolutely no business of mine, I am here to make arrangements and that is all. Now, I understand just how difficult this time must be for you but I wonder if you have had the opportunity to think of how you would like the service to proceed."

Evan shook his head. "Just throw her in the ground and cover her up with soil. That is probably more than she deserves." The man laughed harshly but it sounded false.

"Well," Franklin proceeded with extreme caution. "Burial options are sometimes possible but space in the city is very limited and a burial service can be very expensive."

Evan spat derisively. "I'm pulling your leg, mate. We want to do something but it's gonna have to be cheap; that woman cost us enough when she was living, I don't want her sending us to the poor house now she's gone."

"I understand. Funerals can prove to be expensive, which is why we offer a great variety of services, which… are geared towards those who don't want to spend too much. We can stage a ceremony which is both thrifty and tasteful."

Evan took the pricing sheet from Franklin and inspected it closely as he blew smoke over it. "Whatever you think is the cheapest. Me and my brothers are all chipping in but we ain't got much to offer. I know it sounds ungrateful of us kids, but you know when someone famous dies and the Prime Minister and the Queen always say how they are "shocked and saddened?" Well, that ain't us - we knew this was coming for years, even when we were children, and how sad can we be when she lived her life leeching off the lot of us."

Franklin did not like the direction the conversation was going in; he tried to interrupt but Evan had more to say. "Two weeks ago she crashes her car and is begging on my doorstep in the middle of the night asking me to pay for it. She got locked up in a drunk tank every couple of weeks and it was always me paying her fines or covering the cost of some bus stop she smashed up. Then there was her work, I had to phone her in sick all the time because she was too hungover to start a shift at four in the afternoon; Christ knows how she managed to hang on to that shop for two whole years. She was drinking away all her money, so it was always me who was on her doorstep when the bailiffs came round."

Franklin sighed. "Yes, that does seem very difficult indeed and I am deeply sorry to hear that," he took out his notebook and pen; for the first time in his life he felt guilty about flashing a Parker pen that could easily have cost Franklin more than this man paid in rent each month. "I can make arrangements with local crematoriums to ensure that costs are kept to a minimum, it may mean that you have less of a say regarding times and dates of the service however."

Evan suddenly shouted so loudly that it made Franklin jump. "Lucy! Fetch us a cuppa!" from nowhere, a pale, tow headed woman, about Evan's age appeared. "Tea? Coffee? How do you like yours?" he asked Franklin.

"Oh, tea please. Milk, no sugar."

The ghostly woman nodded before peering anxiously out the window at something, as if the prospect of the coming rainstorm was filling her with doom, and then drifted into a corridor where Franklin heard a kettle being filled.

"Lucy's my wife. Been looking after the baby all afternoon and forgets that I'm a grieving man sometimes."

Franklin steered the conversation back to the ceremony. "Now, if we are to find a slot when the crematorium is available, how many guests would you estimate would be in attendance?"

"Not many," Evan said flatly. "Wouldn't be surprised if nobody turned up if I'm honest with you. It'll be me, my two brothers and all three of our wives. Maybe a few people from her work but I'm sure they will all be secretly pleased that she's gone and that they've got a day off. Maybe… just maybe my dad will be there, but I wouldn't count on it. Mum and Dad divorced when I was little and he only heard from her when she was doing the rounds begging for booze money."

Franklin nodded. "I shall suggest that the numbers will be low but no confirmed figure. Now, have you given any consideration to other things, such as the casket or flowers - perhaps some music that she might like."

Evan seemed to think about the question for quite some time. "A casket? Do you mean a coffin?"

"Yes, I do."

"They sound expensive, how much do they cost?"

"That all depends on materials. They begin at about fifty pounds for a cardboard casket and go all the way up to… well, thousands really."

"Thousands? Just to go into a fire?"

Franklin nodded just as Lucy appeared with two cups of tea. On his mug were the words "World's #1 Sexiest Lover." Franklin stifled an embarrassed chuckle and thanked Lucy profusely. She again said nothing and drifted away once more.

Evan was inspecting the list further. "So… A cardboard one, do other people choose those for their… caskets?"

Franklin blew on his tea and nodded. "Yes, they are popular; especially nowadays what with people being more concerned with the environment and all."

"That's a load of old crap isn't it?"

"Excuse me?"

"The environment. It said in the paper that it's all just going to freeze back up again eventually and…"

Franklin did not mean to interrupt but he wanted even less to get engaged in a debate over global warming. "Yes, well. There are interesting arguments all round. They are also popular caskets for practical reasons. They are lightweight and very affordable."

"But you say people use them, right? So it won't look mean if I go for the cardboard one?"

Franklin shook his head. "It won't, I am sure everybody will understand - and they are really quite handsome creations, it's not just a big shoebox, I promise you."

Evan nodded slowly and Franklin was certain he could spot just the faintest tremble of the man's lower lip. "As long as it doesn't make her look stupid, or that we're throwing her out like last week's rubbish."

"I assure you it will not."

Evan slowly composed himself. "There is one more thing. It's a dress, it's like a nightie really. When we were going through her things we found it in her wardrobe and all three of us boys remembered it from when we were kids. She always used to wear it around the house and it always felt really soft."

"I see. Those are very important memories. Would you like her to be dressed in it for the service."

Evan nodded.

"Just to be certain though… the service includes the cremation so you won't be able to get it back afterwards."

"I know that. I'm not thick."

Evan stubbed out his cigarette and Franklin sipped on his tea as the man left the room and returned with a long, cream housecoat made up of small patchwork panels. Evan inspected it closely. "Memory is a funny thing isn't it? I remember the smell of booze on my mum from when I was growing up but there is something so familiar and different about the smell of this - it smells like my childhood."

Franklin nodded slowly, sympathetically. The two men finalised the last of their plans and Franklin finished the last of his tea. As he left, housecoat tucked delicately under his arm, Evan followed him to the doorway. It was only when Franklin had begun the descent of the staircase that he heard Evan call out; "Please take care of her, you know, her body."

Franklin nodded. "I will, I promise."

Just as Evan's eyes became overwhelmed with tears he turned and closed the door firmly behind him.

13.

It was mid afternoon by the time Franklin arrived back at the funeral home and found Meredy face down asleep at the reception desk.

Days were long for the woman, who spent much of her time waiting by the phone for news of fresh bodies on their way to the death chamber or finalising details of upcoming services. On her desk were piles of crossword compendiums, books of Sudoku puzzles, celebrity magazines and romance novels. It was hard to blame her for finally surrendering to the tedium and Franklin was in no mood to do so. He crept softly by her and carried Donna Hawley's housecoat through the death chamber, where he placed it on a hanger in the metal wardrobe.

Rowan was in his office exactly where he had left her, and in the couple of hours since he'd been gone, he was surprised to discover that she seemed to have not even moved from the screen.

"Afternoon, Franklin," she said, not looking away from the monitor once.

"How's it going?" he replied.

"Very well thanks, look," with a click of a mouse button, the woman expanded a small window from the corner of the screen and Franklin stared, bewildered by what he saw. "It's a spreadsheet." she informed him.

"A what?"

"You can use it to plan your time more efficiently, and to add times and dates of all the services to prevent any overlapping."

"Oh, well, isn't that something. Did you phone around the crematoriums and get suitable dates?"

"Of course," Rowan stroked a finger down the screen. "In this column you can see all available dates and times and if you click on each one, you can see where it is."

"Um. Thank you, I think. But it was only necessary to write down the dates and times. I have never once had an overlapped service."

Rowan turned to face Franklin. She looked crestfallen. "I'm sorry, this is just the way my mind works - I like to have everything in place, right there on the screen."

Franklin scanned the befuddling page. He could just identify the manner in which each column responded to dates, while each row, an hour of the day. "Does this really work? I mean, I usually keep it all in a diary that Meredy writes down for me, just pen and paper really."

"Well, that's good too - I can transfer it to your diary if you want."

Franklin was intrigued and wheeled his chair around the table to sit beside Rowan. "No, no. I think it's about time that I moved into the twentieth century."

"We're in the twenty-first century, Franklin."

Franklin chuckled. "It has been quite a while since things changed around here. Do you think you could teach me how to use this?"

"Of course."

"Well, it would be good to have everything in one place."

Rowan sucked a huge, audible intake of breath into her lungs and then added, "I did see something else on your screen while you were gone."

Franklin's jaw drooped in panicked horror. "Crap. What did I leave there?"

"Nothing bad; you just didn't close down your webpage from the last time you used the internet. I didn't mean to pry but as soon as I moved the mouse it was just there."

Franklin could feel his cheeks blushing. "Please, what was it?"

"Just your profile on that dating website. I saw your face and by the time I realised what it was, it was too late as I'd already started reading it."

Franklin banged his head against the desk and covered his face with his hands. "Oh no, that is really embarrassing."

"No it isn't. Honestly. Don't be ashamed, I only mentioned it because you told me to be completely honest with you."

"Couldn't you have lied just this once, or omitted it ?"

"Probably. But, I think I can help…"

Franklin lifted his face from his hands. "Really?"

Rowan nodded and smiled sympathetically.

With that Franklin sat upright in his chair. "What am I doing wrong?"

"You sound too defensive in your bio, it is almost like you are already accusing the women who visit your page of being shallow." With that, Rowan read aloud what Franklin had written about himself while the man in question winced and ground at his teeth.

"I am a funeral director (undertaker) who runs his own business,

if my job is too off-putting or you are making judgments about me

because of it, please do not waste my time or yours in contacting

me. Hoping to find a smart woman who knows how to laugh and

enjoys the lighter things in life. No time wasters please."

"Now, everything you put there is about what you want, what you are looking for. What are you offering? A girl has got to know what she can expect in return because the only glimpse of personality is that you sound very bitter and have been let down too much in the past."

"Well, I kind of have."

Rowan was already deleting the text. "Let me try."

Franklin watched her fingers as she typed, almost too ashamed and torn by anxiety to look up at the screen. Suddenly he noticed that on Rowan's lap she had open a notebook of her own, over which she had scrawled text; crossed out and rewritten several times from which she was copying.

"How long have you been working on this for?"

"Just an hour or so. Here, what do you think of this?" again she read aloud.

"Funny, urbane and handsome are all words that have been used

to describe George Clooney, but that is not to say they can't apply
to me too. I'm a funny guy, a smart dresser and a good listener.

I work as an undertaker, which means that I am tired of spending all
 my time among the dead. Hoping that very soon a special woman
can bring some joy into my life. Could that be you?

I'm looking to meet an intelligent woman who likes to have a laugh
and is as happy spending a night out at a restaurant as she is
spending a night on the sofa with a glass of wine and a good movie."

Franklin squinted at the screen. "I don't get it. Is it supposed to be funny?"

"First of all, thank you Rowan; secondly, it's not supposed to be laugh out loud funny – it's supposed to minimize the fact that you're an undertaker and emphasize the best qualities you have to offer. Think of it as a bad news sandwich; begin and end with the good, stick the bad in the middle. Trust me, this will work. As soon as I saw your age parameters, which are essentially women approaching or in the midst of middle-age, writing it became easy. Any woman reading this in her forties is going to come away only remembering the words "funny", "smart dresser", "good listener" and I've already put the idea of George Clooney into her head, so I've opened her to all kinds of fantasies middle-aged women have already."

"Does that work?" Franklin asked, utterly stunned by his assistant's work. "Isn't it dishonest?"

"Only if you think presenting yourself in the best possible light is dishonest. It's light it's gentle and it doesn't make you sound like an angry lunatic like the last one did." Franklin did not say anything in response but Rowan clicked on the "save" button at the bottom of the page regardless. "Trust me. This is going to work."

Franklin was too torn between embarrassment and shock to respond properly.

"Also, when I looked at your Internet settings, I discovered that you didn't have a password for your wifi. Anybody in the street could log in to "Gallowandsons" and use your Internet for free. In fact, anybody could just pull out a phone outside the building and log in, without having to use a password, and that would halve the speed of your Internet access. So I set a password."

"You did?"

"1776"

"Oh. Well, I should tell Meredy."

"Already have."

"And Peterman."

"Him too. If you set it on your phone, it will automatically log in and you won't have to enter it every time you want to go online."

Franklin allowed himself a release of tension with a casual laugh. "Are you going to reorganize my life every time you use the computer or is this just a one off thing?"

Rowan shrugged her shoulders casually. "It depends on how disorganized you're prepared to leave it."

Franklin began to slide a smile across his face when he heard the doorbell suddenly chime. His immediate response was relief. The Funeral March had been replaced by a simple "ding-dong"

"Meredy is asleep, I should get that. Don't touch anything. You have been helpful enough already."

Rowan offered her boss a cheerful salute as he left the room.

Groggily, Meredy awoke on the appearance of her boss, she grabbed a copy of a magazine and pretended to read it upside down. "Oh," she yelled. "Did the doorbell ring?"

"Don't worry, Meredy, I know you get bored, you don't have to pretend."

Sheepishly the woman righted her magazine and hid a yawn beneath an outstretched hand.

Franklin opened the door and offered his most sympathetic smile, only to discover that nobody was standing on the other side. Puzzled, the man stepped out onto the path and looked both ways. To the left of the garden, Franklin watched as a ginger haired and ginger bearded teenage boy fled from the property and into a mucus coloured mini cooper that had been parked in the adjoining road.

"Excuse me!' Franklin called out, "Is there something you wanted?" The boy said nothing and barely even offered Franklin a glance. "Can I help you at all?'

The boy seemed to shake his head but almost imperceptibly so. Franklin watched as he started the car and sped off out of sight. Returning to the reception and closing the door behind him, he found Meredy sitting upright and staring blearily at the screen before her.

"Any idea who that was?" he asked.

She shook her head. "Maybe a relative, someone who wanted to see one of the bodies and lost his nerve at the last minute."

Franklin stroked his chin. "Maybe. Has anything else happened while I was out?"

"Well, now that you mention it, I received two calls today from a man who asked for you. When I said you weren't here he hung up immediately without giving a name or anything."

"Curious. He asked for me specifically, not just any old "Gallow" from the title of this place?"

"He asked for Franklin Gallow, both times. He sounded quite rude – didn't even say please."

Franklin reflected on this strange encounter. Often grieving friends and family, usually drunk or at least drunk on misery would turn up on his doorstep at all hours of the day, requesting one final look at their dearly departed. It was nothing of importance he assured himself.

But there was something about that boy's face, ashen and pale against the shocking red of his hair and beard that led him to think otherwise. Whatever it was it was certainly not over with.

14.

Franklin drove his sky blue Smart car across the Clifton Suspension Bridge, while Rowan sat in the passenger seat beside him, consulting her iPad for directions.

The bridge, easily the most iconic landmark in the city was once the highest in the world, and though it had been surpassed in length and breadth and eventually height, few had come close to matching it in beauty. The bridge had come to symbolise not just the city itself, but the heroic strife of the Victorian era to think big and create engineering feats that were built to last - the bridge itself was expected to stand for at least a thousand more years. The other, darker claim to fame that the bridge had staked throughout its history was that of a suicide hotspot, second only to Beachy Head in the minds of the public.

White, wire barriers had been erected on either side of the bridge to ensure that only the most determined could hurl themselves from its pedestrian crossing, while a long stone tunnel protected the busy road far beneath from falling bodies.

As she travelled alongside Franklin on the way to visit the family of Henrik Neilson, Rowan could not help but wonder just how many people had ended their lives here - and how many others in the city were thinking of doing so.

"It makes me furious," Rowan said.

"What does?"

Rowan, suddenly taken aback by the fact that her thoughts had escaped through her mouth added, "Suicide. It's so selfish. So many people in this world are confronted by death, they have their lives stolen away from them - to do it yourself because life wasn't enough for you… it is just unthinkably cruel. It's an insult."

Franklin tutted and shook his head. "We can't imagine what the lives of someone living with that kind of depression must be like. There but for the grace of God go any of us."

The family of Henrik Neilson lived in a manner that couldn't be more unlike the grubby block of flats where he had met Evan Farmer two days before. As the little car pulled into the gravel drive it was clear that this was an opulent home built for wealthy people.

It was enormous, deep and tall. A new build, but tastefully constructed of red brick to fit in with the surrounding, more historic homes. Most of the ground floor was made up of sliding glass doors, which provided a panoramic view of the mighty gorge, which tore the city of Bristol in two.

A man and a woman met Franklin and Rowan at the door. They were dressed in black with fierce, blue eyes that were bleary and bloodshot. They had the high cheekbones and smooth skin that Franklin had come to see as typifying Scandinavian types and when they spoke, the lilt in their words was unmistakably akin to the various Danish TV series Franklin had tried to watch but quickly abandoned on BBC4.

"Good afternoon. My name is Franklin Gallow and this is my assistant, Rowan Kaplan who will be taking notes today, if that is ok with you."

The man and the woman agreed and introduced themselves as Robin and Ana Neilson, the parents of the dead boy.

"May I get you anything?" the wearied, sleepless woman asked. "Tea or coffee?"

"No thank you," Franklin answered for them both and they were led inside of the vast, echoing chamber of a home.

The interior was unmistakably Scandinavian but this was not an IKEA affair. Expensive, mirrored countertops abounded while low, sleek and long sofas consumed entire lengths of walls in what seemed to be a completely open-plan ground floor. Rowan and Franklin sat at the end of one of these while the stoic looking parents sat in another across from them.

"Thank you for coming to see us," Robin Neilson began. He was a rugged, striking man with grey hair and shockingly white teeth and rimless glasses through which his piercing eyes stared with intensity; Rowan began to feel rather ill at ease. She had insisted on coming to this meeting, demanding that if she was to learn, she had to witness the entire process, including those parts, which were most emotionally traumatic.

"As I'm sure you can understand. Things have been devastating for us," Robin went on. "This came right out of the blue and neither one of us could possibly have seen it coming."

"I knew something was wrong," his wife suddenly interjected and Robin put one of his huge hands gently upon her knee.

"Now is not the time," he whispered.

Ana Neilson put a hand to her mouth and gazed out of the window into the gorge below, blinking back tears and hiccupping sobs.

"We are dreadfully sorry to hear of your son's passing but I assure you that my assistant and I, and all at Gallow & Sons will ensure that Henrik's service will run as smoothly and professionally as you would wish for him."

"We have talked a little of what we would like to happen," said Robin. "We would like it to be held in a church. We aren't very religious but we do have faith and we would like an honourable service for our son. Flowers, hymns, everything."

"Danish hymns," Ana interjected. "I would like them to be in Danish."

Franklin nodded and Rowan made a note of all of this on her iPad.

"He was a very good boy," she continued. "He was quiet and gentle, even when he was a little boy he was always reading and writing little bits of poetry, in English too - long before we even moved to this country. I would like there to be some of his poetry in the service too."

"Of course. If there are any pieces in particular that you would like to be featured, then please send them to me." Franklin cleared his throat and shuffled uncomfortably on the sofa. "There may be an issue regarding a service in a Catholic church. There really is no other way of saying this but many establishments still refuse ceremonies to those who have committed suicide."

Robin shook his head slowly. "We are not Catholic. It does not have to be in a church at all, I think Henrik would have preferred a cremation anyway, if he had to choose."

Ana Neilson allowed a tear to roll down her cheek before she added. "You must think us the worst parents in the world, that we must have seen some sign of his intention. Living with our son everyday and somehow not knowing that he was planning his own death. Do you know that on his last night, my husband and I kissed him goodnight and went upstairs - he said he loved us, just as he did every night. How could he do that, knowing that he would never see us again, and what he was going to do to himself? How could we not have seen it in his eyes and known that there was all of this blackness inside of him? For weeks and weeks I had known that something was wrong and I had asked him again and again if he wanted to talk but he said no; that it was just problems with his girlfriend but I knew there was something more, I could almost taste it whenever he was around - something was amiss, but I did nothing. I told him time and time again that if anything, anything at all was wrong he could tell us and we would love him and protect him." Now weeping openly she faced her husband. "We failed him, Robin. We let him down when he needed us most."

Robin said nothing but turned from her and gently nodded. Rowan studied the parent's bodies. Arms folded and facing away from each other, legs crossed and angled as far from their spouse as possible. If a wall had been physically placed between them, they could not have appeared more distant. It was distance she knew all too well from her own parents.

As a silence descended upon the room, Franklin turned and softly whispered to Rowan. "I have left my diary in the car, can you get it for me please?"

Rowan did not need to be asked twice. The tension in the room had become so extraordinary that she would not have been surprised to see sparks leaping from the metallic countertops. Making polite excuses for herself, she slipped from the room and retrieved the diary from the dashboard of the car.

Turning, she was shocked by the sudden appearance of a girl. She seemed to be a teenager but her unfashionable pigtails made her look considerably younger. "Hello," said the girl.

"Hello," Rowan answered awkwardly. She tried to walk around the girl but she blocked her path by sidestepping her way into it.

"My name is Lise. I am Henrik's sister."

"Oh. Well, I am very sorry for your loss."

Lise glanced over her shoulder, through the glass doors to where her parents were silhouetted against the sky behind them. The girl leaned in closer to Rowan. "I don't care what they say, I don't care what the police say, Henrik would never have done that to himself. He would have said something to me, I would have known. We shared everything and there is no way he would have left me all alone just to save himself."

Rowan had no means of response so she attempted a simple, "It was very nice to meet you Lise…"

"…I just want somebody to know that he didn't do it to himself; for somebody to believe me. Henrik was murdered, I just know it. Please, please believe me."

Rowan was about to reply when the girl turned on her toes and jogged off into the house. Dumbfounded, Rowan watched her sprint up the stairs through the glass wall from where she heard a door slam.

Rowan had no time to give her answer but she had been fully prepared for the consequences of providing it. She had wanted to say what had been sitting poorly with her since she had seen the bodies of Henrik and Donna laid out before her. Something was simply not right, and she was going to uncover whatever it was.

15.

Most Friday evenings Franklin met his brother Edison at the Tobacco Factory Bar and Cafe. On the alternate weekends when he was on call throughout the night, he permitted himself a half pint, but Peterman was on shift that evening, and he was free the following day, so he would allow himself two or three pints.

The Tobacco Factory was the trendy, urban heart of the revived end of North Street. Exposed ventilation tubes covered the bare ceiling while provocative art adorned its walls; it doubled as a theatre and had garnered a reputation for exceptional productions that had breathed new life into a tired, run-down and largely forgotten corner of the city.

Franklin waited for his brother beneath a huge oil painting of an embryo in a lava lamp and sipped on his pint of Scrumpy cider. It was flat, warm and as thick as pond water - just how he liked it. He pondered for a while on the sadness of his existence; how these weekly meetings had become the entirety of his social life without him even noticing it had happened.

"Evenin' Frank," his brother beamed upon his approach.

"Evening Edison."

Disdainfully, Franklin was reminded that Edison was not his preferred name and the pair exchanged the usual complaints about their father's insistence that the two boys be named after great American thinkers.

"I suppose we have to sit outside because of the old political correctness?" Edison groaned.

"Of course we do. The smoking ban has been in place since 2007 and you still whine about it every week - and it's not even political correctness, I don't think you know what that means."

Franklin followed his brother outside to the seating area. The evening was warm and the days were feeling longer; the once distant approach of summer was drawing closer with every night. Edison lit a cigarette and began complaining about paperwork. He was a police officer and had been one for almost twenty years and during that time, neither his status nor wish to rise through the ranks had increased one bit. He was two years older than Franklin but looked considerably older; too much booze, too many late nights and the general weariness he felt for the frustrations of life and work had all taken their toll, turning the man's once blonde hair silver and his eternally boyish face prematurely wrinkled, giving him a somewhat peculiar appearance, like a man who had somehow aged before his time.

It was Edison who had worked on the paperwork for the two bodies who were due to be buried next Friday. Henrik and Donna had been offered only cursory interest from the police and only then because of their ages. "How's life treating you? That woman was cut up pretty badly," he asked gloomily.

"About as well as can be expected. I just wish we could have a few simple deaths for once - some old people would be perfect; it's always me who has to deal with the tragedies."

Edison shrugged his shoulders and blew a cloud of smoke in the air. "You come highly recommended, I always like to drop your name in when I can. Believe it or not, people tend not to have favourite undertakers, so they will take any advice they can get."

"I suppose I can't really complain about the work, it's just that Peterman gets all of the easy ones." Franklin studied his older brother and elected to confide in him. "I think it has been since turning forty appeared on the horizon, I'm not dealing with it very well…"

"It's nothing, you'll be fine." Edison stubbed his cigarette out in an ashtray, which seemed to signal to Franklin that this line of conversation was over with. The two brothers had never shared much of a bond and talking about feelings and concerns was not something Edison was prepared to start doing this evening.

Franklin steered the conversation back to work and tried not to take the snub to heart. "My new assistant has some interesting ideas about these deaths; I know it's crazy but…"

"…Oh yes, the assistant. I saw you became friends with her on Facebook. She wasn't what I was expecting…"

Franklin raised an eyebrow. "Really? What were you expecting?"

Edison seemed to realise he had probably misspoken but was in no hurry to correct himself. "I mean, you don't see many people like her in your line of business."

"Like her? Thanks Edison, you always remind me how little faith I should have in the modern police service; it sounds as if you have really made strides in racial sensitivity."

Edison pointed at Franklin with the unlit end of a fresh cigarette, "If you're going to talk like that about the police, you had better hope you don't get burgled or mugged anytime soon."

Franklin slammed his empty pint glass onto the wooden table. "Guess what, Edison? I kind of hoped I wasn't going to get mugged or burgled anyway. Rowan is a great assistant, better than I could have hoped for."

"Fine," Edison drew upon his cigarette and when he spoke next, clouds of smoke billowed from his mouth and nostrils. "I just didn't see you as the type to fall for all that political correctness stuff."

Franklin rolled his eyes. Anything his brother found thoughtful or difficult to understand was put down to "political correctness" - a strange, amorphous force that was responsible for everyday annoyances like bicycle lanes, fortnightly bin collections and disabled parking at supermarkets.

Franklin was not quite finished with taking digs at his brother. "While we are on the subject of police incompetence, are you absolutely sure there was nothing more to the two deaths you sent my way? How thoroughly were they investigated?"

Edison held his brother's gaze for as long as possible, once it was clear that no apology was coming he offered: "As thoroughly as we would investigate any deaths that had very clear causes - we already knew all about the woman; multiple incidences of drunken behaviour, she knew the inside of the police station better than I did - she was a whisper away from losing her license forever; how much of a surprise is it that she would eventually wind up killing herself - and that boy; a poet. Need I say more? He had just broken up with his girlfriend so he was a prime candidate, plus, he was Swedish and they commit suicide more than…"

"...No they do not!" Franklin barked. "That's a common myth but it's not true! Anyway, Henrik Neilson was Danish, and can you please stop smoking? You're chaining them - I don't want to be painting up your face in the death chamber in two years time."

This was how the two brothers spoke to each other and the way it had always been. Pleasantries had never been a part of their relationship and the sibling rivalry most children leave behind with adolescence had never shown any sign of diminishing.

The steely silence was broken only by Franklin surrendering first. "I'm going to visit Mum and Dad next week. I'm sick to death of Peterman, I can't work with him anymore."

Edison shook his head. "That old man again? I don't know why you let him get to you so much, I like him."

"There's a surprise, you're just about as unreconstructed as he is."

"Is that why you got an assistant then? Want to train her up as his replacement?"

"No it's not. I found an assistant because I'm tired of having to deal with everything by myself, lugging corpses around the city, arranging every part of a service. I'm not as young as I used to be, and I'm feeling it more and more nowadays."

Ed nodded and the pair shared the briefest glance of understanding before he added; "Growing older is bloody terrible. I hate it."

The conversation for the rest of the evening was across much calmer waters. By the end of the third pint, Franklin yawned and made his excuses and was about to leave when quite unexpectedly his brother, who had imbibed two drinks for every one of his, confided in him in a low and dreary voice.

"D'you know, I wasn't certain about those deaths either. I think they happened within an hour, and just a little walk of each other and in places where no CCTV would record them. They both had post mortems but the officer in charge was certain that nothing was amiss."

Franklin nodded and wished his brother a good night.

16.

The funeral of Donna Hawley was held at 11am on a Friday. Under a stony sky that would not stop threatening rain, the family assembled behind the hearse and the sombre procession began through the city to the crematorium across the Downs.

There were not many mourners, though Franklin had not expected there to be. The three sons and one day worker served as pallbearers, with Evan Farmer the only member of the family appearing even close to tears. Each of the brother's wives followed the cardboard casket into the crematorium to the strains of Celine Dion's "My Heart Will Go On" and as the doors opened, the wispy figure of Lucy Farmer, the silent ghostly woman who had made tea at the grim and smoky flat in Knowle West made the briefest of glances in the direction of Rowan who physically jolted beside Franklin; so otherworldly was her face, her features delicate and soft, her eyes fierce and knowing.

"There's something about that woman," Rowan softly confided once the doors were closed. "She gives me the heebie-jeebies."

"People deal with grief in different ways, perhaps she was closer to Donna than her husband." Rowan seemed nonplussed by this assessment. "There is certainly something quite peculiar about her though, she is very pretty considering…"

"Considering what?"

"Well, Evan doesn't seem like that much of catch to me, if you'd met him in his flat…"

Rowan allowed a slender smile. "That is very snobbish of you… but yes, she's actually a bit of a stunner. Talking of which; how is the dating site going?"

Franklin offered Rowan a wink and hid a grin with the palm of his hand. "This is neither the time nor the place, but yes, it is going very well thank you."

Rowan simply nodded and turned from him. Her attention had been caught by the approach of a short, round figure. A bearded, dishevelled man was approaching. Beads of sweat gathered on his forehead and he was gasping for air when he spoke.

"Am I too late? Has it started yet?"

Franklin inched closer towards the door where he could still hear Celine singing her lungs out. "It hasn't started yet, you can go in but please be quiet."

The man bowed politely and patted Franklin jovially on the shoulder. "Thank you. Would hate to miss out on paying my last respects."

Franklin slowly opened the door and the man slipped inside as gracefully as his bulk would allow. As soon as the door shut behind him, Rowan asked: "Who do you think that was?"

"Work friend maybe? Perhaps a boyfriend? Evan said his father probably wouldn't make it and he didn't look old enough anyway."

Rowan seemed to accept this explanation. "It's sad isn't it? About poor Donna Hawley - nobody here seems to be that upset, what a waste of a life to leave nothing but a mess behind you and to have nobody miss you when you're gone."

"It is terribly sad, but by all accounts, Donna gave out about as much love as she has coming back to her today. I have seen addiction claim many lives and the bitterness it leaves in its wake can be enough to extinguish any kind feeling there might once have been."

"Have you ever directed a funeral for someone who was murdered?"

Franklin nodded his head. "Yes I have." Rowan's eyes narrowed knowingly. "But not this time. Let me tell you something about murder, Rowan - two things really. Murder is very rare; it is exceptionally rare. Forget what you may read about in the news, violent crime - even in a city with half a million people like Bristol, is not an everyday occurrence and when it does happen - on those rare and tragic occasions, it is never as clean or as well thought out as you might imagine. It is ugly and frenzied, it's stupid, vengeful narcissists who act on a whim and think they can get away with it. It is committed by panicked people who don't know what they are doing or how to cover up the mess they have caused and who leave evidence all over the place. People get caught by their own mistakes and nobody gets away with something so terrible."

Rowan just shook her head and turned away from Franklin.

By twenty past the hour, mourners had already begun spilling out of the crematorium, faces now pale and awash with tears. Franklin and Rowan stood clear of them to allow them space and watched as hugs were exchanged and cigarettes ignited.

Evan Hunter was the first to make an approach towards Franklin, letting go of his wife's hand and instead, reaching for his. Franklin shook it and was not surprised to feel how cold it was.

"Thank you for all of this." he said. "I didn't expect much but I think we gave her a good send off. Much better than she deserved anyway."

Franklin smiled politely and offered his condolences. From over the shoulder of the man, he just made out what Rowan had been watching and waiting for. The short, chubby man with the beard and sweaty forehead was the last to leave the crematorium and did so without a word to his fellow mourners. He simply slipped through the open doors and around the assembled crowd before scurrying into his car and driving away, pausing only to offer a kindly nod to Lucy who blanked him completely.

Once the last of the mourners began to file away, Franklin consulted his watch and reminded Rowan that the time had come to return to Gallow &Sons. Today was a busy day after all.

"These days are rather unpleasant," Franklin informed Rowan on their ride back to the funeral home. "It can feel like a conveyor belt one after the other but I'm afraid they do happen more often than you would think."

Rowan seemed disinterested. "It's fine by me, it saves time."

Franklin could sense something unsettled about her. "Are you okay? Have I said something wrong?"

Rowan just shook her head but then with an apparent change of heart said, "Well, yes actually. You talk to me like I am a child sometimes, like I can't understand anything and you have to correct my way of thinking. I'm not stupid and I am not being hysterical about this. Something isn't right - you should trust me enough to at least understand that perhaps I know more about these things than you may assume."

Franklin kept his eyes fixed firmly on the road ahead as the first drops of rain fell from the stormy sky. "Well, I'm sorry you feel that way but you have only been working with me for two weeks and I've been doing this for twenty years - even longer if you count helping my dad out when I was younger. I do have a lot of experience and you are still learning - you can't just invent wild stories because of a hunch - these are people's lives, not some adventure for you to enjoy."

Rowan chewed angrily on her lip. "It is not an adventure and I'm not thinking this way out of boredom. Do you know what the very worst thing about being young is? Why I hate it so much?"

"What? Surprise me, because turning forty isn't a barrel of laughs either."

"I feel like an adult but nobody, absolutely nobody will ever take me seriously or even listen to what I have to say."

Franklin sighed and then nodded his head. "You are right. Nobody cares what you have to say right now - but one day they will."

Rowan let out a cold, belittling laugh. "Really? Will they? Or is that just what happened to you because when you were nineteen you grew up to be a white man and therefore everybody has to pay attention to what you have to say?"

"Very true," Franklin confessed. "I'm sorry."

The two drove the rest of the journey back to Gallow and Sons in silence. Once there, Rowan was alarmed to see just how speedy the turnaround between services was. No sooner had the hearse arrived in the garage, the steel door to the death chamber was pulled open and the day workers were sliding Henrik's red oak casket into the back of the awaiting vehicle.

In no time they were back on the road to Leigh Woods where the hearse met the extended Neilson family at the glass house across the suspension bridge. The rain was now falling in mournful sheets as dark umbrellas opened and a procession of grief stricken people trailed from the building, led by Ana and Robin who clutched onto each other in desperate fits of lamentation.

From inside the hearse, Rowan watched as their daughter Lise, her face hidden beneath a black hat and dark veil, bowed her head sorrowfully and watched the ground before her, incapable of even bringing her eyes to meet the casket that lay in the back of the vehicle.

The crematorium the family had selected was not the same as earlier but one on the outskirts of the city that was built to accommodate larger gatherings than the more intimate one they had experienced before. It was designed in much the same way, vaulted in the manner of a church but bereft of any religious imagery with huge glass windows providing views of the rolling hills of the surrounding countryside that on a sunny day would have looked breathtaking, but instead today ran with thick, heavy bolts of rain.

The mourners must have numbered over five hundred to Franklin's best guess. The Neilson's had suggested such a figure but he had thought it unlikely; so often families will over estimate the manner in which their loved one had touched the lives of others but in this instance they had, if anything, been conservative.

"He was a popular chap." Franklin offered, as the doors to the crematorium were closed and he and Rowan had escaped from the rain into the hearse.

"It would seem that way. It doesn't make him a better person though."

"I know that. I have known fine people with barely anybody at their services; some people are just more outgoing I suppose, better at making friends - it looks as if there were a lot of people his age in the crowd."

Franklin was not wrong. Unusual for a service of any size, the range of ages of those in attendance veered from the very young to the very old, each one bearing that same expression upon their face - a kind of contorted agony that went far beyond the look of grief Franklin was so familiar with; this was an open wound and a self inflicted one at that - each of the guests asking themselves what they could have done, what they should have noticed to stop him doing something so final.

"There are a lot of people," Rowan commented thoughtfully. "Surprising for a suicidal poet, don't you think?"

"I think you'll find the profile of the average suicide victim is a lot more complicated than you imagine."

The service lasted over an hour - a stifling and unbearably painful slog, caused by the fact that the service was in both Danish and English, with extensive readings of the man's own poetry.

"In and out, that's what I want," Rowan said. "No fuss, just a couple of songs and then off to the pub to get smashed. Easy."

Franklin smiled. "Me too, but I have never once been to a funeral that has truly been for the dead - these services are for the family and friends to say goodbye and their wishes may be quite different."

The rain was still tearing at the sky in angry strikes that beat upon the roof of the hearse when the mourners began leaving the crematorium. One by one their umbrellas opened like black flowers in some morbid garden and soon the car park was filled with people who bore expressions akin to those he had seen on the faces of people on the news who had witnessed some terrible atrocity - a look of shock and confusion, fright even.

"There's Lise," Rowan pointed out the figure of the sixteen year old girl, without an umbrella but too heartbroken to even notice the weather; her eyes were still fixed upon the ground where huge puddles washed over the tops of her shoes as she walked, her cheeks pouring with tears and rain. "She looks angry. I think she knows what it's like to have nobody take her seriously too."

Franklin caught Rowan's eye and shook his head slowly. "Not now, Rowan - and I said I was sorry."

Rowan seemed confused, something had caught her attention. "Franklin, quick, look!"

Franklin followed her gaze and peered through the rain soaked windscreen into the crowd of assembled mourners. It did not take him long to see what had distracted her so completely.

There, once again slipping through the doors of the crematorium was the short fat man with the beard. Hurriedly he ran through the onslaught and into his car, where he sped off without a word to his fellow mourners.

"What in the world?" Franklin gasped.

"So somebody knew them both? Why would he be at the funerals of two people who aren't connected in any way?"

Franklin's mouth had fallen open. "More importantly, who the hell is he?"

17.

Back in the death chamber, Rowan waited anxiously while Franklin paced back and forth about the room on the phone to his brother. She listened intently to half of a conversation, trying to fill in the moments of silence.

"It was definitely the same guy, we both saw him.", "Maybe you're the ones who made a mistake.", "Just take another look for me, just in case something was missed."

After hanging up, Franklin twitchily returned the phone to his pocket and folded his arms gruffly across his chest.

"Well?" Rowan ventured.

"He thinks I've gone mad. I just despair of him sometimes, he can make feel so bloody small!"

"Are they opening up the investigation again? Can he do that?"

"He can put in a request apparently, but nothing more. He's absolutely useless," Franklin fell into a metal chair beside an empty stretcher. "He thinks he was just a funeral tourist."

"A what?"

"I've seen them before; sick bastards with an obsession with grief. They like to visit funerals and pretend to know the victims - some of them are just there for the free booze at the wake."

"But that man can't possibly have been one of them, can he?"

"I don't know. I don't think so. Usually those ghouls hang around for as long as they can, milking it for all they're worth; it's like a game to them. This man was just in and out and gone in no time."

"There must be something we can do, surely?"

Franklin just shook his head thoughtfully. "We can go home. It's been a long day and I'm sick of death and misery. There's nothing more we can do today so we might as well bugger off and lock this place up."

"By home do you mean upstairs?" Rowan asked.

Franklin rubbed his face with his palms, "Dear Lord, it sounds depressing when you say it that way. I really can't escape can I?"

It was late afternoon by the time Rowan left. She retrieved her bicycle from the office and pedalled away into the crisp, post-storm air. Her parents wouldn't expect her home for a couple of hours, so there was plenty of time to visit the park on the way - just to be close to her sister again - it had been a while and she felt as if she needed it.

Brandon Hill was a sprawling, hilly park that overlooked the entire city. It was a pretty, tree lined escape to solitude from the cacophony of urban living over which a mighty edifice, Cabot Tower rose - a huge brick structure, built to mark the rocky friendship between the UK and the US during the Victorian era. When she was a little girl, her older sister Ruby told her that it had once been the home of Rapunzel and even now, Rowan could not help but imagine the captured damsel letting down her hair from the top of the turret to her waiting prince below.

It was on a bench beneath an apple tree, now bereft of most of its blossom that Rowan rested her bike and sat watching the little lights of houses blink into life as dusk set upon the city while she fed nuts to a squirrel that had come to sit beside her.

It had been here that they had sprinkled Ruby's ashes. It had been here that the two girls had played in the summer sun as little girls, nibbling on picnic sandwiches and drinking coke from the bottle while their parents watched on adoringly. It had come to mean little to Ruby as she grew older, but as Franklin had told her; these rituals are rarely for the dead, more for the living and how they wish to remember those they have lost.

Rowan could not help but think of her own sister's funeral - almost two years ago, and how little she had felt at the time; it was not unlike that sensation of stubbing her toe and feeling nothing but numbness but knowing full well that pain would soon be coming in aching waves that would consume her - and come they most certainly did; because once she had found herself capable of understanding that her sister would never return, that she would never see her again and that there was nothing - no deal or bargain that could ever bring her back, the sorrow fell upon her like a curse, forever robbing her of the chance that she would ever again feel real happiness, unburdened by grief, like they had enjoyed on those long summer days in the park.

Just like Lise Neilson; her life would forever be in the shadow of the brother she had lost, her sibling like a ghost haunting her and asking why not her instead? The dead, Rowan thought had it lucky; they had not the curse to miss anyone once they were gone.

A buzz from her phone was enough to bring Rowan back to the realm of the living, she read the text message from her mother, asking if she was okay and coming home soon. Rowan checked the time on the screen, she was not late but she knew her parents liked to keep track of where she was - at home she may be nearly invisible to them but they wanted to make sure she was safe when not confined to her room.

Rowan informed her mother that she would be home soon. She understood why these messages were necessary but despised them nonetheless. Every time she felt that familiar vibration of her phone in her pocket, she was queasily reminded of the night her sister had died - messages she had kept locked away inside its memory as well as her own.

"Have you heard from Ruby? She hasn't come home yet."

"Don't want to worry you but still can't get hold of Ruby. Her phone is off."

"Can you please give us a call, have you heard from Ruby? We're getting quite scared now."

"Dad is out in the car looking for Ruby. Please call us if you see this message."

When she finally found the messages and had called her mother, she was already in tears - not yet of grief but of an all-encompassing terror that had seized every cell in her body.

Rowan left Brandon Hill and cycled home to her parents. It had only just turned into night but both of her parents were already screaming at one another. With only the briefest acknowledgement of her existence, her mother and father resumed their fight whilst she helped herself to cold samosas from the fridge. The kitchen was kept impeccably clean - eerily so and Rowan did not like it one bit. Once the house had been messy and chaotic, piled up dishes left in the sink, the laundry basket overflowing with clothes but now the house was manicured from top to bottom with surgical precision, as if attempting to scrub the sorrow from the carpet itself. Her mother never stopped cleaning - she was trapped in an endless cycle of sterilisation to keep herself from getting lost in her own mind.

After a couple of hours and once the chaos downstairs had yelled itself into silence, Rowan heard a knock on her bedroom door. Her father opened it gently and poked his head through. "Can I come in?"

Rowan shrugged her shoulders. "It's your house. Do whatever you want."

Oscar Kaplan had once been a striking, proud man with a pristine beard and a head he kept shaved bald. He was the kind of father other girls at school giggled to each other about - tall and handsome and always arrestingly dressed in fine suits; the teenage girls had fawned over him like some exotic specimen of masculinity. Two years had turned his beard shaggy and withered, his head now bore temples of grey hair - his eyes once sparkling and intelligent now looked nothing more than tired.

"How's the job going?"

"Fine," said Rowan, with practiced nonchalance.

The man cleared his throat and stepped into the room. "I went into Tesco today. Thought I might see you there, was going to ask someone but I didn't know if you would want to be bothered."

Rowan looked up from her iPad to see if her lie had been discovered. "I was out the back… doing a stock count."

"Oh, I see."

"You shouldn't ask for me when I'm working, I don't think it looks very professional."

"Very well," he said as he moved towards her and sat on the edge of her bed. Rowan cringed at his closeness to her. It had not been long ago that such casual intimacy would have been welcome, a friendly hug or even one of his huge hands squeezing protectively at her shoulder, but then, there was a time that lying to her parents about her work and offering them a hasty story about a new job in a supermarket to save herself from the trouble the truth would have found her in, would have been hard for her to pull off. A lot had changed in two years.

"Your mother and I were talking about next week and the anniversary. We weren't sure what we wanted to do and wondered if you had any suggestions. Maybe you'd like to say something for…her."

"You were talking? Is that what that racket was downstairs?"

"I'm sorry, Ro, it's just next week. I promise things will get better soon, they have to eventually. All the books say the first two years are the hardest."

"That's great to know," Rowan huffed. "Only a few days left and it will be like she never existed."

Her father bristled at these words. "You know that isn't true. She will always be a part of us; of this house. We will never forget about her but maybe we will be able to… start thinking of the future… of our lives, what has changed and how we move on."

"How can we though, Dad? Nothing can ever be right again. You can't even bring yourself to say her name and you want us to start thinking about the future?" Rowan turned her iPad screen to face him and the image from her Facebook profile of the two girls smiling and drinking cocktails seemed to hit him like a bullet.

"Don't do that to me, Rowan," the man's eyes welled with tears. "Not just yet - I can't look at her."

Rowan swallowed her guilt at her father's reaction. "Well I have to, and I don't want to move on or pretend it never happened. There is a wound in all of us and we cannot fix it or make it better, we all just have to stumble through life with the pain."

The man stood up from her bed and wiped his eyes on the sleeve of his shirt. "I see. We all have to do this our own way." Turning from her, as if ashamed of his tears or his reaction to his dead daughter's face, Oscar Kaplan left her bedroom without a word and closed the door behind him.

Once she was certain he was not coming back, Rowan returned to her iPad. She tapped on the screen and brought up the two windows she had minimised. One was the

Facebook profile of Henrik Neilson, whose name had been unique in Bristol and easy to find. His page had become a morbid book of remembrance with friends and family from around the world leaving hundreds of messages of loss and sorrow, all written directly to the man as if he could ever read them. The profile of Donna Hawley had been harder to track down and her page was bereft of any such heartfelt farewells.

Rowan flipped open a notebook and consulted the group of friends both of them had added. One by one she listed them in a column in the book - certain that somewhere in this cavalcade of stranger's names, she would find somebody, anybody to link the two together.

Once she was done, she looked up Lise Neilson and began writing the message to her she had planned all evening.

18.

On Monday morning, Franklin awoke anxiously. Before getting out of bed, he checked his phone to see if there had been any messages sent in the night, half hoping that she would have cancelled their appointment. There was no such text. His laptop informed him that he had received six messages on the dating website overnight but since he had heard from Verity Duke, he had felt increasingly disinclined to reply to them.

After eating two crumpets over his kitchen sink and dressing for work, Franklin made his way downstairs to the reception where Meredy, as always, was every bit as punctual as he and was waiting patiently by the door. For some time Franklin had tried offering her a key to let herself in, but she had always declined. She was never happy being by herself at the funeral home, knowing dead bodies were only mere feet away from where she sat at her desk.

Franklin was more surprised to see Peterman waiting alongside her. "What are you doing here on time?"

"Second Monday of the month - it's payday."

"Oh I see. The only day you show your face before 10."

Peterman muttered irritably to himself when Meredy presented his cheque in an envelope. He opened it and examined the amount suspiciously; once he was certain the payment was adequate he grunted a word that could possibly have been "Thanks."

"There's something I wanted to say to you both and it's probably nothing to worry about at all," said Franklin. "But I've been noticing a few strange things of late - we had a few phone calls from a stranger last week and a mystery man turned up on the doorstep too. Like I said, I'm sure it all has a simple explanation and I don't want to make a big deal of it for fear of you thinking that I have completely lost my mind, but if either of you see anyone strange around or spot anything... out of place, then report it to me at once."

Meredy gasped excitedly, Peterman merely grumbled to himself.

"How deliciously weird!" Meredy enthused, "You can't just leave it there, you have to tell us more!"

"I wish I could but it's just... anomalies more than anything else; you know how the human mind has a way of looking for patterns where none actually exist?" Franklin saw that neither person in the reception knew what he meant. "Well, this is probably one of those occasions - putting two and two together and getting paranoia instead."

Peterman's expression could not have been more withering if Franklin had soiled himself in front of him. "If you don't mind, I have my cheque and will be going."

"Very well," Franklin relented, for there was little use in trying to persuade Peterman to show interest where he had none, "but there is one more thing I've been meaning to ask you."

"Oh?" Peterman was already backing out of the door.

"It really isn't fair on me - or Rowan, that we always end up with the violent deaths. Rowan hasn't even worked on an old person yet because you keep on nabbing all of the naturals."

Peterman laughed dismissively. "How is that my fault? It's only that your brother is always fixing things at the police station that you end up with all the young 'uns. If it weren't for him this place would probably have gone out of business years ago."

The comment smarted, but mostly only because it was true. Thanks to Edison, Gallow & Sons had developed a reputation for dealing with terrible, unnatural cases that other funeral directors were happy to do without.

"Be that as it may," Franklin continued, undaunted. "Next violent death is yours, Peterman - I think Rowan has earned a natural death at this stage."

Peterman sneered at this suggestion, not because he had enough of a heart to care too much for the recently bereaved, but because cases of sudden, unexpected death were usually harder to plan. There were no wills or requests for funeral traditions from the departed; just shocked and empty relatives trying to make some sense of the abomination that had befallen them. "I thought you did the bad ones because *you're the best*."

After ignoring him completely, saying his goodbyes and making his excuses, Franklin headed out for his morning walk along the harbour side, reassuring Meredy, as he always did, that he would not be gone for long.

The morning was bright and breezy. The oppressive heat and humidity that had built over the course of days preceding the funerals had dissipated with the storm and had left in its wake a cool and very welcome spring freshness. On his walk, Franklin spotted a few house martins - the first he had seen that year and their welcome return cheered his anxious heart in between near compulsive checks of his phone, repeatedly fearing that she had called or cancelled, while he tried to deal with this queasy sense of anticipation that rose like waves of panic through his body.

Once at the harbour side, Franklin ordered a coffee from the Crepe and Coffee Cabin on Prince's Bridge - a tiny cafe that claimed to be the smallest in Britain. The warmth through the cup helped ease the nervous chill he felt in his fingers but the effect of the caffeine seemed to only heighten his disquiet.

The previous evening he had found himself once again engaged in conversation with Verity Duke - the woman he had always regarded as his one true love; the one who had not only got away, but had left his life entirely for the best part of twenty years. Somehow, through the ease of exchange between computers, Franklin had found himself agreeing to talk to the woman the following morning; she had half a day off and her work schedule was so erratic that it was not easy to tell when she would have an available window again. At the time it had seemed like a wonderful idea but now, in the literal light of the day, Franklin was regretting his decision. Simply too much time had passed, he was certain he would somehow find a way to humiliate himself.

At the very least, he wished he had offered to phone her instead of wait for her call - aside from it seeming the more gallant option, having control of the situation himself would have reassured him somewhat.

Already he feared what the conversation would entail. He knew she was a teacher and therefore had succeeded in life to a degree much higher than he had accomplished. No wife, no children and an inherited job from his father were not likely to earn him many bragging rights. His evenings were taken up by playing video games, watching TV and reheating takeaway food, while the only living creature he had found to reciprocate any love or affection was his ailing cat who lived her life somewhere between his dismal home and death's door.

Still, Franklin could not help but reminisce about those years they had shared together. Renting adjoining bedrooms in an adorably squalid student house with four other people. During term holidays the others would return home, and Verity had once too, but he never had the heart to ask why she had stopped going back. Quiet nights they would spend together, chatting enthusiastically about their coursework, about politics or about nothing at all, while Franklin gazed adoringly at her from across the sofa, trying hard not to let the love show on his face, for fear that if he were found out this magical spell between them would be torn asunder.

The phone suddenly sprung to life in his pocket, jarring Franklin out of his daydream. Seeing the name "Verity Duke" on the screen sent him into a frenzy of terrified panic. He knew how to answer his phone, he had done it a thousand times, but somehow his brain had frozen like a contestant on Mastermind who suddenly can't remember his own name.

When he eventually tore himself from his seizure Franklin answered the phone with a friendly "Hello" which came out much higher pitched and breathless than he had intended.

"Hi, Franklin," she said. Her voice, so familiar and warm, was enough to allay all fears as it propelled him through time to those days in their flat in London. "I'm sorry if I'm a bit late - to be honest I was really nervous."

"I think you're right on time," Franklin reassured her. "I was really nervous too!"

"What is that all about? It's so strange isn't it - I mean, we left things pretty good last time we saw each other didn't we?"

"Yeah. Sure." That had not been how Franklin had remembered it but he was glad to forget that moment forever.

"God, doesn't it seem like a long time ago? Can you believe it's been almost twenty years?"

"It's impossible isn't it? And terrifying." Franklin could not help but smile broadly at the sound of her voice. Verity had always been a master at hiding her privileged upbringing - masking her poshness beneath a studied drawl that she only let drop when she was drunk. There were no such attempts at working-class affectations now, but the soul of her voice, the rich crispness of it remained intact.

Soon the conversation was flowing with casual ease. She asked him about his work and he relayed with a submission of pride his lack of success.

"Well, at least you're doing something," she reassured him. "There's no shame in what you do, you should be proud of yourself."

"So, you're a history teacher? Can't say I'm surprised, I think it was obvious you were going to end up working with kids."

"Well, thank you. I'm thinking of moving to a state school though, it feels time to move on."

"Where to?"

"I thought maybe a comprehensive. I'd like to help people who are a little less privileged for a change.. Don't give me that look!' Verity chided.

"What do you mean? You can't see me!"

"I know you, Franklin – class warrior to the end, but we don't always get to do exactly what we want."

"There's nothing wrong with working for a private school. I'm not quite as radical as you once knew me!"

"Really? That's a shame. I was rather fond of the Franklin Gallow who read Marx and was going to overthrow society with a revolution of ideas."

Franklin winced at her recollection of him. He moved the conversation to the smoother waters of her parents.

"Dad's dead," she said bluntly. "It happened five years ago."

"Oh Verity, I'm sorry." Franklin said earnestly, the sense of moving between bear traps with his topics was causing him to strain inside again.

"Don't be. We knew it was coming for quite some time. He was always an older dad anyway and I suppose the one good thing about going away to boarding school when you're eight is that you learn that your parents aren't always going to be there for you."

"Nevertheless, I'm sorry for your loss."

"Well, at least he got to know Alf before he died."

For a moment Franklin envisioned the American sitcom about an alien puppet before he remembered that her son was called Alfred.

"Well, that's something I suppose. How is he doing?"

"Very well. He is sitting his exams soon and is already starting to look at universities, in fact, he was thinking about Bristol and has been there for a little while, staying with friends. Actually, Franklin, that was what I wanted to talk to you about."

Franklin had not prepared himself for this uncomfortable route of conversation. He was sure she was going to ask him about job opportunities at the funeral home. The simple mathematics of the boy's age suddenly loomed towards him out of the confused mess of his mind. "He must be... eighteen then."

There was the sound of a deep intake of breath on the phone, and when her voice returned it was shaky and distant. "I told him to wait until he was eighteen if he ever wanted to meet you. Franklin, you're his dad."

The coffee and the phone slipped clean out of his hands and fell to the floor.

19.

Rowan immediately regretted her decision to meet Lise at Bristol Museum. She had never noticed quite what a gallery of death it was until that morning; cabinet upon cabinet of petrified animals, stuffed and preserved behind glass, fossils and skeletons, portraits of people who had died centuries before. She cursed her foolishness.

She had arrived early and shuffled wearily about the vast main hall of the building, beneath a huge replica of a box plane and by the elegant stone staircase that Rowan hoped she would be able to whisk the girl up to a suitably bland exhibit. She had messaged her on Facebook the evening before and had had received a near instantaneous reply.

"Hi Lise. I am Rowan, the woman you met very briefly at your home last week. I was one of the people arranging the service for Henrik, I hope you remember me. I was wondering why you suspected that your brother's death was not suicide. Please don't be alarmed but I would like to know any information you may have."

Rowan had been very careful with the wording of her message; she instinctively knew that this was a deeply irresponsible move on her part and that it could land her in a lot of trouble if Lise reacted badly to a relative stranger reaching out to her under such circumstances, but the girl had been reassuring and level-headed:

"Thank you for contacting me - nobody will take me seriously and they all think I have lost my mind. Do you have information yourself? Can we meet? I don't want anyone else knowing about this."

So the date and time was set. Lise had recently finished her Easter holidays but her parents and the school had agreed that she was in no fit state to return for the last of her education, or the GCSE exams she would be sitting later on in the month, and would therefore return in September.

The very moment that the huge Wills Tower that stood high and noble over Park Street peeled its enormous bell to signal the hour, the automatic door to the hall slid open and the tiny girl crept inside. Her eyes met Rowan's and they marched across the marble floor to one another.

"Good morning," the girl began, attempting to hide her shyness by focusing her stare upon her feet. "I didn't know if you would be here."

There was almost nothing of the girl, she was thin and small and her face, while beautiful, was disarmingly angular; shaped precisely like a skull as if she had little more than skin stretched over it. She dressed in a plaid skirt and blouse with long socks which came up to her knees; her hair was once again in plaits and the sight of this sixteen year old took Rowan back to the weeks after the death of Ruby and the enormous strain her own existence had put on her; the peculiar need to dress like a little girl again, to have her parents protection - to halt the passage of time.

"Of course I'm here. You can trust me, I promise." Rowan had never heard herself speak like this, like an older sister or a young aunt, more surprising was just how easily she slipped into this protective role. "Shall we go upstairs? I know somewhere that nobody will see us if you are worried about being spotted."

Lise nodded.

Part of the top floor of the museum was dedicated to pottery from Bristol - thousands of individual pieces of beige and grey earthenware on plinths and display boards. It was quite the dullest permanent exhibition the museum housed and this morning, just like almost every other morning, it was bereft of visitors, save for Rowan and Lise.

"I've never been up here," Lise commented as they climbed the last flight of stairs into the bright, white apex of the building.

"It's always empty; dinosaurs are clearly a much bigger draw than terracotta. There's some glassware up here too if you're interested…"

"Glassware? Really? You didn't say there would be glass!" the two girls allowed themselves an unexpected chuckle, which immediately lifted the cloud of tension that had settled over them. All it took to bring it back was the girl's words: "So you saw my brother then. I mean, afterwards?"

Rowan stopped in her path. It would have been easy to suggest that she worked solely in an administrative position at the funeral home but she knew that Lise deserved the truth. "Yes, I did."

"How did he look?"

Rowan gulped but her mouth had run dry. "He looked… very peaceful, like he was asleep really."

Lise could only offer half of a smile. "Thank you. My dad was the one who identified his body and he wouldn't say anything about it to me. I just wanted to know that he was… at peace, you know?"

"I promise you we looked after him well. We afford all of the deceased a huge amount of dignity and he was treated with the respect he deserved."

Lise nodded thoughtfully. "I suppose that is something then."

"My sister," Rowan began. "My sister died almost two years ago and so I understand, I was close to your age when it happened. God, can you believe I will soon be the same age she was, and then, it seems so wrong for this to happen, be older than Ruby."

"I'm sorry to hear that. Does it ever… stop, the pain I mean?"

"I think it does. It can't go on forever. I find it easier to think that, at the very worst, when it hurts more than you can possibly imagine, you will physically endure the pain, you will survive. Crying helps a lot, I have found."

Lise shrugged her shoulders. "I haven't cried once yet - is that a terrible?"

"Not at all, it really isn't - I don't think there is any right way to go about things, but I think… it will happen eventually." Rowan patted the girl gently on her shoulder and she didn't seem to mind.

"So, what makes you think that there is more to my brother's death than everyone else does? Why are you the only one who believes me?"

"A couple of things, I don't know how much you want to hear but…"

"…Tell me everything you know, please?"

Rowan could not deny the frail little girl. "Very well, I will. Do you know that on the night your brother died, there was another death, just a little further down the river? They probably died within an hour of each other. The police say it was an accident and there was nothing to link the two deaths. She was a middle-aged woman who drank a lot and supposedly fell into the water."

"That is strange but I don't see what it has to do with Henrik."

"She was called Donna Hawley and we directed her funeral too, it was on the same day as Henrik's. There was a man - a fat man with a beard, about forty I would guess, and he was at both funerals. He must have known both of them... He left before we could find out who he was."

Lise's eyes widened as the realisation of what this meant sank in. "So, somebody knew them both?"

"We've told the police about it. They are looking into it; trying to work out who the man was and track him down."

Lise blinked and her bloodshot eyes looked for a moment as if they might produce a tear. "Oh God. Do you think I was right? I don't know what is worse really. It is horrid to think of him killing himself because he hated himself so much - and that none of us ever knew, or is it sadder to know that he wanted to live and somebody murdered him?"

"I'm really sorry, Lise. We'll get to the bottom of this eventually; in the meantime, I think it's just a case of waiting. If the police don't come up with anything, I was thinking that perhaps I could look into things, just casually, I don't want to pry or to hurt anybody, but something strange appears to have happened and I don't quite know what yet. You said you didn't think he had any reason to kill himself."

"Ellie," Lise suddenly blurted.

"Sorry?"

"They all blamed it on her, his girlfriend Ellie. They had been together for three years but had split up a couple of weeks before that night. Everyone says it was her fault because she dumped him - but Henrik told me everything; we were really close like that. The pair of them were breaking up every couple of months and getting back together the next day. This was longer but he was the one who broke it off this time around."

"Did he say why he split up with her?'

"They had a big row over at her place and Henrik just said he'd had enough - she didn't even make it to the funeral, which everyone hates her for, but what is she supposed to do? Turn up and have everyone blame her for him killing himself? Do you know what the worst part is? Everyone is saying that he was an artist, and that is just what artists do - I hate that; this sick notion that creative types are unhinged and that poets are always doing away with themselves - he wrote poetry because it gave him joy. This wasn't stupid stuff that idiotic teenagers write, his poems were about the joys of life and the happiness he felt for everything. His poems even rhymed! Suicidal poets don't write rhyming couplets!"

Lise took a deep breath, which was Rowan's cue to interject. "I don't suppose you did what I asked? Did you get it?"

A fragment of suspicion passed across Lise's pink-flushed face. Her passionate defence of her brother had clearly brought some colour to her cheeks. "I did, but I want you to promise to only keep it for a week and no longer, I don't want to lose it. You must know how precious it is now. Anyway, if my mum and dad found out it was gone, they would kill me." Lise cringed at her own misplaced words. "Please take good care of it and tell me everything you find out with it. I don't know what you are looking for... but I trust you."

"Thank you, Lise."

With that, Lise reached into her handbag and produced the item Rowan had requested; Henrik's mobile phone.

20.

Franklin scrambled about the floor, desperately attempting to retrieve his coffee and phone in his suddenly uncooperative hands. Once he was certain he had a firm grip on them both, he allowed himself to stumble sideways into Millennium Square where he found a bench to fall on.

"Verity? Are you still there?" his own words reverberated madly around the chaos of his mind.

"Franklin?" she replied at the end of the phone.

On the big screen TV that was fixed high above and before him a science documentary was being screened in the morning sun. Vaguely Franklin recognised pictures and words and he found that if he sat still and focused on it, the madness began to dissipate.

"I thought you'd gone," she continued. "I didn't mean to shock you, but I thought you had to know – not just because of you being Alf's dad, but because he wants to get to know you."

"Verity, why are you saying this? I don't have a kid. You would have said something before - I would know."

"Franklin, calm down, I can hear you panting over the phone. It's not a big deal, I promise you."

"Not a big deal? I have a son? Why are you being so unreasonable? Why are you telling me this? Are you trying to make fun of me?"

"I am doing no such thing; I'm simply stating the truth."

"And he's mine?" Franklin ventured, cautious not to sound accusatory.

"Sorry? Trust me, it could only have been you. Do you remember the last week at uni? The party at Heather Tomlin's flat? It may surprise you but I wasn't sleeping with half of London at the time - there was only you. That year at least."

Franklin could remember that night, it was not a vivid memory but enough of it remained to let him know that it had been real, despite the alcohol and the pot.

Heather Tomlin had been a mutual friend; a rotund lesbian who wore her fatness like a badge of honour in tight fitting jeans and buttoned down shirts. The pair had adored the fearlessness with which she took on her life and her parties had become legendary both for their free flowing booze and liberal attitudes towards soft drugs. They had been invited before and had both declined but in the closing weeks of university had concluded that one final blow out was a perfect ceremony to bid the last days of their education goodbye.

It had not been the first time they had experienced each other – a few drunken nights had involved gentle, casual fumbling, kissing and trembling fingers reaching just below the waist, but this had been the first and only time the pair had dared to surrender fully; it was as if the world were ending as university finished - everything they had known was coming to a close and the big, scary world of debt and responsibility loomed just over the horizon. That night was the full stop at the end of a sentence that had gone on for three years. It was supposed to matter.

"But," Franklin found himself blurting. "I didn't think it could happen on your first time."

Verity huffed derisively. "Are you twelve?"

"No, no, no. I mean, I know it can happen now but at the time I thought you got one... like a freebie."

Verity laughed, this time not unkindly and somehow Franklin found himself laughing with her. "Oh Franklin, half the people alive in the world today only exist because their parents thought that was true."

Franklin took a deep breath. "So what is he like?"

"He's perfect. He's an artist - a sculptor, believe it or not. No idea where he gets it from and I'm damned if I understand it half the time, but people who know what they're talking about think he's good."

"Does he look like me?" Franklin was unsure why that felt relevant, but it did.

"He's a redhead if that's what you mean."

Franklin found himself smiling at this revelation. "Poor kid."

"I think he quite likes it, he's never been one to fade into a crowd - he's always been outstanding in one way or another."

"So... what do I need to do? I don't have much money saved if this is a... thing, I mean, I can send you some money if you need support."

"What are you talking about? Alf is eighteen and we've coped just fine without you for all these years. It's only now, and only because he showed an interest, that I tried looking for you."

"Oh. Well, I'm sorry that I wasn't there. It must have been tough."

"Yes it was, especially for the first two years, but if I'd really needed you, I would have found a way to track you down. I was determined; as soon as people told me how hard being a single mum was it was as if a gauntlet had been thrown at my feet - I knew I wanted to do it alone and I have no regrets at all, he's a great kid Franklin. Maybe if he'd shown any real interest in you I would have looked for you but he didn't until now. I think he's scared of moving to university - he won't say it himself but I know it's true; I think he wants to know who he is."

"Does he hate me?"

"Of course not, he doesn't know you. There is one thing he does want from you though."

"Oh?" Franklin asked, not even trying to hide the tremor in his voice.

"He wants to meet you."

21.

Rowan left Lise at the museum, where the girl was happy to while away the rest of the morning in peace. It was a comfort Rowan knew very well. In the weeks following the discovery of her sister's body, she had found herself so exhausted by people's constant demands to talk, to share her feelings and their eagerness to tell her that they were here if she needed them, when in truth all she wanted was to have some time to herself, to try and forget about what had happened, if only for a minute or two.

The ride to Southville was an enjoyably easy one. Bristol was an incredibly hilly city which had nevertheless garnered a reputation for cycling; its young, largely student and environmentally conscious population had taken to this form of transport in their thousands and Rowan had found herself merrily joining in. She released the brake at the top of Park Street and allowed herself the sensation of speed as she tore down the hill and past the harbour side. She was at the house in no time at all.

Her idea had come late the night before; if Henrik and Donna really did know each other then surely there would be some way of proving it? Her only problem was how to do so - and then, just as she was drifting in to sleep, something loomed out of the darkness; an idea so perfect that were it to work it would prove their connection beyond doubt. That was when she had messaged Lise.

Donna had lived on the ground floor flat of a house on Beauley Road. She could not recall the number but she and Franklin had driven past it on the way to her funeral and she knew it had a bright green door and a scruffy front garden covered in bags of uncollected rubbish.

The old Victorian building loomed before her. Its curtains were open and through the bay window she could make out a scene of messy abandon. Clothes were scattered everywhere, empty wine and vodka bottles littered the floor while an ashtray overflowed on to a coffee table. There appeared to have been some attempt to clear the chaos as several cardboard boxes had been brought to the house and had been partly filled with belongings - no doubt her family had begun the laborious task of sorting through her meagre possessions.

From her jacket pocket, Rowan produced Henrik's phone - a very new looking iPhone that was likely loaded with information about his final hours, though she imagined it would prove to be as useless to her as it no doubt had been for the police. There was no sign of a Donna in the contact list, but she had not imagined there would be; that was not the evidence she was searching for.

She went to the Internet settings on the phone and was immediately presented with a list of available Wifi connections in the neighbourhood. She did not know which on the list, if any, had belonged to Donna but the phone most certainly would. A little tick appeared next to one connection: "HawleyBeauley" and the phone made an agreeable "ping" as a link to the house was formed.

Had it not been for the underlying sadness of this investigation, Rowan would have permitted herself a squeal of victory. The phone had clearly remembered the password to her flat. Donna must have known and trusted Henrik well enough to share this with him so that he could use her Internet, presumably because he was often there and needed to use it. Like a dog identifying its owner among a sea of faces, the phone had remembered it and had dutifully returned.

Rowan's first thought was to call Lise but decided against it; she needed more than just this simple connection, moreover, this already seemed like a matter that needed attention from the police.

Instead, she decided to call Franklin.

"Hello?" he answered in a weary voice.

"Sorry, have you just woken up?"

"No, no, I'm at the harbour side."

"Oh, you just sounded tired."

"Oh no, not tired... just, thinking about a lot of things."

Rowan thought twice about pressing him on this; one thing her short life had taught her thus far was that when people really did want to discuss things, they said so. "I was in Southville and..." Rowan looked at Henrik's phone, which she held in her other hand. It had not occurred to her that not only would she have to explain how she had come to have it in her possession, but also how she had exploited the trustful young daughter of the family which could be enough to permanently destroy the reputation of Franklin's business and would most certainly get her fired on the spot. "I was just wondering if my pay cheque is at the home."

There was a moment of silence on the line. "Yes, I think so. Meredy deals with all of that though, you should probably phone work if you want to check it is there."

"Oh yes," Rowan laughed nervously down the phone. "I hadn't thought of that."

"Is that it?"

"Yes. It was just that I was in the area and I wasn't sure if I was getting paid this month as it hasn't been four weeks yet."

"Well, you could pick it up today but I thought you were in tomorrow. Look, if you need the money immediately, I'm sure we could sort out some kind of cash arrangement, just for this month."

"No, no, I'm fine."

"OK," there was a brief, contemplative silence from Franklin's end of the phone. "Rowan, you know teenage boys. What do they like?"

The sudden change of direction in the conversation slipped Rowan into a easy chuckle. "What do teenage boys like? How old is he?"

"Eighteen."

"Porn."

Franklin laughed heartily, "No! I want to buy a gift for an eighteen year old boy."

"Porn - or booze, don't you remember being eighteen, Franklin?"

"I was never that kind of eighteen."

It was Rowan's turn to laugh. "Why do you need to buy a present for a teenage boy?"

"I'm expecting a visit from somebody soon, thought it would be nice to be able to offer him something he would like."

"I'll think about it. I'm in tomorrow right?"

113

"First thing, if you're happy with that. Four days a week unless we need you for extras."

The two exchanged their goodbyes and then Rowan hung up, relieved that she had at least appeared to carry the conversation off without drawing too much suspicion upon herself. She was just about to climb on her bike and head back home when out of the blue the door to Donna's house opened.

Rowan gasped and turned to find a man standing in the doorway. He looked somewhere in his mid forties, with long, unconvincingly coloured hair that was tied in a long plait that ran down his back with a matching chestnut moustache that slithered across his face. A pair of vivid blue eyes scanned Rowan from top to bottom.

" Can I help you?'

Rowan's mouth fell open. "I don't think so,' she was about to speed away on her bike but knew that would look suspicious. "I'm just a friend of Donna's," Rowan blurted out. "We worked together."

"Oh," the man nodded slowly, his eyes never leaving her face. "At the supermarket?"

"Yes, at the supermarket," she breathed a sigh of relief as she had completely forgotten where Donna had worked. "I just thought I would stop by and… show my respects."

"I see, would you like to come in? I didn't know her very well but I understand she had a few friends."

"Oh no, no. I'll get going," Rowan was about to make her excuses but instead found herself asking. "So, do you live here too?"

"Yes, well, no. Not really. I live in the flat upstairs, we just share an entrance door. Barely knew her to be honest."

"Oh right. I used to be around quite often and was just wondering why I never saw you."

"Well, I must admit I didn't know her very well at all. I have only lived here for a few weeks but she seemed like a very… spirited person."

Rowan ventured a smile, which she hoped would be read as knowing. "She did like a drink but we had lots of fun evenings together."

The man raised a bushy grey eyebrow. "Yes, I know. These houses aren't the best at insulating sound; she certainly liked her late nights. She could be rather noisy."

Rowan was feeling brave, even foolhardy. "Did you ever meet any of the people who came around here? There was a man, a friend of ours. I've been trying to track him down but he hasn't been answering my calls. He was a young Danish man called Henrik."

"Henry?"

"Henrik."

The man stroked his moustache as he pondered his response. "I do recall a young chap coming round from time to time. Never had a chance to speak to him, I do like to keep to myself upstairs as much as possible. I'm sure I would have remembered his name if I had heard it; unusual."

"I suppose it is really."

"Speaking of names," the man held out his hand to her. "I'm Art Branwell."

"I'm…" Rowan knew she could not use her real name so settled on the one that was constantly tumbling through her head. "Ruby Kaplan." Rowan took his hand and shook it. It was cold and damp.

"Well Ruby Kaplan, if you do ever find yourself pining for your friend, I'm sure nobody would mind you coming around here. It's just a shame that we had to meet under such sad circumstances."

The flirtatious wink and the flash of brilliant teeth the man offered her made her feel instantly queasy. Why did men insist on turning completely innocent and polite conversations into appeals for sex; especially those old enough to be her father? "Well, I best get going."

"If I see your friend, I'll tell him a Ruby Kaplan is looking for him. If we're talking about the same chap, he always seemed to have a pal with him."

Rowan froze in her effort to raise her bike from the concrete floor of the front garden. "Oh, really?"

"He was a big fella, you know," Art patted his belly. "Probably about my age. Never saw the younger one here without him."

Rowan shook her head in an attempt to feign confusion. "No idea, but thanks."

"You're welcome," said the man who winked at her once more.

Rowan was gone as quickly as her bike would allow.

22.

Franklin woke later than usual on Thursday morning. So reliant had he become on early nights and a regular sleep pattern, he no longer felt the need to set an alarm. The horrors of his daily work certainly took their toll on the man emotionally but the sheer abundance of exposure to trauma had somehow never invaded his sleep - in fact, the only time he was not haunted by the ever-present spirit of death was during the night.

The change had come almost immediately after hearing news of his son. The thought of a child being born with his blood in his veins, without his knowledge, and growing into a young man without Franklin ever being part of his life had permeated his unconsciousness to such an extent that the he would find himself waking with a jolt several times each night and riding his way through a roller coaster of emotions from unbridled sympathy for the boy, deepest regret for what he had lost, and then finally, utter terror that the boy had returned.

It had been Felicity who had woken him. Hungry and no doubt confused as to why the human was not up at his regular hour, the cat had pawed and prodded Franklin until finally he blinked into bleary life. Confronting the clock on the bedside table was enough to send him into a wild panic; Felicity, in a rare show of speed and agility leapt from the bed as Franklin threw himself out of it. Fifteen minutes was all the time he had to be ready and unlock the door downstairs.

He managed it by only overrunning by five. Still feeling somewhat disorientated and his hair still wet from the shower, Franklin fumbled for the keys and unlocked the door to the reception, all the while apologising profusely through the glass to Rowan and Meredy who had been cheerfully engaged in conversation.

"Good morning," his receptionist said. "Bloody hell, Franklin. You look a mess!"

The two women chuckled together, despite being suddenly very self conscious of his somewhat bedraggled appearance - his shirt untucked, his cufflinks undone, his belt nowhere to be found, he could not help but be touched to see Meredy and Rowan apparently getting on so well.

"I'm sorry, I only just got up."

"Late night was it?" Meredy asked with a sly smile that unsubtly implied that he might have had company the evening before.

"I wish I could say it was; just a strange night of sleep is all."

Meredy took her place behind the computer that whirred into life with the touch of a button. Rowan stood obediently beside her boss and asked: "So, what is the plan for today?"

"I was thinking of giving you something to do by yourself if you think you're ready."

Rowan nodded enthusiastically. "Of course,"

"Mrs Freeman, I was wondering if you'd do her makeup for a quick viewing the night before the service."

Rowan blinked disbelievingly. "You want me to try doing the makeup by myself?"

Franklin shrugged his shoulders and offered the platitude that he knew worked best on his assistant. "Why not give it a try? We all have to learn someday and there's no time like the present."

Mrs Freeman was the elderly woman Franklin and Rowan had been organizing the funeral service for over the course of the week. Peterman had been true to his word and had offered the next "natural" to Franklin rather than taking her on himself. It had been a blissfully straightforward affair for a woman who had died peacefully in her mid nineties and he and Rowan had for the first time together, come as close as it was possible to actually enjoying their work.

"I'm heading off to Bath for the morning so you two have the run of the place. I'm assuming Peterman isn't likely to show up anytime soon?"

"Who knows," Meredy grumbled. "He comes and goes as he pleases nowadays."

Franklin sighed. "This is absolute nonsense; we're supposed to be a business not a social club - Peterman has two bodies out there and he's barely had any contact with the families. I've had enough of this!"

Franklin only then noticed how Rowan had changed. She looked smaller and younger, her eyes soft and thoughtful. She had taken a step away from him. "How long will you be in Bath for?" Her voice was tiny.

"I'll be back by one o'clock, I should imagine."

"So I will be… working with Mrs Freeman by myself?"

"Yes, but you've seen me work on the makeup before, and you've had those practice goes on your arm with the airbrush," suddenly Franklin realised just what Rowan had asked him. "Oh my goodness, I'm so sorry Rowan, it never occurred to me that this would be your first time alone with a body. Don't worry about it for now, I've been a total buffoon. Wait for me to get back, play around on the computer in my office or something."

Rowan was shaking her head. "I think I can manage it. It'll just be a little strange that's all. Like you said, I have to do it sometime."

Franklin gave a single bob of the head. "Only if you are absolutely sure you can; if it is getting too much for you, leave her and when I get back I can watch you while you're doing it. She's already undressed - but she has a paper apron on. It's just face and hands."

"I think I can." Rowan said, though it seemed mostly to herself.

"How come you're going to Bath?" Meredy asked, as if trying to remind the other two that she was still there.

"Visiting my parents, hoping something will get done about Peterman."

"Good luck with that," she smirked as she returned her attention to the computer screen. "Although, I'd put on a tie if I were you, I don't think they let people in the city unless they're dressed nicely."

Meredy was joking of course, but Franklin nevertheless found himself doing as he was told, and as soon as he was dressed in a manner more becoming, he left the funeral home for the train station.

At Temple Meads station, Franklin bought himself a ticket and a vegetable pasty and boarded the train just as it was about to leave the station. It was only half full so he was able to find a window seat, through which he watched as the industrial outskirts of Bristol fell away in an instant to rolling green hills and farmlands of the British countryside. It was a distance of only fifteen miles between the cities of Bristol and Bath but to drive through the complicated one-way systems and multiple traffic lights could take up to an hour, so the train was always preferable and he never grew tired of the vista that unfolded before him.

He knew that the most pressing piece of information he had to impart to his parents was the existence of his son, Alf, but he had no idea how to even approach that subject - this was to be a business meeting first and foremost; concerning his father's drunken and unreliable friend Mr Giles Peterman.

Despite his father having retired from active work at the funeral home, he was still the owner and the condition of Franklin working there and living in the flat above was that his dad, Malcolm Gallow, would have final say regarding all major decisions; specifically regarding Peterman who the old man knew was far from a model employee. This could prove to be a difficult conversation and the only thing that was going to further complicate it was for him to bring up an unknown prodigal son.

As the train pulled into the busy, attractive station, with its Bath stone facade and glorious views across the impeccable city skyline, the music Franklin was playing on his phone faded away and the sound of ringtone replaced it in his earphones. Stepping from the train he answered the call from his brother.

"Hi Edison," Franklin yawned, he still hadn't had a coffee and his body was feeling the effects of its absence.

"Morning Frank. I tried calling you at the home but your receptionist said you had gone to Bath."

"Yes, just arrived."

"Are you visiting Mum and Dad or is this a work thing?"

"Both. Got some things to sort out at the home - have to run it past Dad first."

"Well, if you're not too busy, we're releasing another body from the morgue today. This guy was a hit and run on the Portway and his…*husband* is fine with you taking him." Franklin rolled his eyes at the disapproving way he had said "husband" as if the concept were an unfathomable and faintly comical one, but he opted to let it go.

"OK, when will he be ready."

"Well, I was going to book that in with your receptionist but seeing as you resent my help with your business so much I thought I'd check with you first."

Franklin was in no mood to play games with his brother. "Will three be too early?"

"Three is fine, you know the drill by now."

"Of course."

"Good. Give my love to Mum and Dad, tell them I'll be there to visit soon."

"*Will* you be there to visit soon?"

There was a nasty chuckle from Edison's end of the phone. "Not a chance."

The brothers bade each other farewell and Franklin began the ascent up the hill to where his parents lived, from the foot of which, one could easily see the dwelling that belonged to his family thanks to its latest addition.

Upon the railings of the old Georgian terrace house a tall pole had been fixed from which fluttered a gigantic American flag. The sheer gaudiness of the colours against the tasteful stonework that the city had been constructed of was angrily vivid in the morning sun. Franklin found himself staring incredulously at it for an inordinate amount of time before he rapped on the door to his parents' house.

His father answered the door, wearing his bald-eagle patterned pyjamas and a tatty looking dressing gown. "Franklin!" the man exclaimed joyously as he threw his arms around his son. "What a splendid surprise! Sarah! Guess who's here!"

Malcolm Gallow was a thin-faced, bespectacled gent who wore all the eighty years of his life with the kind of natural dignity not even a pair of pyjamas could tarnish. His hair was white and distinguished, his face surprisingly smooth for his advanced years. The man patted Franklin on the back and invited him inside.

The living room was dressed in the American-themed paraphernalia his father had begun collecting when Franklin was only a small boy. It cluttered almost every surface, tiny flags on sticks, model representations of Mount Rushmore and the Statue of Liberty alongside sombre declarations to "Never Forget" over miniatures of the Twin Towers. Upon the mantel sat a framed photograph of Barack Obama, which, while a peculiar choice for a man who could never vote in a US general election, was a marked improvement on the George W. Bush image it had replaced - at least to the liberal-hearted and socially conscious Franklin.

His mother, a round woman with long, white hair and pretty grey eyes was eating a piece of toast in her nightie when she saw her son appear in the doorway of the room.

"Good heavens!" she beamed and leapt from her seat on the sofa to embrace him. "I suppose you saw that monstrosity outside?" she whispered into his ear.

"I hope you aren't referring to my flag, are you Sarah?" intoned his father, and his mother offered Franklin a knowing wink.

"The council says I have to take it down," Malcolm complained.

"I'm not surprised. It can't be within planning regulations, the whole place is a world heritage site." Franklin responded.

"Bloody jobsworths, that's what they are. Where's their sense of patriotism?"

Franklin couldn't help but laugh. "Patriotism for Britain, Dad, not America."

The man simply grumbled to himself in response. Finally he offered his son a cup of coffee, which Franklin gladly accepted, and irritably clomped his way to the kitchen.

"Is he being terrible about that flag?" Franklin asked his mother.

The woman simply nodded. "You know what he's like, he isn't happy unless he has a project on. We have had people from the council around twice and letters through the door most mornings but I'm… past caring; I love your father but when he gets himself in pickles like this, I just choose to sit back and let him deal with it all."

Franklin offered her a sympathetic smile. They chatted warmly until Malcolm returned, brandishing a mug of coffee upon which the words "Don't Tread on Me" were printed, over the image of a coiled rattlesnake. Franklin took a seat on the sofa beside his mother. "I'm here to talk business for a bit."

His father nodded and he too took a seat in an armchair. "Shoot!"

Franklin smirked at the unlikely Americanism the man had no doubt learnt from a TV show. "It's about Peterman."

His father shifted uncomfortably. "Go on."

"Well, he's always late, if he turns up at all - he's scruffy, he's short with the families and… he's still drinking a lot. I've given him so many warnings but nothing ever changes. I think it's time we let him go."

Malcolm raised his eyebrows. "That's rather hasty, don't you think?"

"We have a reputation to uphold, Dad."

"Has he had any complaints lodged against him?"

"No."

"And he manages to get all of his work done too? He's never been late for a service yet?"

"No." Franklin could hear his teeth grinding inside his head.

"Well, sounds like he is doing his job just fine then. Are you sure this isn't just a grudge thing? I know the pair of you don't see eye to eye on much."

"On anything."

"Well, he's an old man and he likes working. The only reason he hasn't retired is because he wants something to do with his time. He's not like me and your mum, he doesn't have anything worth coming home to, he likes to stay busy."

"He has his booze to come home to," as soon as he said this, Franklin realised how much like a petulant child these words made him sound.

"That may be so, but he's managed to do all of his work without the help of an assistant, which is rather admirable, don't you think?"

"How did you know about Rowan?"

"Edison told us about her on the phone, we looked her up on Facebook. How's she working out?"

"She's great, much better than I could have hoped for. Wait, you're on Facebook?"

His father nodded his head smugly. "We both are."

"I'm on Twitter," his mother gleefully informed him.

Shaking these words from his head in disbelief that even his parents had entered the world of social media, Franklin persisted with singing the praises of his new employee. "I know I should have mentioned that I was looking for someone, but I just really felt - well, I've been feeling that it's pretty lonely working all by myself; I've got nobody to come home to either so it's nice to have someone to talk to during the day. She is learning everything so quickly and she's interested in it all and I just like having her around, it gets boring talking to corpses all day long."

His father tutted and shook his head. "Isn't she a little young for you?"

"It's nothing like it, I just like having a friend; it has nothing to do with anything else. You'd really like her, she's going to be something one day and I want to be one of the people who helped her get there. The mind of that woman is extraordinary."

His parents exchanged doubtful glances across the room before his mother intoned: "Perhaps if you had someone to come home to, you wouldn't feel so lonely. I met Ken Buchanan's mum the other day and do you know he's been married for almost twenty years, with the third baby on the way."

"Who is Ken Buchanan?"

"You went to school with him. Primary school."

Franklin rubbed his eyes, inside him he felt his secret worm its way up his throat from his stomach. Before he knew how to stop it, it was already in his mouth. "Well, guess what. I have a son."

The mouths of both of his parents dropped open. A stunned silence held the room hostage until his father roared: "That is tremendous news!"

Already they were on their feet and before he could say another word, both of his parents had him in a vice-like grip around either shoulder as he sat and attempted not to spill his coffee.

"When is it due?" his mother sobbed through tears of joy.

Franklin could only shake his head. "About eighteen years ago."

The hug was broken instantly. Franklin looked up to see both of his parents towering over him.

"It was a one-night thing, ages ago, when I was just leaving university. I've only just heard from his mother this week and apparently she has a son; he's called Alf."

Another silence, only this time it was broken by a huge hail of laughter from Malcolm. "Thank God for that, we're too old to be looking after a little kid!"

"Aside from you and Edison," his mother informed him. "I've never been fond of babies. All those dirty nappies and late nights. I think you dodged a bullet there."

And then the embrace began again. The suddenness of the revelation had startled Franklin to such a degree that he had started shaking - but the hug was sincere and the words were comforting; he held them closer revelling in the knowledge that no matter what he did, or how many mistakes he made in his life, his parents would be there for him, with open arms and cups of coffee.

23.

It was only when Franklin was safely on the train from Bath, that he fully understood how much the weight of his revelation had been bearing down upon him - and what a joyful relief it had been to feel it lift.

He had never thought his parents would react terribly, but secrets had a strange way of nesting inside Franklin; he found it a dark and miserable burden to foster within one's soul. His parents - two people who were always there when the storms became too much to bear, had been both reassuring and loving.

"We'd love to meet him one day," said his mother.

"He can't blame you; you never even knew he existed," added his father.

On leaving, his mother had given him the last remnants of a tin of Belgian chocolates and she and his father had walked him across the city to bid him farewell at the station; an act they rarely had the strength or compulsion to do now they were comfortably settling into an age they regarded as "elderly."

Franklin had grown tired of the limited musical options he had uploaded to his iPod, so instead opted to listen to the radio. As the train rattled comfortably onwards to his home city the static from the local radio station began to spew the news headlines.

A warm voiced man with a light, radio-friendly Bristolian accent recounted the events of the past twenty-four hours. It was the usual stories of corrupt councillors, plans for a music arena on the outskirts of the city and a location based piece on the effectiveness of speed cameras. It was the fourth item that hauled Franklin from the slumber that had settled upon him.

"Police have named the victim of a hit and run incident at the weekend. Forty-six year old Ben Stirling was struck and killed while out jogging on Saturday evening and was found early in the hours of Sunday. Avon and Somerset Police have appealed to witnesses who may have spotted anything unusual on the Portway, close to the tunnel that runs beneath the Clifton Suspension Bridge, after 10pm on Saturday night to urgently call Crimestoppers on..."

The fourth item on the news was a poor showing for a man robbed so violently of his life - a couple of decades too old to be the top story, Franklin sighed to himself as the news reporter took on a more jovial tone and moved on to an item of yet another sighting of the Bristol Crocodile in the Avon River.

Franklin could not help but wonder how this poor man was likely to look. Pedestrians struck by cars were never pretty and that was without the irresponsible driving he imagined would be associated with a hit-and-run. He wondered if it would be better to suggest Rowan stayed at the funeral home rather than accompany him to the mortuary.

After the twenty-minute stroll from Temple Meads Station, Franklin was both pleased and surprised to see through the glass door that Meredy and Rowan were seated on the sofa, mugs of tea in their hands, chatting intently together. As he let himself in they curtailed their laughter and tried to compose themselves for their boss.

"Sorry Franklin," Meredy offered apologetically as she stood up and returned to her desk. "We were just having a little natter."

"Not at all," Franklin smiled. "I know it's a pretty slow day." Franklin did enjoy watching such friendships form and could not begrudge either one the chance to escape the drudgeries of yet another day surrounded by death in its many guises. He could also not deny that snap of jealousy he often found at the ease at which people seemed to become friends; that closeness and kindness, that shared silliness, was a sport he could only enjoy as a spectator - those long nights with Verity on the sofa, drinking cheap wine and laughing themselves hoarse at the terrible people on "Changing Rooms" were now just a bittersweet and distant memory of a friendship long past.

"How was Bath?" Rowan asked as she sipped on her mug of tea.

"It was good... It was eventful. I had some news to share with my parents." Franklin thought that if he had to share his secret he might as well get it all done in one day. "It turns out that I have a son."

Rowan and Meredy gasped.

"An adult son..." Franklin quickly interjected before they too began asking about dates and who the mother was. "I didn't know about him until... well, yesterday, in fact. It's been a bit of a shock to be honest."

"Franklin Gallow!' Meredy exclaimed. "You dark horse. You were the very last person I would ever have imagined to have a secret love child!"

Franklin chose to take her words at his kindest reading of them. "Thank you, I think."

"What's his name?" she went on. "How old is he? Where does he live? Oh my, is he angry with you?"

"His name is Alfred Duke but I think he prefers Alf, he's eighteen; he lives in Cheltenham with his mum but he's coming to Bristol in October for university." Franklin was surprised how quickly he was able to recall these details but then, they had been rolling nonstop through his head since he had first learnt the news. "I don't know if he's angry with me - but he does want to meet."

Both Meredy and Rowan murmured cautiously to themselves.

"What? That's good news isn't it?"

"Possibly," Meredy suggested.

"Probably not," Rowan added.

"What? He's extending the olive branch, he wants to get to know his old man." the two women looked unconvinced by this suggestion. "It's not my fault anyway!" Franklin almost felt like stamping his foot petulantly to emphasise his sudden sense of indignation. "I never knew he existed - if Verity had told me I would have been there from the start to.. you know, help out."

Rowan was shaking her head slowly. "It's not that simple. He could still resent you, it won't matter if you have a valid excuse or not, the fact is that you weren't a part of his life growing up - that can be a pretty deep wound to stitch up with a single meeting."

"And he's a teenager too – a teenage boy," Meredy chimed in. "Everybody says girls are harder in adolescence but my eldest, Crystal, was the sweetest thing as she turned into a woman- never had any problems at all, but then came Hayden - he took to puberty like he had been thrown into the army; everyday it was a different challenge, some outrage, some disaster. Boys can be tricky - it can be hard to know what they're thinking because they don't always know how to express themselves. Crystal – she could scream the house down when she was mad, but Hayden; he just felt the weight of the world like a burden, suffering in silence…"

Slightly floored by these insightful yet devastating pronouncements on the future prospects of meeting his son, Franklin bleated only a dismissive, "I think it's time we all got back to work, don't you?" as he walked between the pair, Franklin was certain he caught sight of a worried glance shared between them.

Franklin pushed aside any sense of agitation as he typed "1-7-7-6" into the keypad of the death chamber and asked Rowan, "How did you get on with Mrs Freeman?"

"I think she's ready for her big show," she answered softly. "I'll let you be the judge."

Upon opening the door and being hit by that familiar gust of cold and smell of antibacterial cleaners, Franklin caught sight of the elderly woman lying in a cool blue nightie on the steel bed in the centre of the room. He could not believe what he was seeing - the woman, impossible to imagine now as a corpse, looked near beautiful. Her grey skin, once so thin it appeared almost translucent was as rich and as warm in hue as if blood still passed through her veins. Her lips, slightly parted in the centre to show just a glimpse of tooth and to suggest a tranquil smile were soft and pink and looked moist and alive.

"How did you do that to the lips? They always look so dry when I do them."

"Chapstick," Rowan answered casually. "I just put it on thick over the lipstick and it seemed to do the job."

"I would never have thought of that. What a marvellous idea!"

Rowan allowed herself a proud grin.

The rest of the makeup on the woman's face was so subtle and finely applied that it was almost as if none were there at all - as if somehow Rowan's efforts had breathed some kind of youth and life back into Mrs Freeman's body; the face, framed by long grey hair that fell in waves on either side looked more blissful and contented that any dead person he could recall having made up himself.

"This is staggering," Franklin effused after stumbling for the right word to use. "How on earth did I ever manage to do without you? Mrs Freeman's family will be so… well, as this is the last time they will ever see her, I cannot imagine a more dignified way to remember her."

Rowan was nodding slowly. "Thank you, that's very kind of you to say… but, I'm not going to do this every time."

"Sorry?"

"When I came for my interview you said you were going to train me up in every aspect of the job. Just because I have a talent for this… I don't want to end up as your makeup girl."

Franklin held out his hand. "It's a deal - the whole show or nothing at all."

She shook it warmly. "Deal."

"Well. There's no time like the present."

"Do you know that you only ever say that when we're about to do something horrid."

Franklin nodded sympathetically. "I have a feeling this is going to be pretty horrid. It's a body collection from the police station mortuary. Mid forties guy, hit-and-run - he might be a bit smashed up."

Rowan shrugged her shoulders. "Well then… No time like the present."

Rather than the hearse, which had long high windows to best view the casket and flowers, the pair climbed into a navy blue van bereft of any markings. The back was completely empty and free of light - the retrieval of a body was not a matter for public consumption, this was to be done discretely and quickly.

As Franklin drove them beneath the high suspension bridge and through the tunnel towards the police station, Rowan asked Franklin: "Is this where the accident happened?"

Franklin was taken aback. "Yes it is, how did you know?"

"The police put up a sign back there asking if anyone saw anything."

"Oh, I see."

The tunnel was long and lit by dusky orange streetlamps, which gave the length of it a moody, dirty air. Rowan tried to picture how it would have happened - a man on the Portway, the long, serpentine road that slipped through the Avon Gorge, beneath the high cliffs either side and beside the dark and silty river. The tunnel had been built to protect vehicles from the mighty Clifton Suspension Bridge, 75 metres above their heads, a place once favoured by suicides who had often plummeted to their deaths on to the tarmac below, sometimes taking other lives as they smashed into the road.

Once they arrived at their location, high on a hill overlooking the city, the sight of the building took Rowan aback - this was unlike any police station she had seen before. No concrete and steel monstrosity from the sixties, this was instead a Victorian brownstone fortress, replete with turrets and battlements, everything, short of a portcullis and drawbridge to say, "beware" and "keep out." It stood grand and ominous against a slate grey sky. Franklin gradually turned the van around and then curiously, Rowan thought, he backed it slowly up against one of the walls of the building until it gently touched. "Perfect," he said, intriguingly to himself.

Franklin led her not to the main entrance, but to a tiny side door, almost too small for an adult human to comfortably fit through. He pressed the doorbell once and Rowan heard it buzz inside the station.

"Is that you, Franklin?" asked a scratchy voice over the intercom.

"Certainly is, Ray."

"Just a second."

There was a frosted glass pane in the door to the mortuary through which Rowan could see a dark figure below the ground, silhouetted against an icy blue light and drawing closer and higher until the door creaked open. Rowan was almost disappointed to find the man rather ordinary looking, middle-aged with receding hair but not as ghoulish as she had pictured. Perhaps, she wondered, she had thought of undertakers in the same was as morticians once.

Franklin shook the man's hand. "Rowan, this is Ray, the mortuary technician. You might get to see a fair bit of him over the years. Ray, this is Rowan, my new assistant."

The pair shook hands and Rowan was pleasantly surprised that the man did not seem to react either to her age, her race or her gender and instead offered her a welcoming smile and a small bow.

"Follow me," he began as he led the two of them down a set of stone steps and into a steel room of strip lights and that familiar smell of cleaning products in an unventilated space. "I'm sure your brother has filled you in on some of the details. A pretty straightforward case this one, but rather a sad one - I hate the ones my age, it does something terrible to you doesn't it?"

Franklin mumbled in agreement.

Rowan saw that the set of lockers in which the corpses were held was almost exactly the same setup that Franklin used at the home; only this was on a larger scale and able to accommodate far many bodies than Gallow & Sons could. Stacks upon stacks of little doors lined the walls and Rowan couldn't help but wonder how many held corpses - just how many people died in unexpected or suspicious circumstances every single day in a city of half a million people?

Ray produced a key and unlocked one of the little doors at chest height to the man. Franklin wheeled over a steel framed stretcher and raised it to a suitable height so that the body could be slid from the locker and out into the room.

The figure, obscured beneath a maroon coloured plastic cover that was zipped all the way down its length, looked large and wide. Before Rowan had time to prepare herself, Ray had unzipped the bag and exposed the corpse from head to chest. Rowan let out a little squeal of horror - it was not that he was horribly broken or battered, for neither was true, it was that he was clearly the same fat, bearded man who had attended both Henrik and Donna's funerals.

"Don't mind her," Franklin said to Ray. "She's new and still a little squeamish."

"Sorry," Ray apologised. "If I'd have known."

Rowan simply shook her head but still could not speak.

Franklin and Ray checked the number on the body bag along with the one which the corpse had been booked in with, then they checked details against a photograph of the man in life to ensure it was the right person before both men signed a series of forms that released the body into Franklins care.

From the elevated bed, the corpse was slid into a lift, which would transport him upwards to ground level. Ray, Franklin and Rowan ascended the stone stairs into the late afternoon light.

Still not quite believing what was happening, Rowan numbly assisted Franklin from inside the van to haul the stretcher that held Benjamin Tramor's body inside in such a way that anyone looking would see only a van which had parked a little too close to the wall and have no idea that a corpse was being passed between them.

Once they had bid farewell to the mortuary attendant and the van had finally pulled away from the police station, Rowan finally allowed her eyes to meet Franklin's.

"I know, I saw it too," Franklin said to Rowan's enormous relief. "What the hell are we going to do about it?"

24.

The silence seemed to fill every inch of space as the van bounced down the hill towards the Portway, only the delicate patter of light rain falling on the windscreen and the occasional shriek of wipers going laboriously back and forth could be heard.

The pair had not spoken since they had acknowledged that the corpse they were now in temporary possession of was unmistakably the same man who had first linked two seemingly unrelated fatalities, a coincidence maybe, had he not now joined them in death and in doing so provided evidence of something far more sinister.

Incapable of standing the crushing force of the quiet, Rowan turned the dial of the radio and it hissed into life. She could not have chosen a worse time, for as the van turned into the tunnel which had been the last place Benjamin Tramor had known in life, the local news were reporting on what little was known of his death.

"...are currently visiting mechanics across the city and inspecting cars which match those seen on the Portway CCTV cameras at the time of the incident. Police are asking the public to be alert to any recent damage seen to cars in their neighbourhood."

The report then cut to a police officer with a gruff, somewhat disinterested voice who informed the listeners that: "We as yet have no reason to suspect that this was a case of dangerous driving, it is possible the driver could have thought they had hit a large animal or something. It was a dark night so he might not 'ave seen 'im."

Franklin turned the radio off, irritably. "Nice to know they're putting their best men on the job - did they just wake that policeman up before the interview?"

"But is he right? Would a car really sustain much damage if it hit a person?"

"Oh yes. I hit a muntjac deer last year on the Downs. First time I'd ever seen one and bam, it messed up the entire front of my car - those things are tiny and Ben Tramor, well... he was no small man - you'd have to hit him with quite a force to kill him and I can't imagine the car would end up looking too great."

"What happened?"

"Well, the driver must have been going at one hell of a speed when.."

"…No, I mean what happened to the deer?" her voice heavy with a concern that took Franklin by surprise.

"It died," Franklin replied.

"Oh."

"It was quick though, it can't have known what happened… I wasn't right for days and couldn't go out driving at night for ages without thinking about it."

The note of sympathy for the deer seemed to be all she needed to hear. "So. Do you think there's any chance now that all three of these deaths were just a coincidence?"

Franklin thought for some time. "Well, there's a chance of course that this is all just terrible luck – unlikely, but unlikely things happen every day. If we thought that all three were murders then why commit them? Did they all know something? If so, what was it that they needed to be silenced for and who else knows? If anybody else is in on the secret then I imagine they would be in very serious danger indeed. Here's the other thing though that is rather odd - Henrik was killed, if he was killed, in such a way as to make it look like suicide, and if Donna was killed, it was done in a way to make it look like an accident - two ways to minimise the odds of the police getting involved. Why then kill poor Ben Tramor in a manner that is going to arouse suspicion?"

It was Rowan's time to think against the silence. "Perhaps all three were meant for the same night. Imagine that Henrik, Donna and Ben were all supposed to be killed on that Saturday, but for whatever reason, Ben is the only one who doesn't turn up to his appointment with murder. Ben knew the other two were dead, we saw him at their funerals, but what if the killer got desperate and had to get messy. What if there was no time to plan a clever method, just get in the car and run him over…"

"That could well be the case," Franklin concurred as the car turned into the driveway of Gallow & Sons. "The only thing missing is a way to connect Donna and Henrik. If we could prove the pair of them knew each other then the police would certainly have to link all three together."

Franklin seemed to be struggling to contain a giddy excitement at this parlour game of speculation but in Rowan it induced a stabbing pain of guilt. She had that evidence; she knew very well that Donna and Henrik were connected.

He said nothing more to her as he stepped out of the car and into the drizzle where he pulled out his phone and made a call. Rowan followed in order to listen to as much of it as she could.

Franklin gave Meredy a wave through the glass door into the reception where she sat. His brother's line was ringing.

"Frank!" Edison beamed at the other end on answering the call. "I've been hearing all about you from Mum and Dad."

"They told you already?"

"Yes, of course they did. You bad boy - absent dad and all. I always thought that was more my style than yours."

"Edison, I haven't got time for this, something significant has happened. Do you remember me telling you about that man at the funerals, last week?"

"Not really."

"The Danish kid who killed himself, and the woman who fell in the harbour; she was drunk."

"Oh yes. Look Frank, I went through all of the records and…"

"…Listen to me. The man who went to both of their funerals is dead. I've just picked up his body from the police station - he's the hit and run you told me about."

There was brief pause. "Shit."

"Quite."

"Frank. You're saying something pretty big here if you're saying what I think you are."

"Triple murder, is that what you mean?"

"You said it, not me and you can't go throwing accusations like that around like confetti. Believe it or not, the police do know what they're doing."

Franklin snorted derisively.

"I don't care what you think, Frank, we work bloody hard to keep the streets safe and we don't take too kindly to being told that we aren't doing our job right."

"Even when you're not?"

Edison continued undaunted. "I looked through those files, and there was nothing, absolutely bugger all connecting the two of them together. People die all the time, it's sad but it's part of life. It's just the law of averages, stuff like this will happen once in a while and you've just got to… just try not to… just stop seeing patterns in random noise."

"You don't sound so sure, Edison. What if the pattern is so clear it can't just be chance."

"I've got to go now Frank."

"What if there are more murders?"

"I'm hanging up the phone." and with that he was gone.

Franklin stared dumbly at his phone in disbelief, incapable of comprehending the hoops of denial his brother would so gleefully leap through without ever touching the sides, just so he would not have to be proved wrong - just so he didn't have to do any more work. The hand on his shoulder hit him like an electric shock; it was Rowan.

"Was that your brother? What did he say?"

"He thinks it's all some absurd coincidence, he won't listen to reason. Without anything linking Henrik and Donna it just…"

"…I'm sorry Franklin!" Rowan blurted out, her voice wavering on the edge of hysteria. It cut Franklin dead in the tracks of his train of thought.

"Sorry? What for?"

Holding back tears, Rowan cried, "They did know each other. I have Henrik's phone and I went round to Donna's house. The wifi is still running in the house and… his phone latched right onto it, it knew the password and everything. He must have known her well."

Franklin's mouth fell open. "What?"

"I'm sorry, I should have said something but…"

"Is this fun for you? People are dead, Rowan."

"No it isn't, of course it isn't!"

"How in the world do you even have his phone in the first place?"

"His sister gave it to me - Lise, you know, the one with the plaits? I contacted her on Facebook because she thought he was murdered too and I promised I would help and…"

"You did what!" his voice rose in such a storm of unbridled rage that garden birds that had settled down to roost for the evening in the tree above him took flight. Franklin did not care that the woman was already in inconsolable floods of tears. "You contacted the daughter of a client, to get the property of a dead man? Do you have any idea how much trouble you are in? How much trouble *I* am in? You exploited a grieving child to get access to her brother's phone? That is the most irresponsible thing I have ever heard!"

"I know Franklin, but please!"

"Do you know that if this case were reopened, that evidence would be enough to get it thrown out of court? Exploitation of a minor!" Franklin was unsure if this was actually true but it sounded like the kind of safeguard that would have been in place. "Not to mention the reckless damage to my business, if people knew what you had done I'd probably be ruined."

"I know!" Rowan screamed through her tears.

Suddenly a third voice joined the rabble. "Franklin! Step away from that girl at once!'

Franklin turned to see Meredy standing in the doorway of the reception. The rotund woman then came bowling over towards him at such a pace and with such angry strides that the man could not help but take a step backwards. He had never seen her look this ferocious before.

"I don't care what she's done or what you think she's done or anything else - I won't just stand by and watch a fully grown man bully a young woman who is obviously in distress. Have you no shame?"

Meredy pulled Rowan into her chest where her sobs grew softer and less desperate.

"I won't stand for you talking to your employees like that, Franklin; I won't have it," she berated as she poked angrily at the air in front of him with an accusatory finger.

"Well, she's not my employee anymore," Franklin mumbled as he stuffed his hands into the pockets of his suit trousers.

Meredy just shook her head disdainfully at him. "Whatever she's done - I don't care what you're accusing her of, you don't ever talk to anybody like that again. Understand?"

Though he tried his hardest not to, Franklin couldn't resist the urge to nod. In that moment he suddenly realised that perhaps the friendship between Rowan and Meredy, had at least been from the point of view of his receptionist, one of maternal care from a woman whose children had all grown up and flown the nest - and one thing Franklin had learned in his profession was that one of the most frightening forces known to mankind was a mother protecting her child.

"Now come on Rowan, we'll get your bike out of the office," Rowan nodded and let Meredy guide her back to the reception with an arm across her shoulder. "I'm going home early today," she called back to Franklin who could find no way to argue otherwise.

When they returned, Rowan assembled her Brompton bike into its familiar shape and received a hug and a gentle kiss on the cheek from Meredy. She was no longer crying now but her shoulders were still heaving, as if she were not far from starting again. It had been years since Franklin had felt so utterly ashamed of himself.

"Rowan," he called softly as she cycled up the path towards him. She just shook her head and went on.

Franklin so rarely lost his temper and the shock of it had caused a guilt so raw he could feel it like glass embedded in his skin. Perhaps it had been brewing inside him since Rowan and Meredy had discussed the possibilities of his and Alf's first meeting, added to the boneheaded deductions of his cretinous brother and finally over spilling with Rowan's tearful confession.

Yes, she had been foolish but she hadn't been evil. For all of her perceived maturity, Franklin sometimes forgot that there was something vulnerable in that young woman, something damaged that he had never quite been able to fully understand. He felt sick with himself.

He watched from the garden as Meredy heaved on her long overcoat and left without saying goodbye. He pulled out his phone and was about to hit redial to inform his brother of this strange and irresponsible turn of events when it suddenly occurred to him that he would still not listen. So often, those caught out in their own mistakes chose not to own up to them; they instead opt to deny the facts even stronger. Would it really do any good to land Rowan in even more trouble? If the police didn't care, maybe it was up to him to at least find out what he could from Ben's husband.

He replaced the phone in his pocket and returned inside as the sky grew darker. He opened the steel door to the death chamber and wheeled the trolley bed over to the van, transferring the body to the freezer by himself.

He could not shake the sense of shame, so decided that rather than phone Rowan on her way home, he would instead compose a heartfelt and earnest message of apology to her and send it privately over Facebook. On opening his laptop and logging into the site from his living room upstairs, Franklin scrolled through his meagre list of friends until he found Rowan's name. As he opened her profile the first thing he saw was that there had been a posting.

A girl named Orla Birken had offered a video; the still frame of which showed a beautiful, dark skinned woman with shocking red streaks running through her fountain of luxurious hair. When he clicked on the video, an introductory title faded onto the screen.

"Ruby Kaplan: Down Town," and then a moody, sexy voice began, a voice full of the joy and despair of life - a voice that didn't just come from the heart, but came from somewhere deeper, denser. It was a voice so captivating that watching it, Franklin could see the faces of the patrons of the boozy, gloomy looking blues bar as each one in turn fell in love with her until all of them - and he, were utterly spellbound. It was a song that Franklin had known all of his life, but it had never seemed so brooding or so sensual to him before.

When the video was finished, Franklin sat in silence, awed by the devastating talent of Rowan's older sister - until he spied the rest of the message Orla Birken had left.

"I can't believe it's two whole years tomorrow since the angels took you away. I love you and I will never forget you."

25.

When Rowan awoke on the morning of the anniversary of her sister's death, it was not to the familiar, gentle whir of her phone alarm, but instead the aggressive drone of bass from the next-door room. Something, she knew at once, was terribly wrong.

The room had been, and still was, Ruby's. It had been left virtually untouched since the evening she had died, with only the occasional visit from a tearful parent to assure it had not been forever abandoned. The walls still covered with the posters and photographs of a teenager's life cut tragically short, a nineteen-year-old frozen in time, who would never grow up - and never return home.

Pulling on her dressing gown and creeping anxiously from her bedroom, Rowan saw the remnants of her sister's life scattered haphazardly about the corridor. Her mattress and bed had been hauled from her room, the bare frame now stood upright against a wall while her bedding lay like a crumpled corpse upon the floor. Framed pictures and trinkets that once sat on her dressing table littered the carpet like flotsam after a flood. The sight was too strange, too surreal for Rowan's tired eyes to comprehend - and then there was the music, thumping from the empty bedroom.

Still dazed, yet somehow certain that this insane turn of events was related to the almighty row she had heard her parents having the night before, Rowan gingerly tried the door to the room which opened to reveal her mother in a now almost gutted room, standing on a chair in a t-shirt and a pair of knickers and attacking the wallpaper around the ceiling with a garden trowel.

The room smelled of tobacco smoke and booze. A bottle of gin, now almost empty, stood on the sunset orange carpet in the centre of the room, while the woman, singing drunkenly along to the radio with a cigarette between her lips, hacked away at the wallpaper, tearing it away in strips, pulling it apart in frenzied motions, revealing the girlish pink paint beneath that Ruby had once so expertly papered over.

"Mum?" Rowan called out, now certain that this was some troubled dream from which she had not yet found means to escape from. "Mum!"

The woman turned woozily and the chair wobbled beneath her. "Morning Ro," she slurred.

"What the hell are you doing?" Rowan marched across the room and switched the radio off. The room was suddenly gripped by silence, the attack on the room no longer a bizarre fantasy of a troubled mind but on the life and legacy of Ruby herself.

"We can't leave this room like this forever. I thought I'd turn it into a gym."

"What? Why are you doing this?"

"I'm sick of this room, it needs changing."

The woman was pouring with sweat; it ran down her gerbil cheeks in thick streams. Her eyes, tired and intoxicated glared at Rowan across the room, dark holes in a sea of red.

"Where's Dad?"

"He left us," the woman said casually as she returned to the wall. "Said he needs some time alone. I know what that means - it'll be the last we ever see of him, you mark my words. They're all the same, men."

"What do you mean?" Rowan could not believe this.

"He left last night. I don't care - we can get on just fine without him."

"You don't look like you're fine at all. Have you gone to bed yet? Did you drink all of this?" she asked as she held the bottle aloft.

"You put that back where you found it, Ro', I'm not finished yet."

"Yes you are, mum. Get out of this room and leave me to fix it."

This just caused the woman to roar with nasty, drunken laughter. "Fix it? Fit it! How will you do that, it can never be fixed. She's gone forever and we just have to forget about it all. You can't fix it because she's dead and she's never coming home. I kept this room like this because I always thought, somewhere in the back of my head, that she would be back, but she's gone and I hate her for it!"

"Don't say that." Rowan demanded with just enough defiance in her voice to let her mother know that she should go no further.

"I do - I hate her for what happened and I hate her because she... she has it so easy. She caused this and she never had to grieve."

Rowan stared dumbly around the room, the walls, now almost stripped of the seductive, moody purple wallpaper seemed to already be washed clean of the enchantment Ruby still held upon it. "Mum, please stop. Just stop and go to bed."

The woman's eyes narrowed suspiciously. "Aren't you supposed to be getting ready for work?"

"I have a day off," she lied.

Another snort of cruel laughter. "I might have known. You can't even hold down a job at a supermarket - this has to be a record for you. Three weeks is it?"

Rowan leant against the doorframe and watched as the desecration of her sister's room continued unabated. "I'm leaving now," she said as her eyes began to pool with water. "I don't know when I'll be home."

The woman gave no response.

Rowan returned to her room and pulled on a pair of jeans and a crumpled shirt she had found in a charity shop, it had been made for a man and was too large for her but she enjoyed the shapeless way it hung, the way it hid her body in a formless tent of excess fabric and uncomplicated plaid. She neither checked her reflection nor packed anything to take with her before she went once more to her mother.

"I'm going now," she called to the woman.

"I heard you the first time," she spat. Rowan was just about to turn and leave when her mother decided to add, "Do you know what?"

"What?"

The woman did not turn from the wall. "I wish it had been you instead."

In the ferocious stillness that swelled into the room, Rowan could only offer, "So do I," before she turned and headed for the front door. She was half way down the stairs when her mother turned the radio back on.

As she was pulling on her Doctor Marten boots, the doorbell rang. It was an unwelcome intrusion on what should have been a richly deserved door slam, but nevertheless she opened it. Franklin Gallow stood sheepishly on the step, a bunch of daffodils nestled in his arm like a baby.

"I'm sorry," he blurted. "I was wrong and stupid - and cruel, I was just..."

"Fine." Rowan conceded. "Do you have your car with you?"

"Um... yes."

"Please, can we just go somewhere today? Somewhere... nice."

Franklin looked confused, but seemed to understand that this was no time to either argue or ask questions. "Where do you want to go?"

"Take me to the beach. Weston Super Mare."

"Your wish is my command."

Inside the womb like safety of the little Smart car, Franklin seemed more inclined to pry.

"Are you alright, Rowan? You seem distressed, is everything ok?"

"I'm fine. I'll be fine,"

The car entered Gloucester Road. Franklin nimbly played with the satellite navigator on his dashboard until it wove a path through the city to the beach for them to follow.

"Thank you for the flowers," she said, looking down at the bunch of daffodils on her lap.

"It's the least I could do. I'm not usually like that, really I'm not. Meredy has worked with me for years and she has never seen me like that. I slept horribly last night, I think everything with Alf was just... stressing me a bit."

"Does this mean I'm not fired anymore?"

I don't think you ever were, not really anyway. Pretty sure you could have wrung me through a mangle at one of those no win, no fee places - have me up for unfair dismissal or something – but that was not why I apologised."

"What's happening at the home today?"

"I gave Meredy the day off. Peterman's running the place so I'm fully prepared for the building to be burnt to the ground by the time I get back. There's not much to do really.

I'm seeing Ben's husband tomorrow to make some arrangements."

"Can I come too?"

"Of course, if you want to. You might spot something I miss."

Rowan caught his eye in the rear view mirror. "You mean as far as the arrangements are concerned?"

"Well that, yes, anything else that might be of interest too."

Rowan offered him a gentle smile and he responded in kind. Soon the bustle of the city had made way for trees and open countryside as the car sped towards the coast. The pair sat in almost complete silence as Rowan revelled in the kind feelings she felt for her boss, the genuine warmth that could only come in the calm of a subsided storm. It was enough, almost, for her to forget about her mother frantically stripping Ruby's room bare and the devastating thing she had said to her before she had fled.

As they approached the beach, Rowan wound down the window to let the salty air fill the car. "I haven't been here for years," she said.

"Me neither."

Weston Super Mare was a town built on the edge of the Bristol Channel, a silty wash of grey water that spilt across colourless sand beneath a sky the colour of Tupperware. In its heyday, the town had been a destination for day tripping Victorians from the city, who boarded the trains in their hundreds to escape the grime and dust for the more tranquil pursuits of picnics and donkey rides. It had never recovered those times and was now but a ghost of the glory days; an artefact of history. Before summer, almost all the shops, those selling buckets and spades and rock and ice cream, were boarded up. Chains locked playgrounds and fountains were turned off. It was a brooding town, waiting for the season to return.

Franklin parked along the promenade and bought a ticket for the day. Rowan, placed her daffodils on the ledge behind her seat and joined him by the low wall between the pavement and the beach.

"It hasn't changed a bit," Rowan informed him.

"I suppose it hasn't."

"We used to come here when we were kids - Ruby and I."

"Oh. I think I did too," the man sighed heavily. "Rowan, I saw that message on your Facebook wall. I had no idea, I really didn't. I'm so sorry about Ruby."

Rowan simply stared out to sea. "The third of June...Two years today. It doesn't seem possible."

Franklin squeezed her shoulder tenderly. "I suppose it can't. Do you mind if I ask how it happened?'

"Of course," she replied. "But first you're getting me some chips. I'm starving."

Franklin nodded with a sympathetic smile.

The only place open and serving food was manned by an elderly gentleman who seemed surprised to find these two stragglers asking for chips before noon. Nevertheless, he seemed keen on the company as he started the fryer and chatted to the pair. He served their food in polystyrene trays and smothered their chips in tomato ketchup, before he bid them a merry farewell. Franklin and Rowan walked down a slipway onto the beach. The chips were hot and greasy, the ketchup sweet and cheap. It was the most delicious thing Rowan could remember eating in months.

"I like it here," she said as a cold wind blasted from off the sea and squawking seagulls gathered above them.

"It's rather bleak," Franklin offered.

"I know. It's just what I needed."

"So," Franklin did not want to press her on the matter but felt compelled to do so. "Ruby."

Rowan just nodded. "She was murdered. Two years ago this evening."

A chip fell from Franklin's mouth and a gull swooped down to claim it before it even touched the sand. "Oh my god, Rowan, I am so sorry. What happened?'

Rowan just shrugged her shoulders. "Nobody knows, not for sure anyway. She was stabbed - twelve times. In the chest and neck; she was at a gig with her band in St. Pauls in some nightclub - it's closed down now; nobody wanted to go after that happened. She said she was meeting somebody but nobody seems to know who. They found her body on a patch of grass just outside of Leigh Woods."

"Rowan, I had no idea. I saw that video and I thought it had been an accident of some kind. She was good..."

"She was better than good, she was magical. Now those little videos are all we have to remember how great she was - she was going to be something, she was born for it, she was destined for it."

Franklin could only nod in agreement. He had never in his life witnessed a song of such emotional courage; she had not simply sung a song about the joys of urban nightlife, she had turned it into a hymn of freedom. She had become it - a mere vessel through which the song in its raw, unvarnished perfection could move.

"They took my dad in for questioning, and they even arrested her boyfriend but nothing could stick. They still don't know who did it. A little while back we were hearing from the police all of the time, saying that they were following leads and that they had more evidence, but now we haven't heard from them in months. They've given up."

"I'm sure that's not true."

It must be, Franklin. They don't care anymore - the press were never that interested to begin with, just another black girl, probably into drugs or a hooker, definitely up to no good and asking for it."

"I'm sure they'll find them. It really is very rare that murders aren't solved."

"Is it? The police don't seem too concerned about catching whoever killed those three people in Bristol, why should I believe that they will be any different with Ruby?"

There was no answer that Franklin could offer. "I suppose this explains why you met with Lise, then."

Rowan shrugged her shoulders. "I think you're right. I feel like I need to do something, I can't just let this killer go."

Franklin was unsure if she meant the killer of her sister or the three other victims. In a way, he decided, it made no difference; she was doing whatever she could."

"How were the chips?" he asked.

Rowan smiled as she popped the last of them into her mouth. "Absolutely perfect. Just what I needed."

The pair walked together for some time, with nothing but the sound of the breakwater to whisper through the silence.

26.

Rowan opened her front door and slipped out into the morning sunshine. Franklin was already waiting for her in his Smart car, he waved through the passenger window almost childishly and she responded in kind. She was dressed in the formal blouse and dark skirt combination he had grown accustomed to. He would never have said so, but there had been something disconcerting about seeing her the day before in an oversized shirt and a pair of jeans - a slovenliness he realized had reflected the inner turmoil of her suffering.

"Morning," he said as she sat in beside him. "How was it?"

"Mum's still asleep – hung over; I don't think she even knew I came home yesterday, if she did, she certainly didn't care."

"And your dad?"

She shrugged her shoulders. "Haven't heard a word from him. Maybe this really is it - is it strange that I feel nothing? I really don't care if they stay together or not."

Franklin turned the key in the ignition and the car purred into life. "I don't think there's any right way to react."

"Did you know that most parents divorce after the murder of a child? Two-thirds of them?"

"No I didn't," said Franklin as the car filtered onto Gloucester Road. "That's actually very sad."

Rowan shook her head dismissively. "Maybe it's for the best. There's a whole lot of blame involved in the fallout."

She had not revealed to her boss what her mother had said to her the previous morning; nor did she have any plans to do so. It was not that the words had been so unspeakably unkind, but because Rowan and her mother had known, silently, like an unspoken pact, that they were true.

"Tell me about Ben's husband. His details are in there," Franklin nodded to a notebook on the dashboard and Rowan flicked through the pages until she found the last page of writing in Meredy's girlish handwriting.

Rowan waited for the satellite navigator to finish its instructions in a robotically female voice before she read: "William Calverston, 44 of Redand, Bristol..." she began.

"...Bill and Ben?" Franklin allowed himself a little chuckle. "Who are they?"

Franklin just raised an eyebrow to her. "Never mind, you're too young."

Rowan carried on, undaunted. "He and Ben had been in a civil partnership since 2009. No children. William wants a cremation and a simple service with no religious content."

"Sounds straightforward enough."

The car turned off Blackboy Hill, and into a narrow culse-sac where Franklin immediately began fretting about the likelihood of getting a hearse around the tight roundabout at the end of the road. The house itself was unassuming and grey with a door which opened straight onto the pavement.

Parking and getting out of the car, Franklin spun on his feet at the sound of a shrill whistle. Gliding slowly past was a sports car with a man hanging out of the driver's window who called out to Rowan, "Nice tits love, give us a feel!"

Franklin was stunned but Rowan looked unfazed. "What in the world…?" he asked, his jaw agape as the car sped off.

"What, that? It happens all the time."

Franklin's eyes darted about in a sense of bewildered confusion. "To you?"

"Don't look so surprised."

"I didn't mean it like that."

"Franklin, it happens to girls all the time. If you're under thirty and walking down a street, some guy is going to want to tell you how much he wants to have sex with you."

"When did this start happening?" Franklin asked, certain that it must be some youthful invention along with Twitter and happy slapping.

"They started doing it to me when I was about 13."

Franklin was still shaking his head. "That's disgusting."

Rowan nodded her head casually. "You don't need to tell me."

Still out of sorts, Franklin rang the doorbell and an electronic rendition of Westminster Quarters played within the house. The door opened to reveal a ghost of a man. Grey skin with red eyes encircled by dark, puffy folds. The grieving man was probably handsome, but his face registered nothing but loss and sleeplessness. He wore a dressing gown and slippers.

"Good morning, Mr Calverston. My name is Franklin and this is my assistant Rowan."

The man just nodded and stepped aside to allow the pair of them in. The house was dark as the curtains were still drawn. William fumbled around in the gloom to drag one open, and a shaft of light fell upon a small living room with a pair of sofas, over one of which a duvet and pillows had been scattered and thrown asunder. Rowan was convinced that the man had been sleeping only minutes before. A half full glass of water rested on the coffee table beside the sofa, beads of bubbles clinging to its sides.

"I'm sorry about the mess," William mumbled. "I have taken to sleeping down here... the bed feels too big at the moment."

Franklin nodded sympathetically and sat down on the unoccupied sofa. Rowan joined him and found herself gazing around the room; it was small but in a way that was cozy rather than cramped ,and despite the bedclothes and William's protestations, it was neat and welcoming.

"First, let me begin by saying how desperately sorry I am," this was Franklin's classic opener. Rowan was sure he must have used it a thousand times or more.

The man just nodded.

"Now, I know that this is a terribly hard time for you but many people find the act of arranging a service can prove to be quite a distraction when..."

"...Do you know anything about the house?' William interrupted.

"Sorry?"

"The house is in Ben's name and I was worried it was going to go to his family or something. His sister would love to turf me out onto the streets like yesterday's empty milk bottle. See, we didn't get married, because we weren't allowed to, so we got one of them civil partner things - it's just the same, and they said I could call him my husband, but I thought, you know in law and all... We were gonna get it upgraded to a proper marriage but it takes money and we're a bit skint at the moment," William seemed to reel in horror at his words. "*I'm* a bit skint now."

Franklin, not missing a beat and suggesting to Rowan that this was not the first time such a question had been asked of him replied, "We actually don't deal with the estates or wills of the deceased but I do know that in law you will be given the exact same rights as a married couple if you are in a civil partnership. You will be his next of kin."

The harried man sighed with relief. "Didn't want to have yet another thing to worry about."

"So," Franklin continued. "About the service. We offer a variety of packages that begin at very reasonable rates and go all..."

"...Do you mind if we go outside? I really need a smoke," he blurted.

"Of course," Franklin agreed and he and Rowan followed the man through a narrow corridor and into a sparse kitchen where a door opened onto a tiny courtyard with a single plastic chair and a flowerpot as the only decorations. William sat and pulled a packet of cigarettes from his pocket, offered them both one and after they had declined, lit his up and began to speak. "Ben hated me smoking, that's why I always had to do it out here. I reckon that can change now but I don't think it will, seems disrespectful don't you think?"

"I think it's entirely up to you," Franklin suggested, cautiously.

"See, he hated my smoking but I hated his eating. He put on a ton of weight these past five years and only just started to lose it these past few weeks. He started jogging in the evenings after work," the man laughed coldly to himself. "I always said the food was going to kill him and he said the fags would do for me; so we had an agreement to turn a blind eye to those things. Seems so stupid now but it was the exercise what killed him in the end. Fuckin' maniac, hope they catch the man what done it soon." William's eyes widened as he turned to Rowan. "Sorry, didn't mean to swear."

Rowan just shook her head kindly.

"That's the other thing he hated - swearing. You know, when you're with someone though, you just put up with that stuff because... because, he made me happy." William turned away from them and wiped his eyes on the sleeve of his dressing gown. "It all seems so pointless now - getting

152

worked up over things; the eating, the smoking. He spent money like we could afford it, his car got smashed a while back and he just took the other driver's money as compensation at the scene, but it weren't even enough to cover the costs properly. What a waste of time that all seems now; wasting our time together over stupid things that didn't amount to squat now he's gone."

The silence that fell on the courtyard was instantaneous. Rowan looked over at Franklin who shuffled awkwardly on the spot.

"Look, Mr Franklin," the man finally went on. "I ain't got much to give you but I want to give my man a good send off. If we can do it cheap but classy..."

"...We can find a way, I promise you."

The man nodded and tried a grateful smile. "Thanks."

After presenting them with Ben's old suit, which the man tearfully informed them, had been the one he had worn at their partnership ceremony. William seemed disinclined to go on after that, so, when Franklin asked if there was anything more, he simply shook his head and walked them to the front door.

Hands were shaken and farewells and sympathy offered. As Franklin and Rowan turned to leave, William asked, "Is he doing ok there?"

"He's fine. I promise," Franklin said warmly. "We're taking care of him."

"Good and thank you. They made me look at the body and it was horrid."

"I'm so sorry," was all Franklin could give and the man slowly closed the door.

After affixing the suit in its bag to the hook on the passenger side of the car, Rowan and Franklin set off onto Blackboy Hill where Rowan almost blurted, "I don't think he did it."

"Huh?"

"I don't think it was him that killed Ben, or the others."

Franklin kept his eyes fixed on the road ahead. "Neither do I, but go on."

"There's no way he would bring up the will so early on - it would only cause suspicion, plus, if he was actually guilty, don't you think he would have checked all the legal implications *beforehand?*"

"True," Franklin agreed. "But you're assuming that the motive was money."

"Well, what else could it be? You look as if you know something..."

"Rowan, it seems awfully tasteless having this discussion with the dead man's suit hanging up next to you."

Rowan huffed irritably. "No less tasteless than discussing his murder with his corpse in the back of the van the other night."

Franklin could not argue with that. "Well, do you remember him mentioning a car crash?"

"Yes. What of it?"

"Donna's son mentioned that a few weeks before she died she was involved in a car accident and he was surprised that she hadn't had her license revoked... If she was drunk at the time of the crash, and by all accounts she was *always* drunk, she would have every reason to not want to involve the authorities. William said Ben settled at the scene, maybe Donna did too, because she didn't want to lose her license. Maybe it really wasn't her fault."

Rowan pondered this for a moment. "So you mean... Ben and Donna crashed into each other and then paid for the other one's repairs?"

"Well, there could always be a third person involved."

"You mean Henrik?"

Franklin simply stared at her until she responded. "I do have a little theory myself. Something from Henrik's phone that I noticed a while back."

"Oh?"

"Have you ever heard of Manhandlr?"

"I can't say I have. What is it?"

"It's an app. You download it onto your phone and it locates all the other men using it in the area who are up for a little..."

"...Love and affection?" Franklin said with a smile.

"Something like that. I didn't think much of it at the time because, lots of people get stuff like that just to play around, but Henrik had it on his phone."

Franklin released a quick burst of a gasp. "So you think..."

"Maybe, Henrik and Ben had met each other for a little playtime."

As the car sped onto Whiteladies Road, Franklin found himself constructing a series of events in his head that he dared only speak of once they fell into place. "Let's just say that there was a crash. The night before he died, Henrik broke things off with his girlfriend - maybe he had realized he was gay and *maybe* he was having an affair with Ben and had been for some time - he might not have been ready to tell the whole world yet. That man definitely looked overwhelmed at the funeral..."

Rowan jumped in. "That means that if there was a crash, involving Donna in one car, drunk, and Ben and Henrik in the other. All three of them would have something to hide and would probably want to settle at the scene rather than let an investigation have their secrets revealed."

Franklin held a hand out to Rowan and the pair high fived before mutually sensing that this was far from an appropriate act in the circumstances.

"Do you think we can go to the police with that?" asked Rowan.

"Well, as a theory it's a strong one, but the problem is it's just a theory. We've not a shred of evidence to back it up and Edison could knock it down in a blink. Perhaps it's time we delved a little deeper."

Rowan could barely hide the smile that began to form on her face.

27.

It had been a curious day for Franklin; that morning he had decided that enough of an interval had elapsed between Donna Hawley's funeral and the time it was prudent to give her ashes to her son, Evan. He had found early on in his career that doing so immediately after a service was too much for many. Once the funeral was over to have the remains of a loved one in an urn was simply too huge a trauma. He had done the same with Henrik's ashes the day before and it has been as difficult as he had expected He had wanted to get all the unpleasantness out of the way in one go, so had tried contacting Evan but nobody had answered the phone until that morning.

Lucy Farmer, Evan's wife – the pale and ghostly creature who had drifted through her mother-in-law's funeral- picked up the phone and agreed that as Evan was at work, she would be there to collect them.

He met her on the landing outside of her flat at noon and presented the urn in a white box. Lucy had gingerly opened them and peered inside the cylindrical, wooden container.

"Good God," she had whispered into it. "Is that all there is of her?"

People rarely believed that an entire body could be reduced to so little. It was quite astonishing on a cellular level just how much of a human corpse was made up of nothingness. Franklin was also aware that this was no time to point out such a piece of interesting biological trivia.

"I can't believe she's gone," Lucy whimpered. For a moment her eyes met Franklin's and she seemed to be pleading with him; it was then that she said a most curious thing. "I can't help thinking that this… all of this, was my fault. I *know* it was." She held his gaze, almost challenging him to respond.

"What do you mean, Lucy?"

She simply shook her head and said, "I need to feed my baby. I'm sorry, I must go." With that she turned and closed the door behind her.

Franklin was momentarily stunned. It took all his will not

to hammer on the door and demand an answer, instead he chose to put it down to one of those peculiar stages of grief that everyone – particularly those who have lost an addict, believe that there should have been *something* they could have done to save them.

Nevertheless, he could not shake off her words long into the evening.

On any other Friday night, Franklin would be meeting his brother at the Tobacco Factory for a few pints and their regular bouts of animosity disguised as brotherly affection. This however was a working evening and he was busily preparing the visiting room for Mrs Freeman's guests. The gathering was scheduled for seven o'clock but he and Rowan had allowed themselves a good couple of hours to get everything ready for what was often a difficult, sometimes brutal, confrontation. For many, with the inevitability of death - came the reality that not even the strongest bonds of love are enough to keep those around us alive forever. Ordinarily, he would have felt compelled to warn Rowan of these simple truths, but he had learned very quickly that she, more than anyone, knew them to be real.

"Is Meredy gone?" Franklin asked as Rowan entered the parlour. She was dressed in the same all-black ensemble she wore to every funeral and Franklin was dressed likewise, including the service-standard top hat that offered him an air of solemnity.

"Just now."

"OK, let's get the body then."

From the death chamber where she waited in her oak casket, lined with vivid purple satin, Mrs Freeman was wheeled into the room and the pair of them hoisted her onto the wooden plinth in the centre. Rowan immediately set about touching up her makeup that had only slightly diminished since it was first applied.

The flowers had arrived earlier that afternoon and Franklin began placing them in arrangements around and about the casket. The room had a high ceiling and a window took up one entire wall, so that during the day, the space would be flooded with light and beautiful views out across the flower brimming garden; the remaining walls were all lined with wood and unfurnished by any decoration. There was not a trace of religious imagery, for though there was a little annex called the "All Faiths' Prayer Room" Gallow & Sons was conspicuously secular.

"I think she's ready for her close-up, Mr Franklin," Rowan beamed as she stepped away from the casket. Franklin, smiling at his assistant's wildly anachronistic reference inspected her work.

"Superb," he concluded. "Though I didn't imagine anything less."

The old woman looked resplendent. Perhaps more vivid than any corpse he had ever seen; were she to suddenly open her eyes and gasp into breath Franklin would not have been surprised.

Finally a framed photograph of the woman - a grinning portrait of a wizened but handsome elderly lady with a cake in the shape of a "90" upon her lap, was placed at the side of her casket. Franklin consulted his watch: seven o'clock precisely. "Time for the show," he said.

The mourners began to arrive shortly afterwards. As expected, most of them were about her age or only slightly younger. These visits had become a ritual for the aged - a reminder perhaps that death was not as fearful as those dark nights of the soul may make it seem. Once the parlour had begun to fill significantly, Franklin popped the cork on a bottle of sparkling wine and Rowan went about the crowd with a tray of glasses, offering Franklin the occasional bemused glance once it became clear just how jovial the mood in the room was becoming. Chattering voices, even laughter, could be heard until finally a voice - an old but distinguished gentleman's voice piped up with: "Can I offer a toast to Ellie Freeman. I think we can all say that we're going to miss her very much. She drank like a fish, smoked like a chimney and swore like a fucking sailor. To Ellie Freeman and all who sailed in her!"

"Here, here!" the room erupted into a chorus of laughter followed by the chink of glasses. "To Ellie Freeman!"

Rowan scurried over to Franklin. "Did you hear that?"

Franklin had his arms folded across his chest and a grin upon his face. "Well I never! It takes all types."

Rowan helped herself to a glass of wine and raised it to the casket in which Ellie Freeman now rested. "Good on you, Mrs Freeman - what an awesome way to be remembered; as a bad influence all the way to the grave."

"These viewings are very few and far between nowadays, if they happen at all it's just a quick viewing before the funeral. I suppose it's quite a nice tradition really."

Rowan nodded thoughtfully. "I never saw Ruby before the service," she revealed.

Franklin, who was not used to his assistant's candor in reference to her sister's death could only offer, "Oh?"

"I wanted to, but I'm glad they didn't let me. She was pretty bad and that's not what I want to see when I think of her. I want to see that picture of me and her getting hammered in the south of France."

"I like that picture too," Franklin added, recalling that joyous wide-eyed smile on Rowan's Facebook page.

After an hour or so, the visitors began to file out until only a handful remained. The chatter remained light and casual for the most part, with only a smattering of watery eyes about the room, though even as handkerchiefs dabbed at cheeks, the laughter continued as guests recalled more scandalous tales of this woman's life.

As the last of the mourners departed, some the worse for drink than Franklin was expecting, he and Rowan waited by the door to shake hands and bid a good night and a safe journey home. Ellie Freeman's funeral was to be held the following afternoon and Franklin was only slightly concerned what kind of state her drinking friends would be in at that time.

The last man to leave was younger than the others, and by the way the guests offered him kind words and condolences as they departed, Franklin concluded that this was likely the old woman's son. His daughter had been in charge of all the arrangements up to this point but had clearly decided this evening would prove too much.

"I am very sorry for your loss," Franklin offered as he shook the man's hand.

He simply shrugged his shoulders. "She had a fair run - 92 isn't that bad is it? Especially someone who lived like her."

The man looked thoughtfully at his polished shoes. "Mum lived life like it was a challenge, like it was something to use up. She wrung every last piece of joy out of it right up until the end." The words pricked unexpectedly at Rowan's eyes; the man turned to her just as she was wiping a tear away. "Were you responsible for her makeup?"

Rowan nodded. Ordinarily she would be offended by the assumption that the only woman left in the room had to be on makeup duties, but she was too touched by the idea of Ellie Freeman, imagining the last years of life for her being like the last dregs of chocolate milk in a bowl of cereal, lifting it up and pouring it straight into her mouth, not letting a single drop go to waste.

"She looks incredible. Better than that - she looks like a film star. Thank you so much."

Rowan somehow overcome by both humility and pride, but could not find words to speak, so simply shook the hand of the silver haired man and nodded her head.

With his departure, Rowan and Franklin were the only living people in the room. They both found themselves wandering over to the casket to gaze upon Ellie one more time.

"I can honestly say I wasn't expecting any of that," Franklin said with a disbelieving shake of his head.

"I made her look like a film star!" Rowan chuckled. "It wasn't the look I was going for, but her son seemed happy."

Franklin offered the dead woman a small salute and whispered, "Good night Mrs Freeman," as he closed the lid upon the casket.

Rowan was not needed any further once the casket was returned to the death chamber but she offered to stay to help clear up nevertheless. The flowers were gathered for the service the following day and placed in Franklin's office and the visiting room was soon returned to its empty state.

"Is there anything else I can do?" Rowan asked.

"I don't think so, everything seems to be in order. Will you be okay cycling home. I can drop you off if you want?"

Rowan just shook her head. "I'll be fine, I have my helmet and my high-vis jacket."

Franklin nodded approvingly. "Quite right."

"Do you fancy going for a pint?" she offered. "I'll pay."

"I don't think so. I fancy an early night, I have my barbershop appointment tomorrow."

"It doesn't have to be booze - just a Coke if you want..."

"...Rowan, are you ok? Are things still bad at home?"

To this she could only offer a half-hearted chuckle. "Things haven't been right at home for two years, but yes, they aren't great right now. Dad's coming round to talk things through with mum."

"Oh, I see. I think you should be there though - it's probably for the best, isn't it?"

Rowan nodded reluctantly. "It probably is."

As she left, Franklin could not help feeling a sorrow deep within him; sorrow and doubt that being there with her angry parents really was the right thing to do. As much sympathy as he had for Mr and Mrs Kaplan, Rowan was the child they had almost forgotten still existed. As she vanished into the darkness at the end of the path leading to the reception, Franklin heard her assembling her Brompton and called out to her, "If you need me, just call."

"I will," she answered as he heard the crunch of bicycle tires on the gravel and the girl sped away.

28.

Franklin was undoing his tie when the phone rang. It wasn't his mobile, which he was fully expecting to ring if things became too awful for Rowan at home, but was instead the work phone downstairs. This happened often, usually a care home or hospital had a body they wanted to be collected quickly; less often it was a mourner, ravaged by nighttime grief who needed to visit their loved one. Either way, it seemed too early for Rowan to have made her way home.

Jogging from his flat down to the reception, his tie still hanging from his collar, he picked up the receiver and in his most professional, most sympathetic voice said, "Gallow & Sons Funeral Home. How may I help?"

There was silence on the line, save for the sound of wind rustling through trees.

"Hello? Is anybody there?"

The line went dead and tiredness made Franklin let his imagination take over. What if there had been an accident and Rowan had fallen under a car. He could see it now, the wheel of her bike still spinning, Rowan, broken beneath the car, reaching for her phone and in her delirium, dialing the business number instead of his mobile.

Panicked, he rang "1471" but whoever had called had withheld their number. It is then that the door chime rang. Through the glass of the reception door, Franklin could just make out the hazy silhouette. With a shaky hand, he replaced the receiver and took a step towards the door.

"Hello?" he called, and then to his own surprise added, "Gallow & Son's Funeral Home. How may I help?"

The figure seemed to turn slightly and then vanished. Summoning strength, he realized what the only likely explanation for this intrusion could be - the anonymous caller from a few weeks ago, Franklin marched towards the door and threw it open.

The figure, a tall, slender man was jogging away down the path. "I can see you," Franklin alerted him. "I know it's you, Alf."

The man stopped running. A long, dark shadow spread

beneath him, as he took a step toward the reception, his face became bathed in the glow from the light and Franklin gasped at their uncanny likeness.

He was a good few inches taller than Franklin and even skinnier. But the eyes were the same seawater green and his hair, somehow even more aggressively red than his own. The youthful skin of a teenager in the last stages of adolescence did nothing to hide the fact that this young man was so very clearly Franklin's son.

"Do you want to come inside?" asked Franklin.

Alf nodded and brushed past him as he stepped into the room.

Closing the door, Franklin could only offer, "Good God this is strange."

Alf shifted awkwardly on the spot. He was wearing alarmingly tight trousers and a scarf that seemed too thin and tied too loosely to serve much function aside from fashion. His black jeans were matched with boots that seemed to be formed from a waxy, dark material that Franklin had never seen before and he was encased in a long, dramatic camel hair coat that came down to his ankles.

"It's good to meet you," Franklin offered him a hand which he shook, meekly. He could not help but notice that the young man was shaking. "Would you like a cup of tea?"

Again, Alf just nodded. Franklin was aware that his son had not yet spoken; a curious idea came into his head that perhaps he couldn't, which he quickly dismissed as nonsense.

Franklin led the way and Alf clomped noisily up the stairs behind him. "Well, this is my home." Alf inspected the living room, which Franklin was very pleased he had tidied earlier that day. From the sofa, where she had curled herself up into a woodlouse ball, Felicity roused and fixed her suspicious eyes upon this strange new presence. "It isn't much but I don't have to travel far to work!"

Alf did not laugh.

"I'll put the kettle on."

In the adjoining kitchen Franklin found himself incapable of remembering simple things such as where he kept the teabags and milk. Finally he found a question to which his son had to offer an answer. "Milk and sugar?"

"Soya milk," was the blunt reply. "No sugar - sugar is more addictive than heroin. Did you know that?"

Franklin tried not to let his eyebrows rise too noticeably. "I didn't know that. I've never been addicted to heroin though so..."

"They keep it quiet because the sugar industry is so huge that if word ever got out, the business would die overnight."

"Oh. I see." Franklin had heard of people like this before; the people who forwarded emails about "what *really* happened on 9/11" and "what the vaccine lobby doesn't want you to know about autism." The slightly unhinged people who claimed to have pulled back the curtain on the grandest conspiracy and had decided to inform the world through the medium of incoherent YouTube videos and badly spelled rants in the comment section of online articles.

"I don't have any soya milk," Franklin intoned; surprised to find himself rather ashamed by this admission.

"Forget about the tea. Did you know that cows are now so pumped full of antibiotics that..."

"...Well," Franklin interrupted. "Your mum told me that you'll be starting university in October. I bought you a present."

Alf seemed to react only slightly to this news. "Yeah? Thanks?"

He had bought it the afternoon after he had discovered Alf's existence. For hours he had agonized over whether or not he should wrap it. Was that too childish? Was thrusting a laptop into his hands too brutal a way of saying "Sorry I missed out on your entire childhood, every birthday, every Christmas, but here's a computer to make up for it."

He had elected not to wrap it but had kept it hidden from view in the knowledge that Alf could appear on his doorstep any day. He retrieved it from the cubbyhole beneath the bookcase and handed the box over to his son.

Alf took it in his hands and turned the box over suspiciously, as if he had been handed a stack of incriminating photographs - or a hand grenade.

"The man in the shop said that make was very popular with students," Franklin offered when no response was forthcoming.

"It's a bit small, isn't it? The screen?"

Franklin looked at the photograph of the little laptop computer on the box. The gift he had so proudly taken home, imagining it to be useful and thoughtful, as well as expensive enough to serve as a means of reaching out to his son, seemed instantly cheap, pointless and even pathetic. "I suppose it is a bit."

"Mum's got me a computer anyway," he shrugged as he handed the box back.

Franklin did not take it and simple suggested, "Well, you keep it. You can sell it if you want."

"Do you have the receipt?"

Utterly lost for words, Franklin returned to the cubbyhole and retrieved the plastic carrier bag he had carried his gift home in. He removed the receipt that still lay in the bottom and gave it to Alf.

"You shouldn't use plastic bags," was all his son could respond with. "They end up in the ocean and turtles eat them thinking that they're jellyfish."

"I know." Franklin mumbled, now almost too winded to defend himself.

To his surprise Alf was now fishing around in his pocket - for one moment Franklin thought that maybe his son had a gift to offer in kind, but instead the boy pulled out a notepad and a pen. "Mum said that this was important. She said I need to know the family history on your side - you know, if there's anything nasty I might have inherited; cancer or Alzheimer's or something."

Franklin thought briefly over his family. "I don't think so. My granddad was mad as a box of frogs by the time he died but he was never that sane to begin with. I think it was the war more than his genes that did him in."

Alf scribbled this information down casually, then as calmly and as coldly as if he were cancelling his subscription to a magazine added, "Now, I don't have any interest in making up for lost time or playing happy families. As far as I'm concerned, we have met now and I've found out all I need to know. I think it's stupid to just try to pretend that we have anything more in common than blood."

"I see. Well... I'm sorry you feel that way. Look, until a

few days ago, I didn't even know you existed and if I *had* known, I would have been there for you, I promise."

"It doesn't matter either way to me," he responded, flatly.

Nodding slowly, Alf turned towards the staircase. "Well, I'd better be going."

"OK. It was nice meeting you," Franklin lied. This had been an utter disaster and nothing like the tearful reunion he had envisioned. "I should get an early night, anyway. I have a service tomorrow."

Alf shook his head and sighed. "That's not for me. When I go, I want to be thrown into the ground. No service, no prayers, no flowers. Nothing. No greedy vultures profiting from of the grief of others..."

The words hung in the air like a noxious stench. "Not everybody wants the same, Alf. It's important for people to say goodbye in their own way."

He just rolled his eyes preposterously at this, even childishly. "Is it important that the funeral industry is a multi-billion behemoth that creates the concept of mourning as a marketable commodity and then packages it and sells it back to those in grief?"

"That's not how I would put it," was all Franklin could manage.

The pair walked down the stairs to the reception in silence, Alf with the laptop under his arm, Franklin with his hands fidgeting as he tugged his tie from his collar.

"Thank you for stopping by."

"Sure.

Franklin opened the door and a cool burst of wind on his damp skin became the first indication of just how much he had been sweating upstairs. Quite out of nowhere, he found himself saying, "I know that this hasn't been the best start and I know you must have all kinds of resentments towards me. Whether I was aware of you or not, I still wasn't there and that has to hurt a bit."

"No," he snapped decisively.

"Well, either way, if you do find yourself wanting to know more, or maybe if you just want to talk or go for a pint when you're at university, you know where I live. Your mum has my mobile number."

Alf nodded as he stepped out into the dark. "Whatever. Maybe."

"You look a lot like me."

"I know," he replied, though to Franklin's surprise, there was no bitterness in his words.

"You got the hair too," Franklin smiled as he ruffled his own. "You lucky thing."

Alf smiled for the first time and to Franklin it seemed almost genuine. "At least I know who to blame now."

"I think you mean thank…"

Unexpectedly the pair indulged in a spot of laughter, both silently admitting that life was not always easy for those possessing such striking and vivid hair - the kind of hair that somehow served as a magnet for spite and bullies.

"Have a good night, Alf. It was nice to meet you."

"Whatever, Franklin."

With that he had gone and Franklin closed the door behind his son. Despite the horridness of their encounter, despite the sanctimonious derisions of his life, Franklin could not help but smile, because somewhere, buried deep beneath the awkwardness and resentment, a little spark of something had begun.

29.

On Sunday morning Rowan found herself led by curiosity to Southville and Beauley Road where Donna Hawley had once lived, in a flat on the ground floor of a row of Victorian terraced houses that sloped and curved high upon the ridge of a hill and disappeared out of sight.

Rowan could not remember the house number but could recall that it had a green door. As she cycled along the street, she relied on memory alone to identify it.

She had been happy for the chance to get out of the house, and had the idea not struck her to spend her day investigating the final weeks of Donna's life, Rowan would have had to find any other excuse to leave her parents behind for the day. There was a thickness in the air, a tension that hid behind the faked smiles of her father as he fried eggs in the morning and her mother laughed at his jokes - just loudly enough for the sound to ring false and hollow through the walls, as she sipped on a glass of water to swallow her aspirins. There was no joy in the eyes of either of them, and that was what Rowan had found so empty about the spectacle.

Friday evening her father had returned. Oscar Kaplan looked crumpled and unshaven – sleeping on a friend's sofa had been unforgiving on the man and it showed in every crease of his usually immaculate clothing. "Your mother and I," he had begun from his position between them on the sofa, "Have decided to give it another go. It has been two years now and this family has been through enough."

He kissed his wife on her red wine stained lips and Rowan shivered at the sight of their insincere display of affection. If this was for her benefit, it wasn't working.

"What are you going to do about Ruby's bedroom?" Rowan demanded.

Her parents exchanged nervous glances before she replied; "We have decided to return it to how it was. It was a stupid decision, I was... mad. We're going to repaint the room tomorrow. I have found wallpaper that matches everything perfectly."

Rowan imagined how this Frankenstein's monster of a room would appear. Even if the likeness were a perfect replica it would never be the same. It wasn't *her* wallpaper. It would never be *her* room again.

Not even trying to hide her disgust at her parents attempt at unity, Rowan left the room without a word and when her father came up later with a sandwich on a plate, she took vindictive pleasure in placing it untouched on the carpet in the hallway. She did not eat until she arrived at Ellie Freeman's funeral the next day.

The funeral was a jolly affair, if funerals can ever be such things. There were rude stories of debauched nights in Amsterdam and San Francisco, tales of dalliances with American soldiers and fifties Lotharios as they awaited entry to the crematorium. Then came the genuine tears of love upon their exit, which Rowan could not help, but find touching in its earnestness.

This morning her distraction would be Donna Hawley. Her plan had been to search for the woman's car to see if there was any evidence of recent work to cover up the damage of an accident. In her head she could see the pieces of a grand - and evil puzzle falling into place and yet she had not a shred of evidence to prove it. Proof of a collision could be precisely what she needed.

Just as she had hoped, the sight of the green door triggered her memory. The curtains that had once hung in the window had been taken down and through the glass she could see that what little furniture had been in the tiny living room had been removed and the carpet torn from the floor. Rowan's heart sank. Her family had wasted no time in gutting Donna's home and no doubt would have sold her car already.

Already on the verge of giving up, Rowan heard the sound of a phone ringing. Instinctively she reached for her pocket but then realized it was coming from inside her rucksack. At first bewildered by this peculiarity, she then gasped with the understanding it was not hers but Henrik's phone that was ringing. Retrieving it, Rowan shuddered at the sight of the name "Lise" blinking on the screen. She elected to answer it.

"Hello?"

"Rowan? Is that you?" asked the timid voice at the end of

the line.

"Yes it is. Wow. It felt very strange seeing your name on your brother's phone."

"Tell me about it, it was much weirder having to call him in the first place. I tried messaging you earlier on Facebook but you didn't answer."

"Oh, I'm sorry. I was busy today..."

"...Don't worry, I was just... It was just that last night I got a strange text from Emma - Henrik's girlfriend. I think she'd been drinking. She had been at a party all night and I think... There were lots of my friends there too. They were posting photos of it this morning and nobody thought to invite me," the tone of the girl's voice was stuck somewhere between bitterness and sadness.

Rowan did not know how to respond; she knew this feeling very well. In the days following her sister's murder there had been kindly texts and even flowers sent to the door but in the weeks after that, one by one her friends faded away, too struck by the horror of murder to be able to look at Rowan, as if she were a living, breathing embodiment of mortality, of violent death. Things could only be worse for Lise, who no doubt had among her circle of friends more than a few who would look at her and think, *she could have saved him* and *why didn't she do something?*

"I'm sorry," was all Rowan could offer. "It will get better." The promise sounded empty and untrue and somehow Rowan knew that Lise could feel it.

"It doesn't matter that much really. I never liked parties," the girl sighed. "It's just that this message said that Henrik was happy - that he had dumped her and that they had split happily and were going to be friends. She didn't want me blaming her because he just seemed so content..."

Rowan nervously chewed on her lip; she could hear her heart pounding in her chest. She knew she had to ask, but she had to do it tactfully. "Lise, this may sound like a strange question but was there any time that you suspected that Henrik might have been..."

"...I think he was gay," she suddenly blurted.

Rowan threw a hand to her mouth. "Really? What makes you think that?"

"Maybe not gay... maybe bi, I don't know. I always had my suspicions, even when I was really small - so did Mum and Dad but they would never say anything to him. Before he died, he started telling me that he was falling in love with someone, but he'd never say who it was. He would always say *this person* and *they are really* but he never said *she* or *her*. Normal people don't talk like that, do they? It was almost like he was trying to tell me; like he was taking steps towards it... Mum and Dad always said that if he was gay, we should wait until he was ready to say so. We're Danish not... Russian, he could have told us and nothing would have changed."

"Why do you think he wouldn't have told you?"

"He was proud," Lise said as her voice began to falter. "He was private and he kept things quiet. We didn't even know for months that he had a girlfriend."

"Did he ever mention anyone? A friend perhaps called Ben?"

There was a pause, full of expectation. "No, why, do you know something Rowan?"

"I was coming to the same conclusion. Lise, I wish I could tell you more but it's just a hunch. Can I meet you later this week? Are you still off school?"

"Please just tell me now."

"How about this evening? I have a friend I want you to meet, I work for him and he will want to ask you some questions too. How about at the Suspension bridge this evening... seven o'clock?" Rowan had found her foot casually toying with a large, smooth pebble that had been placed in the front garden beside a flowerpot, which housed a plastic shrub. It moved with suspicious ease and she was just about to investigate closer when suddenly, to her horror, the green door opened and the same sleazy man with the long plait was standing beside her carrying a black bag of rubbish.

"Lise, I have to go. I'll call you later, okay?"

"Ok. But I want the phone back afterwards."

"Definitely," Rowan hung up without saying goodbye to the girl and immediately felt awful for doing so. There was no time for guilt though as the man, who she now recalled being named Art, was speaking to her.

"Well, well," he grinned with a mouthful of almost

sinisterly white teeth. "We really *must* stop meeting like this!"

"Oh. Hi!" Rowan tried to smile but felt the corners of her mouth wavering.

"Ruby wasn't it?"

"Yes, that's right." Rowan swallowed her remorse at using her sister's name so readily but it really had been the first to come to mind at the time. "I was just here because, I remembered... something. Something I left the last time I visited Donna when she was alive and I was just wondering if I could pick it up."

Art's eyes narrowed and Rowan felt the deeply uncomfortable sensation of scrutiny. "Well," he smiled, his brilliant teeth more like fangs. "Come inside. What was it you were looking for?"

"Do you know... It looks as if her family have cleared everything and it was just a... picture, from work. Just a sentimental thing really."

"Why don't you come in and we'll see if we can find it. I don't think the flat has been completely stripped yet. There's still a chance that..."

"...No, no, it was just a silly thing as I was cycling past."

Art nodded as he opened the lid to the black wheelie bin that stood in the front garden and he dropped the small bag inside. There was something odd about this action - the bag, not even half full that had to be carried out at once. Rowan imagined the man seeing her downstairs and then looking for any excuse to go outside to meet her.

"I thought the bin collection wasn't until Wednesday," she ventured, trying to sound as casual as she could.

The man shrugged his shoulders. "I like keeping my place neat."

"It's recycling this week too, not general waste."

The man laughed dryly. "Well, if only I had you around each week to remind me which day is which, I'd never miss the collection again!"

Rowan felt oddly comforted. The man's motivations now seemed no more sinister than a gross attempt at wooing a woman some twenty-five years his junior. She pressed on.

"I think I actually might have left the photograph in her car. Do you know if her family took her car away recently?"

"What make was it?"

Rowan smiled and threw her hands up girlishly. "I have no idea, I don't really know cars!" her attempt at ditzy flirtation made her feel queasy.

"What colour was it?"

"I can't remember that either, but it was recently in an accident. Got a bit smashed up in fact, do you remember seeing a car that looked like it could have been in an accident?"

The man stroked his moustache. "Can't say I can remember seeing anything like that. You seem troubled though, why don't you come up to my flat and we'll have a coffee, you can talk about your friend and I'll see what I can remember."

"Oh no, that's quite alright I think I'd best be..."

"...Why are you *really* here, Rowan?"

Rowan took a step back as her skin turned to ice. "How do you know my name?"

"Last time you were here, you said your name was Ruby Kaplan; I remembered the name from somewhere so I looked it up online. She was that girl who got murdered a couple of years ago - there was a big picture of her sister, Rowan on the BBC website too. So Rowan, why are you *really* here?"

"I really have to go now. I'm sorry I made up a name it was just... I wasn't thinking."

The man reached out an arm and placed it heavily upon her shoulder. His fingers dug into her skin like claws. A wide grin spread across his mouth but his eyes stayed fix and cold upon her.

"If I were you, I would stay away from here in the future. I don't know what you want but you're clearly up to no good. Now get on your bike, cycle away and never come back. Do you understand?"

"Yes." Rowan whispered, suddenly acutely aware that there was nobody else about on the street.

He winked at her. "Good girl."

With that, she was gone.

30.

Franklin had been enjoying a lie-in, so that when his mobile phone rang he was still in his pyjamas and halfway through feeding Felicity. The skinny, ragged cat purred contentedly around the man's bare feet until he placed the bowl of high-end cat food (the only kind she found suited to her discerning tastes,) whereupon her purrs were replaced by the sound of satisfied greed as she gobbled down her food.

"Hi Rowan," he yawned.

"Franklin, I'm over by College Green, near the Queen Victoria statue. Are you busy?"

Franklin stared longingly over towards the living room where his blanket-laden sofa beckoned him against the backdrop of cartoons on the TV. "Not really. Is it important?"

"Possibly; I suppose, I just got myself a bit worked up. I've had a strange morning."

Rowan recounted her peculiar visit to Beauley Road, beginning with the call from Lise and her suspicions regarding her brother's seemingly fluid sexuality, before going on to the far more worrying encounter with Art, who had clearly done his homework in regards to who Rowan was.

"Are you sure he wasn't just another one of those perverts? Like those men up on Blackboy Hill who shouted at you?"

"Maybe, but this just *felt* different, like he had something to hide, as if he was worried about me; like he had looked me up, not because he was curious but because... he knew something already."

Franklin wandered over to the sofa and sat down. "Rowan, please tell me that you don't think this has anything to do with Ruby?" the silence that followed was made absurd by the cartoon theme song in the background. "Rowan?"

"I don't know. I can't help but think he wanted me gone for a reason."

"You're getting paranoid. No more of this Nancy Drew stuff, Rowan, it isn't safe. If you have your suspicions then tell the police."

Rowan just laughed. "Do you think they'll do anything? Are they doing anything about Henrik, or Donna, or Ben."

"To be fair, they are actually investigating Ben..."

"...Well, they aren't investigating Ruby anymore. Just a dead black girl."

There was no way Franklin could respond to this so he steered the conversation into safer waters. "So what is to be done about Lise?"

" She wants to meet up today - I said you'd come along too."

"Oh thanks, Rowan. I was looking forward to a day when Peterman was on call. I was hoping to have a do nothing day."

"This is serious. It's not until this evening. Seven o'clock at the Suspension Bridge."

Franklin shook his head. "Honestly? Do we have to wear trench coats and disguises?"

"If this is going to be a joke then I'm not..."

"...No, it just felt a little... covert."

"It's only the bridge because it's close to her. She doesn't want to be out of the house too long as her parents worry and she's too young to meet us in a pub."

"OK. I'll be there. D'you need a lift?"

"I'll meet you at yours."

The conversation felt as if it was drawing to a close so Franklin was about to say goodbye, but Rowan clearly had more.

"There is just one more thing that I think you could do to help. You have a smart phone, right?"

"Yes..." Franklin had no idea where this conversation was headed now.

"I tried logging on to Manhandlr on Henrik's phone. He still has it downloaded but it needs a password, I guess he was doing something to cover his tracks. Anyway, I'm giving Lise his phone back this evening and I don't have a smart phone, so I was thinking that maybe..."

"Oh Rowan, please don't ask me to do what I think you're going to ask me."

"I want you to join Manhandlr."

"Yes, that was it."

"Franklin, hear me out. If Henrik joined Manhandlr, maybe his killer was there too. If I was going to try and track someone down, it would be the easiest way to do it - it tells you how far away you are from someone to the nearest metre. You can actually trace somebody by using it."

Franklin found himself looking at his phone suspiciously. Completely unaware that such an ability existed within it. "Henrik was twenty years old... why would he go for some," Franklin chose his words carefully, for fear the corpse resting in the death chamber beneath might hear him, "larger built middle-aged man?"

"Because he was a bear, Franklin!"

"Sorry?"

Exasperated, Rowan sighed. "Bears are big, hairy men. Usually forty plus who lots of gay guys go for."

"What? That's a thing?" Franklin found himself oddly charmed by the concept that truly there was somebody out there for everyone. "You think Henrik was into fat guys?"

"Well, there's a chance - and anybody out there who's also on Manhandlr could track him down if they knew how, what you do is..."

"...Wait a minute, Ben's husband didn't like him being big, but you think Henrik did... so as soon as Henrik died..."

"Yes, yes. Go on," Rowan urged, eager to let Franklin arrive at the same conclusion she had.

"He started exercising again to keep William happy?" Franklin could almost hear her nodding her agreement at the end of the line. "That's what killed him. The hit and run."

"Exactly. I mean... the killer couldn't have predicted it, but, he sounds like the kind of person who takes advantage of an opportunity."

"Fine. I'll do it - but do I have to put my face on my profile?"

"No idea. I have to go, got some reading to do."

"OK, what time should I expect you this evening?"

"Six thirty. Bye."

By the time he responded she was gone. Felicity decided to join him on the sofa; he turned to the ailing cat who was breathing heavily as if fighting off the sleep her meal had induced. "What in the world has become of me,

Felicity?" he asked her, and she merely studied him with watery eyes.

A quick Google search took Franklin to *manhandlr.co.uk,* a garish looking website with a neon green theme accompanied by images of unfeasibly muscular men in public spaces looking at their phones. A black man was wearing nothing but a pair of yellow briefs in a public library; an aggressively tanned and oiled white man was topless behind an office desk. Each image whizzed by as a slideshow and each one seemed to make Franklin more conscious of his narrow, shapeless body than the last.

The website FAQ section provided some comfort. No, he did not have to show his face in the image on the app, though pictures of bums or penises were strictly prohibited. Yes, he could opt out of having his details passed onto third parties, no, there was no fee to join.

Hastily he reached for his phone and searched for the app on the store. Upon finding it, he touched the download button and nervously waited as the bar marked its progress.

After what felt like an interminable wait, Franklin got up, poured himself a bowl of cereal and began pacing about his flat. What if Rowan was right and this really was the key to the killer. Could he somehow know upon sight who it was? Would the killer see him and somehow know where he was?

The phone made a *ping* sound to confirm that the app had successfully downloaded. Franklin approached it with the wariness of a man who was quite certain that an erect penis could explode out of the screen at any moment. Upon agreeing that he was over 18, the first image he saw was a wall of photos, again with that violent neon backdrop that Franklin already knew would be uneasy on his eyes. He scrolled through the agreement before he was asked to provide a photograph. He had thought about this already. Whether it was because of the agreement he had made to meet Lise there, or because it was as impersonal a picture as a Bristolian could offer; he uploaded a photo he had taken a few months back of the Clifton Suspension Bridge. Handsome, classy and bleeding with civic pride.

Next he was asked to provide a name, which the app referred to as a "Handl." That made Franklin feel very old as it made him think of young people with avant-garde spellings spraying graffiti and the kind of boys he no doubt would be screaming at to "get off my lawn" the morning that he turned forty in just over a three week's time.

Looking around his room for inspiration, his eyes fell upon a sheet of paper on his coffee table that he had used to work out the solution for a Sudoku puzzle. It was printed with the letterhead of Gallow & Sons Funeral Home, including the address. The last line before the postcode caught his eye. "Bedminster."

As if juggling the letters in his head, the name presented itself, not as an anagram but a single change of a letter and a space in the middle. He typed his name in as "Bed Monster." He chuckled to himself at his pun.

Once he had pressed enter, he was taken back again to that wall of people. Most were of faces - studiously maintained facial hair and selfies posed in front of mirrors. The closest man to him was, alarmingly, only 28 metres away but as he scrolled down the page the distances got farther and farther until the last was almost two kilometres. Franklin had no idea that so many men in his city enjoyed the company of others so much.

It all seemed fun, Franklin thought to himself - and as a man who was already on a dating website in search of that special lady, he was in no hurry to judge others who might be looking for something a bit more casual. In fact, were any women to offer him a quickie he would certainly not be adverse to a one-nighter. Only when he started to study the faces and torsos of this curious dating game did he suddenly remember that somebody here could well be looking for something far more sinister than a good old-fashioned roll in the hay.

One of them could be a killer - three times over.

31.

Just as he had expected, Rowan turned up at precisely half past six. Franklin opened the door to find the young woman eager to get going.

"I feel terrible," Rowan informed him as they walked towards the Smart car he had parked on the street. "She must be worried sick about what we have to tell her."

"She'll be fine," Franklin tried to convince her but the comment seemed foolish considering that he had yet to exchange a single word with the girl.

The evening was dry and bright; the warmest weekend of the year so far and the residents of Bristol were making the most of the glorious weather. As they drove along the harbour side, pubs had spilt out onto the streets where students sat on benches drinking cider and smoking and generally looking young and cool. Franklin wondered what Rowan made of these people; she was older than some and certainly smarter than most and yet she had seemed disinclined to even consider university. Perhaps her sister's death had derailed her life in so many ways that it was impossible to go back to a time before it had happened; perhaps the call of a funeral home was too strong, for somebody for whom death had visited so intimately, to be distracted by such trifling things as education.

Rowan seemed uninterested by the sights of a city bathed in the early evening glow of peach sunlight and was instead fidgeting around inspecting the contents of the little storage space built into the passenger door.

"What is this doing here?" she asked, as she produced a CD in a case.

"Oh Rowan, please tell me that you're not so young that you haven't seen a CD before."

"I know what a CD is, Franklin, I was born in 1995, not yesterday."

Franklin made a whistling sound as he turned onto Park Street. "1995 - bloody hell. Do you even know who Princess Diana was?"

"I meant why do you have a Kim Wilde CD in your car,

you're an undertaker? I would expect something a bit darker... a bit less... crap."

Franklin laughed. "First of all, you *know* it's Funeral Director, secondly Kim Wilde is most certainly not crap and thirdly; here is the biggest secret of working with dead people all of your life - you need some brightness, be it pop music or kids TV, terrible action movies about giant robots or some god-awful book written for teenagers about girls who can't stop screwing vampires. Everyone needs it - and one day you will too. The only people who can really afford to listen to the miserable stuff are people who don't *really* have anything to feel miserable about."

Rowan just shook her head dismissively. "I'll take your word for it."

"Do you want to listen to it later? I can lend you that CD," he asked hopefully.

"I'm alright thank you. I don't think I even have a CD player anymore."

Franklin tutted as he pulled into an empty spot at the edge of the road. It was close enough to the Suspension Bridge, located at the topmost end of Clifton Village along a terrace of mighty sandstone houses that towered overhead.

They were considerably earlier than they needed to be but neither one wanted to leave Lise Nielsen waiting on the bridge by herself. Aside from the rudeness of asking their only lead in what they were already referring to as "the case," a bridge so closely associated with suicide was no place to leave a girl whose brother was assumed to have killed himself.

No matter how many times he walked across it, Franklin never tired of the majesty of the Clifton Suspension Bridge. Two mighty stone towers stood across the roadway like colossal giants holding aloft gargantuan chains from which the bridge was literally suspended, a hundred and fifty feet above the water line. It never failed to impress Franklin that this incredible structure had been built by the Victorians, nor did it fail to induce in him a mild, dizzying panic as the city beneath him spread unfathomably far below and as far as the eye could see into the hills on the horizon.

Rowan appeared to have no such qualms as she strolled along the pedestrian walkway, running her hand nonchalantly along the barrier before casually noting; "I think that's her there."

Franklin was certain that his eyes were not what they had once been as he struggled to make out the figure standing at the far end of the bridge, let alone be able to identify her. He sighed to himself at the betrayal aging wrought upon a man's body. Not even forty and parts of him were already closing up shop for the big sleep.

As they drew closer, it became apparent that this was indeed the same teenage girl Rowan had pointed out at Henrik Nielson's funeral. The girl who had not taken her eyes from the ground before her, would not look at her brother's casket and seemed silently stewing under a rage that had stolen her life from her just as readily as it had stolen Henrik's.

Her eyes were flushed as if she had been crying; her hair was no longer in plaits but was instead tied back. She wore jeans, a tee shirt and a look of agitated impatience.

"Thank you for coming," she said upon their arrival.

"I said we would," Rowan gently told her. "I'm sorry I had to go so quickly. I've been trying to phone you, I promise."

"I know," Lise morosely murmured. "It's been a hard day... My boyfriend d...dumped me and I haven't been able to stop... to stop..."

With that the girl erupted into tears. It happened so suddenly and so violently that Franklin found himself taking a step away from her. Rowan, in a heartbeat, immediately reached out and warmly embraced her and the girl gracelessly sobbed into her shoulder. He could not have been happier to have her here; had he been left alone with a crying, heartbroken girl, he probably would have fled in fright. Franklin knew he was not heartless but he was also aware that a man hugging a teenage girl would not only make him feel extremely uncomfortable, but would probably make her terrified.

He waited for the tears to pass and wordlessly handed it over to his assistant.

"Here," Rowan said once the hug had finished as she gave the phone over to Lise. "I'm so sorry about... everything.

Trust me though, we are doing everything we can and the phone has been a real help."

"Thank you for believing me... Nobody else does. It's just been horrible." Lise wiped her eyes on a tissue from her pocket. It seemed to already be heavy with tears. "How has it helped?"

Rowan looked over to Franklin and when he did not respond, she opted to share her theory. "We believe that a few weeks before he... died, Henrik might have been in a traffic accident with Ben, the man he *might* have been seeing. It might even have involved more people but we don't know for sure yet."

The news didn't come as much of a surprise to her. "Back in April, near to the start, he had this horrid injury on his forehead. He said he came off his bike, but I was *sure* he didn't take it out that evening, and he was so good at always wearing his helmet. He wasn't a good liar either. Mum and Dad believed him but I knew something was wrong."

"That's all we know for sure right now."

Lise shook her head and her eyes dropped to the floor. "It's like I didn't even know him. How many other things did he lie about? I just wish that... that I hadn't waited, you know, that I had told him that I love him no matter what."

Rowan gently rubbed her shoulder.

"This man he was with, did you say he was called Ben."

Rowan nodded. "We don't know that they were together for sure. It's all just a theory right now."

"Is he a nice guy? Can I meet him? Where does he live?"

This time when Rowan looked at Franklin, he was shaking his head sternly. She chose to ignore him. "Ben was knocked over by a car last week. He died."

Lise's mouth began to tremble. "He was murdered too?"

"I don't know."

"Who else is in danger? Am *I* safe?" Lise's eyes darted back and forth as if visions of her own untimely death were flickering before them.

"You're fine. I promise."

"It was that guy on the news wasn't it? The hit and run guy. I saw it on the TV."

"We don't know *anything* for sure yet."

"And the police still aren't doing anything at all? They still don't believe my brother was murdered?"

"They don't yet... But they will, I promise." It was the second such promise Rowan had made within a minute to which she could offer no guarantee.

It was not long before the girl made her excuses and all but ran back to her home in Leigh Woods. She had said that she would not share this encounter with her family but Franklin was almost certain that she would; this was simply too terrible a burden to rest upon the soul of one so young.

"Well done, Rowan," Franklin hissed. "I think we're well and truly screwed."

"What?"

"You shouldn't have said any of that. I was hoping we would get a little information out of her, but no, all you did was give her a load of things to worry about - and to tell her parents about."

"She won't. Anyway, she has a right to know; she was in such a state and it isn't fair that she doesn't know everything we do."

"Rowan, she was dumped by her boyfriend. She'll be over it in a couple of days."

Rowan's jaw fell open in shocked anger; she jogged up to Franklin who had already starting heading back to the far side of the bridge. "What the hell do you know, Franklin? She's a teenage girl filled to the brim with hormones - she will probably never love anyone, or feel anything as strong as that again. When your heart breaks when you're 16, you actually think it could kill you. The poor girl is already a mess and the worst thing that people like you do - who know next to nothing about how relationships actually work, is dismiss her feelings because she's young and you think anything she feels can just be wiped away clean the morning after."

Franklin was taken aback, partly because he had not expected this sudden torrent of bitterness, but mostly because every word Rowan had said rang true. No emotion in the world was as overpowering as that of an adolescent in love, and nothing hurt more than the brutality of that love being torn apart. "I'm sorry," he begrudgingly agreed. "You're right."

Rowan was silenced; she had not expected him to give in with so little resistance. "Well... Good for you."

"However, you really did say too much and it could well get us into a lot of trouble."

"Why, because she might tell her parents?"

"Yes that... but also, we don't know if she is telling us the truth."

Rowan's eyes widened in horror. "You can't seriously be thinking that..."

"...I'm just saying, from now on, we trust nobody. Somebody has killed three people, somebody connected to at least one of them - probably somebody we've already met."

32.

The following Friday evening Franklin found himself hurriedly marching along North Street from the funeral home. He had returned from a collection of an elderly patient from the Bristol Royal Infirmary, a man who had succumbed to cancer mere hours before. The details of his stay at the hospital, that he had not been visited by any friends or family throughout his illness was already boding ominously towards a sad funeral, with only Franklin, a representative of the council and a vicar in attendance.

There had been a time when he had convinced himself he was destined for the same fate. No wife, no children, not even any friends to speak of, his parents long gone. Now things felt a little less foreboding; he had a friend in Rowan, whether Alf liked it or not, he technically had a son and just that afternoon he had received a reply from a woman on the dating website who seemed neither distressed by his work, nor worryingly excited by it.

The Tobacco Factory was packed as it so often was on a Friday night. Much of the crowd was there to see a production of "As You Like It" which was to be staged upstairs. He found his brother standing at the bar already surrounded by a throng of people, three deep waiting for their turn to hurriedly down a pint before the curtain rose.

Edison spied Franklin and wordlessly nodded towards the garden. He followed his brother as he carried two pints of cider outside to a picnic table and took his seat.

"Evenin' Frank," he said.

"Good evening, Edison," Franklin replied as he removed his suit jacket and placed it beside him.

It was a beautiful night. The weather had been warm for the past week, scorching the last of the daffodils and filling the dusky air with the smell of barbecue smoke. Overhead, house martins swooped and pirouetted against the cloudless sky and Franklin immediately felt a thousand miles from the long day he had endured.

"Cheers," Edison invited and the two brothers chinked their glasses together. The kiss of Ashton Press cider had never been so welcoming to Franklin. Edison followed his first gulp with an aggressive belch.

"So how was the hit and run's funeral?"

"Dire," Franklin replied. "And his name was Ben."

"Bad one then?"

Franklin nodded. "Remember when we were kids and that old woman kept visiting her husband in the middle of the night to cry until morning?"

"How could I forget?"

"William wasn't far off from that. He was a mess; the whole family was a mess, it's just so awful when that happens. We could hear them all the way to the hearse from inside the crematorium."

"William? Was that his... friend?"

"If you mean his husband, then yes."

Edison just nodded. Franklin was a little taken aback to not be accused of being a member of the "political correctness brigade" or of trying to make him feel like an old fool. Instead he finished his first cigarette, which he had smoked at an alarming speed and began fidgeting with the box before starting on another. Something was troubling Edison, but they were not the kind of brothers who asked about each other's feelings, nor felt compelled to share them.

"We still have no leads," Edison complained. "We've tried everything, gone around to all the garages, spoken to all the mechanics, the scrap dealers and car traders. Nothing matched up with the damage we see after hit and runs. They've got records and everything so we know they're not lying... We've been really thorough. We're *always* really thorough. I know you think we don't do anything all day but it's bloody hard work being a cop and sometimes you just miss something. It doesn't mean you're crap at your job though."

Franklin just raised his eyebrows in an attempt to show understanding as he drank his cider.

"You see, Frank, there's a lot of odd things about this incident - very strange stuff. We know that guy, Ben, got hit at a place by the tunnel, but there's no glass at the site, there's always glass, it's weird it not being there, because it's almost like... Did you see what the body was like? All floppy and all?

They said at the hospital that he carried a donor card and they were going to ask his... his husband about donating organs but they were no good, they were all squashed."

"What does that mean?" asked Franklin, genuinely bewildered.

"Well, I have this theory. It's a nasty one that only came into my head because you were being so suspicious about the deaths. Did you know that it *is* possible to run someone over and leave almost no damage to the car?"

Franklin shook his head.

"What you do is, you drive up behind them - not very fast at all, ten, even five miles an hour and knock them over, then just drive right over them and they'll be... crushed to death. You know what that means though?"

"It's no accident." Franklin replied, recalling the sickly sensation of shattered bones as he pushed and tugged Ben into his wedding suit. His torso was like a bag of soup.

"Right. What a way to go," Edison was shaking his head miserably. "It explains a lot though, like why it was there, on the Portway, where there are no cameras,"

"Like Henrik and Donna," Franklin added, to which his brother offered no resistance.

"I think you might have been right all along. Someone did all three of them - the hit and run was our only lead, but the roads were near empty at that time of night. He must have followed him, stalking him and he must have planned it because he picked a route using minor roads so he never got caught on any cameras," he added. "We missed it - and you were right."

"Not just me," Franklin added, trying his best not to gloat at this one-upmanship. His mobile phone had received a text message. "Rowan has just arrived."

"Rowan?"

"She's my assistant. She wanted to meet you."

To this, Edison screwed up his nose and took a swig of his pint. "I knew you'd start shagging her soon enough,"

Franklin broke off from the conversation to text her that they were in the garden. "I'm not shagging her, Edison. She's my friend - and you should be thanking her for doing your job for you. Now watch your mouth and show a little respect." To Franklin's surprise, his brother made no response.

Rowan was soon joining them at the table. She had changed out of her funeral attire and was back in jeans and a plaid shirt, which appeared to be her most casual "not at work" look. For some reason she was simply standing beside Franklin as if waiting for her cue to speak. She eyed Edison with something that seemed alarmingly like suspicion.

"Rowan, good to see you. This is my brother, Edison."

"Ed," he corrected her as they shook hands.

"Thomas Edison," Rowan remarked.

Edison nodded as she sat beside Franklin. "He was an inventor. Made the light bulb."

Rowan put her glass of red wine down. "Thomas Swan invented the light bulb; Edison just stole other people's ideas and electrocuted people's pets."

Franklin chuckled. Rowan turned to him and added, "Benjamin Franklin owned African slaves."

To this, Edison laughed and chinked his glass against hers. "I like this girl!" he grinned.

Franklin simply rolled his eyes. "Talking of Edison stealing other people's ideas, my brother seems to be on board with the triple murder theory... finally."

Franklin explained to her the oddities around the hit and run and Rowan sat quietly taking in this new information.

"No accident," she echoed when he was finished. "Did you tell him about our theory?"

"Not another theory..." Edison moaned after he had upturned his glass to finish the last dregs of cider.

"Who are the two people who have been right all along?" Franklin snapped. "We have this idea that Donna, Henrik and Ben were all involved in a car crash. Sometime in early April..."

"...Wait? How?"

"Being observant and listening to people," Franklin responded coldly. "Sometime afterwards, the three of them stayed in touch - in fact, we think Ben and Henrik were already having an affair and that Donna was probably drunk, that's why it wasn't reported. Somebody paid them money at the scene - a lot of it and they decided to leave without saying another word. There was a fourth person at the crash who had something to hide and didn't want anybody else finding out."

Edison was shaking his head but seemed to be doing so with very little enthusiasm. "It's just speculation, nothing more. We need evidence." With this he belched, only this time silently and into his balled fist; a move Franklin could only take as the closest thing his brother got to refined manners around a woman. "There is a bit more... a *lot* more in fact. I wasn't going to say any of this to you but I think it's important. First I need a pint though."

Franklin got up to go to the bar, leaving his assistant and his brother together at the table.

Rowan saw her chance to speak to Edison. "I can't help thinking I recognise you from somewhere," she began cautiously.

Edison just shrugged his shoulders. "People say I've got one of those faces - I'm about quite a lot so you might have just seen me around. They say I look like Franklin too." Edison lit another cigarette and tried to change the subject. "So how is the funeral home treating..."

"...You don't look like him at all. No, it's from somewhere else, maybe years ago."

"Beats me."

The conversation returned to simpler topics until Franklin returned, balancing two pints and a glass of red wine between his slender fingers.

"So what else was there?" Franklin asked after drinks were handed around and thanks offered.

"It was just a hunch, but you'd been so determined that I had to have a look. When Donna drowned her phone got ruined and Henrik's didn't have any calls in the recent history so we didn't have anything to link the two. Last week I got in touch with the phone companies to see if I could get some records. It turns out that Donna did get a text message that evening, it was from Henrik."

Franklin and Rowan gasped in unison. What did it say?" he asked.

"It was "Come and join us for drinks, we're on the harbour side." Something like that."

Franklin narrowed his eyes. "Did it say "us" or "me?""

Edison seemed to think for a moment. "Definitely "us.""

"Ben and Henrik," Rowan interjected.

"Here's the thing though. According to the records, it was sent right about the time we think Henrik died. So if he was murdered, the killer could have used Henrik's phone to invite Donna over and push her into the water. The alcohol content of her blood wouldn't have given her a chance of calling for help."

"I can't believe you didn't check Henrik's phone for text messages *before* you gave it back to the family." Franklin berated in such a manner that Rowan felt it was aimed as much at her as it was at Edison.

"*Perhaps*," Rowan offered, "the killer had already erased the text from Henrik's phone by then."

"That's right," Edison agreed. "We always check, even with suicides - just to see if there were any last texts or calls or something like that; family or girlfriends, and there was nothing - the phone was empty."

Rowan simply nodded once in Franklin's direction to remind him that yes, she had thought of that when the phone had been in her possession.

"I shouldn't be telling either of you any of this. In fact, they're trying to keep the fact that the case has been re-opened, a bit of a secret. We're informing the families in the next couple of days but other than that we're keeping the press out of it. The last thing the city needs is to think there's a serial killer somewhere, and the killer himself... well, people who make these kinds of plans - you know, the really well thought out ones, can act a bit hasty if they think their time is running out."

"Hasty? How do you mean?" asked Franklin.

"He means the killer might have more murders planned," Rowan answered.

"She is *smart,*" Edison remarked as he waved his cigarette in Rowan's direction. "We could use a mind like that on the force."

"Clearly," she smiled. "I'm quite happy where I am though thank you."

Franklin hid his smile in his pint of cider.

"The pair of you have done a good job," Edison continued. "But no more of it, okay? It's a dangerous thing to get involved in and it requires experts from now on. Forensics and that sort of thing, people who know what they're doing. I know you don't think much of the police, but once we have a lead we know where to go."

"Have the forensics looked at the evidence so far?" asked Rowan.

"Yes, but the scissors we found at the scene had no fingerprints on them... not even Henrik's, so he was wearing the gloves when he slashed him."

Rowan and Franklin exchanged a conspiratorial glance. "You said *the* gloves," Franklin pressed. "Not *a* pair *of* gloves."

Edison was now flitting his eyes between the two of them. "Ok. I'm only saying this because it's weird and I don't want you to think this means you can go gallivanting off on another adventure - cause if you do, I can have you done for interfering with a police investigation."

Both nodded obligingly.

"Well, at St. Mary Redcliffe's Church, there was a glove near to Henrik's body. We found Henrik's fingerprints on the outside of it, so it seemed as if the kid may have grabbed it off of the killer when he was dying. Probably got lost in the dark."

"Were there any other fingerprints?" asked Franklin.

"No, the inside was fabric lined so we couldn't dust for prints, but right at the bottom of one of the fingers the forensic guys found a tiny, microscopic piece of fingernail. They ran a DNA test and it matched up with some drug addict we arrested for suspected dealing a few years back."

"Who was he? Did you arrest him?" said Franklin.

Edison shook his head. "Here's the weird thing, he died just before Christmas last year."

Rowan shivered at this news and from the corner of her eye saw Franklin pull his jacket back on. The evening had become dark and the temperature was dropping. A chill wind rushed over the beer garden as if to remind them that summer was still a way off yet.

Soon the conversation moved on to less morbid subjects.

For Franklin this meant the ongoing struggles with Peterman, for Edison it was the usual complaints about paperwork and the endless sensitivity seminars he was expected to attend, "politically correct nonsense," he was quick to dismiss them as. Rowan sat in silence; calculating ideas in her mind before finally speaking up once it seemed as if the evening was drawing to a close.

"Who was the man whose DNA you found? Can you remember his name?"

Edison seemed too drunk to suggest that she stay out of the investigation. "No, I heard it earlier this week but it was one of those weird ones that the long distance runners have at the Olympics."

"An African name?"

Edison gulped down his cider and nodded sheepishly to the black woman, certain that he had said something offensive. "I think so - I handed him over to Franklin, he dealt with the funeral."

"I think I remember," Franklin added.

Eventually it felt as if the night had run its course and the cold wind was starting to bite. Edison was going to move inside for a final pint but Rowan and Franklin said they'd had enough. They said their goodbyes and stepped onto North Street, elbowing their way through the crowd of theatregoers who had gathered to smoke during the interval.

"Well, that was all very interesting," Franklin began. "My brother isn't very good at keeping official police business private, which is good for us."

"I can't believe it," was Rowan's response.

"I know, we barely had to say anything and he started..."

"...No. I can't believe he didn't recognise me. As soon as I saw him I knew who he was, and when you went to the bar, I gave him every chance to remember me, but he didn't."

"What are you talking about?"

"Your brother. He was one of the men who interviewed me after Ruby was murdered; he even came to take my dad away for questioning. He's supposed to be working on it still but he didn't even know who I was; that's how much he cared about me..."

"Oh. Rowan, I'm so sorry, I'm sure he just... I don't

know. My brother's a bit of a git but I'm sure it doesn't mean that they've given up."

"It doesn't matter, I'm fine. I promise you."

"As long as you are,"

"I am. So what now? We're supposed to give up on the case altogether?"

"That's what he said,"

"I feel kind of disappointed, you know. Tragic as it all was, there as a certain thrill in the adventure of it."

Franklin could not disagree as the pair strolled up North Street towards the funeral home. "Still, it wouldn't hurt if we just looked up the name of that dead man on the records..."

"...Just out of curiosity, nothing more." Rowan agreed.

Franklin and Rowan quickened their steps until they were all but galloping back to Gallow & Sons.

33.

It took the pair longer than it ordinarily would to reach the far end of North Street. It was not late but it was dark, and the post work revelers, eager to make the most of a sun drenched Friday had started drinking early - filling pub gardens and lining pavements to smoke. By now the ones who knew their limits had started staggering home or towards waiting taxis, filling the streets like hoards of the undead.

"G'is a kiss, Ginger!" one intoxicated young woman cried out to Franklin as he and Rowan wove their way between the stumbling masses. The woman then turned and threw up against a garden wall.

"It's mayhem tonight," Franklin noted, as they hopped over a fresh stream of urine that trickled out of a nearby alleyway.

"I've seen worse," Rowan informed him.

By the morning, the mile long stretch of North Street that separated the trendy area of Southville from its less salubrious neighbour, Bedminster, would be strewn with the detritus of a night of debauchery. Pools of vomit mingled alongside upturned polystyrene food containers, doner kebabs sprinkled liberally among chips and broken glass. Once there used to be blood too - and Franklin had seen what he was sure was a tooth one morning, but that was rare nowadays; the south's attempts at gentrification had not reduced the alcohol intake of the populace, but now they seemed to be more of a hazard to themselves than anyone else.

On reaching the ordered silence of the funeral home, Rowan and Franklin found a teenage boy attempting to unbutton his flies in the front garden.

"Bugger off!" Franklin called out to him as they strolled up the path, and the boy, oblivious to where he was or who was calling him, swayed woozily away at the man's command.

The home was shrouded in darkness, and looking up at the building, curtains drawn upon the dead, shadows cast against the moonlight, Rowan for the first time found herself a little frightened by it. It was not so easy to forget that this was a place where death was welcomed, where grief was raw.

She shuddered in silence as Franklin unlocked the door to the reception, stepped inside and switched on the light.

The whole length of the corridor leading to the viewing room at the back was drenched in white, fluorescent light and instantly Rowan felt secure in the familiar surroundings. Even things which had seemed alarming on her first day of work; the soft smell of detergent that clung to the air and the echoing squeak of shoes on the wipe-clean floor, felt safe - this was not a place to fear, in many ways it was the place she felt most at home.

"The files will be in my office," said Franklin, and Rowan followed him through to the tiny space next door to Peterman's death chamber. She instinctively switched on the computer and it hummed into life. "All my files are on paper," Franklin reminded her.

"Of course they are," she sighed.

As with everything else downstairs, Franklin's office was kept to a meticulous standard. Bookshelves lined the walls with their contents ordered by subject, with little labels informing him of what each section represented. "Poetry Readings on Death," to "Funeral Customs by Nation," and "Funeral Customs by Religion/Tradition."

His records were kept in three filing cabinets, each arranged by year, stretching back decades to before Franklin had even been born. 2013 had clearly proved to be a profitable year for Gallow & Sons as it took up an entire drawer and a half just by itself.

"I had forgotten how busy we were last year," Franklin said somberly. "Here we go," he sighed upon finding the record in question. It was kept in a paper sleeve with the man's name and the date of funeral. Inside, loose sheets were held together with a paperclip, into which two photographs had been placed. One was of the man alive and youthful looking; a coal black man with wide, kind eyes and hair in a wispy halo around his head; the other taken in the death chamber - his hair now plastered to his face, the face itself gaunt and drawn, his eyes open but hollow.

"That's what heroin will do to you," Franklin told her, a slight note in his voice led Rowan to hear a fatherly warning that might as well have been followed by a: "*so don't you ever try it.*"

"He was twenty-eight?" Rowan gasped, barely able to comprehend that it was the same man in both pictures.

"It's terrifying. I remember the service - barely anybody there at all. You see that a lot with addicts, they eventually drive everyone away and people just have to let you go. You become beyond saving."

"Like Donna Hawley," said Rowan.

"Exactly," Franklin suddenly found himself thinking of the ghostly woman, Lucy Farmer, he had handed the ashes to. What was it she had said again? Why did it suddenly seem relevant?

"Manto Makeba," Rowan read aloud from the information sheet. "Born in Pretoria, South Africa. Moved to England as an infant with his mother... Died December 18th, 2013..."

"Does it say anything there about how he managed to murder two people from beyond the grave?" Franklin asked with a wry smile.

"Strangely enough it doesn't..." Rowan drew a long breath. "This is going to sound ridiculous, but are you sure it was the same man in both photographs?"

Franklin looked at Rowan. "Are you suggesting that I can't tell one black man from another? That's racist." Rowan just laughed. "Anyway, it says he was positively identified by his mother. I remember her, she was so *angry* with him."

"Okay, I'm going to ask something even more insane... Was he cremated or buried?"

Franklin threw his hand to his mouth to stifle an outraged laugh. "Are you suggesting that he wasn't really dead and somehow managed to crawl out of his grave to commit a double - no, triple murder?"

"Franklin, at one point, I thought Donna Hawley had been eaten by the Bristol Crocodile, I'm not letting any possibility go unexplored."

"Well, he was cremated - and on top of that, if he was playing dead he would have had to have been bloody good at it because he went through a full autopsy at the mortuary." Franklin shook his head disbelievingly. "And for the last time, there really *is* no Bristol Crocodile. It's just a few logs in the water and bored journalists; nothing more."

"Fine, be like that. The truth is that his DNA was found at a murder scene. I'm just saying that maybe... the man who was cremated wasn't the same man the police have on record as a match. Maybe they were the ones who screwed up."

Franklin closed the folder and returned it to the filing cabinet. "This is getting us nowhere. Every time it looks as if there is some kind of rational explanation for just one tiny part of this mess, something comes along that blows everything open again."

"Well, we can't give up now, can we?"

"Why not," Franklin was shaking his head. "I don't think there's anything more we can do. I don't think there's anything more we *should* do. We don't have the resources at our disposal to crack this, but we've helped out. That should be enough."

Neither one looked satisfied by this conclusion. She would never admit it, but this investigation had meant a lot to Rowan. It had felt in some small way that the injustice of her sister's murder was being lessened - that if somebody could be punished for killing another, some part of the imbalance of the universe could be restored. She had needed this, and she was certain the same was true for Franklin. A man surrounded by death all day long had to find no excuse to want to fight it.

"We need to let this go," Franklin went on. "It was an interesting distraction, but these are people's lives we're playing with. We'll be interfering with the police - we'll be getting ourselves into danger."

Rowan looked disappointedly towards the filing cabinet. "You're right," she lied. "No more sleuthing."

"It's for the best, I promise."

Rowan just nodded. "Well, I suppose I best head home. My parents don't like me staying out too late."

"I hope you're not cycling back,"

"No. I'll get the bus. Full of drunks at this time of night, but at least it's quick."

"Do you want me to walk you to the bus stop?"

"No, I'm fine. But thank you."

Upon her leaving, Franklin wandered uneasily up the

stairs to his flat. The cider had been strong and he'd had four pints of the stuff and was feeling every drop of them. He changed into his pyjamas, hung his suit neatly inside his wardrobe, and turned on the TV to whatever dross talent show he could find to switch his brain off.

After grabbing his laptop and flopping sideways onto the sofa, he opened up the bookmark to the dating website to see if Angela had contacted him. She had.

The first message had come only the day before. She was a full figured, forty-two year old brunette with an interest in photography and a flirty, sexy smile. Along with a handful of pictures of herself, she had included a small selection of images she had taken; cityscapes and interesting looking people milling about the urban sprawl of Bristol city centre.

"How was the funeral?" she had asked.

"Best day of my life," he replied. He considered adding a smiley face at the end but decided he was too old for that nonsense so sent it unaccompanied. He waited a little while for a response but she was clearly not online at that time. It was a shame because over the course of the past 24 hours, the pair had struck a kind of rapport, the likes of which he'd not encountered for quite some time. At the very least it was nice to have somebody ask him how his day went - nobody ever asked him that.

After waiting impatiently for a response, Franklin eventually decided that messages never arrived when he looked at the screen, so he should give it a while before returning to see if she had replied. Almost immediately, on closing his laptop, his mind started wandering to the murders. *No.* The case was over as far as he was concerned and for that he should be glad. He had helped open an investigation that could prevent further murders from happening; it could even lead to the culprit being arrested. *Yes.* For that he should be pleased.

None of this rationalizing stopped him from picking up his phone and opening the Manhandlr app. *Just to see* how his alter-ego Bed Monster was faring in his world of online dating - if he happened to find another clue or see the face of a killer staring back at him from the screen, so be it.

Bed Monster, with his scenic view profile picture and

empty biography page had received no attention whatsoever. Franklin scrolled down through the menu of available males in the area, inspecting each one in turn for some sign of a killer in the midst of horny Bristolian men. Maybe, somewhere there he would see the face of Manto Makeba and Franklin would know that somehow the man had survived, not only his death, but his cremation, and was back, taking lives across the city. It made as much sense as any other theory Franklin had up until that point.

Instead he saw another dead man. The sight of his face, cheerful and round and optimistic, as if at that very moment when he was taking a selfie in front of his bathroom mirror, he was imagining what a long and fulfilling life he had ahead of him, turned Franklin's blood cold.

His name was BenT. He had been online for eighteen minutes. He was 1.8 miles away. The face of the man was unmistakably that of Ben Tramor; the man who had been killed in a hit and run accident almost two weeks ago. The man Franklin had seen cremated that very afternoon.

34.

It took a little while, staring at BenT's face, for Franklin to be aware of the sense of dread, and something close to panic that had come upon him.

Unmistakably the hit and run victim, the man on the phone screen beamed a benign smile of contended happiness while his brief biography informed any would-be suitors who this gentleman was; "*Just here for a laugh. Looking for mates not dates. How about a drink sometime?*"

The queasy sense that something badly wrong had happened, that the common laws he had always depended on - that the sun rose and fell each day, that the dead did not return to the living, felt abruptly less dependable. First a dead man's glove appears at a murder scene, then another makes his presence known via a dating app with a neon green tick beside his smiling face to inform onlookers that he was currently online. Online and *alive*.

Franklin knew instinctively that this kind of paranoia was for the weak of mind and that he had to pull himself together and think rationally, but this did not stop his anxious fingers from quivering as he clicked on the "*further info*" button at the bottom of the screen.

A new page opened, this time asking for location data to be allowed, and suddenly the phone launched a brief animation of a map of Bristol being zoomed in from the heavens, steering northwards from Bedminster to the lofty heights of Clifton Village. Here, a pair of semi-circles joined each other to form a whole over a row of houses on Royal York Crescent - one of the most prestigious streets in the city; the elegant sweep of tall Edwardian houses that overlooked Bristol and far away into the countryside that surrounded it.

Franklin was momentarily stunned. Was it really that easy to find somebody's location? He just had to ask and this suddenly sinister piece of software would guide him there immediately? It was chilling in its simplicity - Franklin had long heard tales of how modern devices were steadily leaking the private information of individuals with each new model and update, but had yet to see it demonstrated quite so starkly. That people really would surrender their privacy for the sake of convenience - or a quick shag with a total stranger.

Franklin's first response was that he should get in his car and drive up to the house, if for no other reason but to confront whoever was running the machine at the other end, but he knew he was too drunk to drive, and worse, once there he would be a danger not only to himself but to the case. Whatever he decided to do next would require him to be sneaky and to have patience.

With his forefinger and thumb he zoomed the map in closer to reveal the particular house that the app was guiding him towards and, on the back of a takeaway pizza menu, he jotted down the house number that the programme had alarmingly chosen to reveal to him.

Something at least seemed to make sense at this point. It had never occurred to him before how the killer would have been able to draw Henrik out of his home in the middle of the night. What would stop a would-be murderer using the real Ben's photograph and setting up a false profile on Manhandlr, perhaps making it identical to one already set up by the man himself. From there he could talk to Henrik whenever he wanted, who would have no idea that he was talking to the man who would kill him.

Franklin could now visualise the night of Henrik and Donna's murders with such clarity it could have been a reconstruction. The killer, waiting for Henrik to come online, woos the man out with the promise of a late night tryst - perhaps even a daring encounter in a semi public place. He had heard that along with the edges of the vast Downs on the peak of the city, the heavily wooded roundabout just before St. Mary Redcliffe church was notorious for people - particularly men, who engaged in late night, al-fresco sex. The daring young man, eager to try something new, was inadvertently walking to his own death as he left his home that night.

From there it was simply a matter of hiding in the shadows of the mountainous church and waiting, watching that circle draw closer on the screen of his phone until he was ready to pounce. It was risky and he could have been seen, but killers must always take risks. A hand over Henrik's mouth, the young man might have thought this to be no more than a wilder experiment in sex than he had imagined, until the blade slashed at his wrist. Falling to the ground, taking one of his killer's gloves with him as he sank, Henrik would have bled out until he died, perhaps still unaware what had happened to him.

Once dead, the killer would have searched Henrik's pockets until he found his phone. From there he sent a single text message to Donna, informing her that Henrik and Ben were out for the night and wanted to see her. If Henrik's downfall was sex, then Donna's was most certainly alcohol. The killer must have known that on a Saturday night, when the woman was not expected at work the following day, she would be deep into her bottle of vodka and powerless to resist the urge for more. He waited for her response then wiped the phone of its previous text history.

The murderer must have planned his route beforehand to minimise areas where he might be caught on CCTV, nevertheless, he would not run for fear of drawing attention to himself. Instead he strode purposefully through the mainly residential areas of the city, around the back of the harbour side where the cameras were trained only on speeding cars, not pedestrians. His black clothes would have helped obscure not only himself as he paced across the city, but the blood that had no doubt splashed upon him from the violent death he had just inflicted.

From there, he might even have seen Donna's approach as she drunkenly stumbled across the footbridge towards the Floating Harbour. Perhaps he was tempted to run to her at once and fling her over the edge, but she no doubt would have screamed and drawn attention to them both before he could haul her into the muddy water below. She had to die in silence and it had to look like an accident. He instead slipped through the shadows ahead of her until he found a place beside the water, away from the prying lenses of the cameras that lined Bristol in their thousands. Then, it was just a matter of waiting.

Crouching in the dark, with only the sound of his own

heartbeat and perhaps the slosh of the water and the creaking of masts as the boats rose and fell with the gentle ebb of ripples on the harbour; the far off sounds of nightclubs booming bass, and the drunks screaming and singing until her graceless footsteps drew closer and closer until...

A single, ferocious push and the woman was sent toppling into the blackness. If she had found time to scream it would have done her no good as instead her lungs would simply fill with water. The splash she made was probably louder than he had anticipated but they were both far enough from those who were sober enough to acknowledge it.

Surfacing, she must have known her fate was sealed, stunned and unable to breathe, death would probably have come quickly to her in the frigid May harbour. Perhaps she would have been too drunk to know anything at all and would have slipped away as quickly and peacefully as those many nights where sleep had not taken her, but the friendly warmth of alcohol had instead.

Snapping from his imagination as suddenly as if he were waking from a dream, Franklin found himself shivering with the awareness that this was where all the clues had been leading him. That this was the only version of events where every piece of the puzzle fit in place with the kind of elegance only a carefully laid plan would allow.

At once he closed Manhandlr and phoned his brother. It rang for an agonising amount of time until eventually Edison answered, his voice groggy from sleep and slurred from drink.

"Frank? What time is it?"

"It's..." Franklin had lost track of the hour. "Just gone two."

"What's wrong? Are Mum and Dad okay?"

"They're fine. Look, I think I know where the killer lives, I just don't know who he is."

"What are you talking about?"

Franklin explained his most curious night and the even stranger reappearance of Ben Tramor. Edison seemed a lot more awake when he'd recounted his tale.

"Wait Frank, you were on a gay dating site?"

"I was doing research..."

"Ah, crap. I've seen this happen before. There were a couple of guys from work who said they were just researching something on one of the work computers. Few months later, they're both marching in that gay parade in Bristol - in their uniforms and everything. Look, it's not up to me what you do with your life but that was just political correctness gone…"

"…Shut up, Edison. Did you listen to anything I just said? The killer lives on Royal York Crescent, I even know the house number."

"Because he had the same picture on… what was it? Man Hunter?"

"Manhandlr."

"Well, he probably just stole someone else's picture to hide it from the wife. People do it all the time online; nobody's who they pretend to be are they?"

"But…" Franklin was suddenly lost for words. He remembered back to when he had called himself an "events organiser" on his dating website profile.

"Frank, if you tell me the address, I'll get someone to look into it tomorrow but I don't think we can even question him. There's another guy on the force who lives up on Royal York Crescent. Maybe he can doorstep him in the morning."

Franklin was about to agree when a new and terrifying thought came into his head; a memory of the grey haired policeman sitting in his uniform in an unmarked car outside of the Farmer's flat when he had gone to meet Evan and Lucy. "This police officer who lives on Royal York Crescent. He wasn't responsible for dismissing the case as an accident and a suicide in the first place, was he?"

There was a long pause on the phone before a thin voice replied; "Yes, as a matter of fact he was."

"And he has no doubt been eager to close it now it has been re-opened?"

"Look Frank, it's one thing to accuse the police of incompetence it's another to say that one of us is responsible."

"Answer the question Edison."

"Then yes, he has been saying it's a waste of time."

"Are you working tomorrow?"

"No, but I really don't want to get involved in…"

"...We're meeting tomorrow, for breakfast. I'll pick you up first thing."

There was an annoyed huff at the end of the line. "Fine. But you'd better be on to something here. Accusing a fellow officer of murder is pretty much the quickest way I can think of off getting fired."

"Don't worry, I know what I'm doing."

With that the two brothers hung up their phones. It was late and Franklin was tired and drunk so he opted to spread out under a blanket on the sofa, prompting Felicity to move at her top speed - a sluggish crawl, to clamber onto his chest where she purred and patted her feet before curling into a contented ball.

Just before sleep took hold, Franklin found himself opening up Manhandlr one last time. BenT was still there, still smiling and still online. Downstairs the same man's ashes lay in an urn in the darkness of the death chamber.

35.

As promised, Franklin was at his brother's house the following morning. Edison lived in a modest dwelling in the heart of the district of Redland. Along the leafy terrace of Victorian houses, all occupied by middle income families, who cared for their front gardens and chatted merrily to one another on the daily school run; all of them except for Edison's, the front garden of which was completely barren and uncared for. Edison was not one to make friends easily, least of all with people who he only knew due to a fluke of geography. He was never rude to his neighbours, but a dismissive "morning"' as he marched to his car every day was usually enough to keep them at arms length.

Upon ringing the doorbell, Franklin waited patiently for his brother to respond. Eventually Edison did appear, bleary eyed and wearing a crumpled shirt.

"What time did you go to bed last night?" were Franklin's first words to him.

"I found half a bottle of gin in the fridge when I got home," was his reply. "It's every Englishman's right to have a lie-in on a Saturday. I think it's in the bible."

Franklin forced a smirk. "It's 9am. It's hardly the crack of dawn."

Edison rubbed his eyes. "Give me a second," with that he jogged upstairs. Franklin waited until he heard the sound of a toilet flushing before his brother reappeared with a couple of bananas. "Here," he said. "Breakfast."

Edison's car was littered with old chocolate wrappers and crisp packets. On the passenger seat a small pile of The Sun newspaper were scattered, which he picked up and hurled into the back. An ashtray, overflowing with cigarette butts rested in the partition, to which Franklin offered a withering look of disdain; if Edison had spotted his reaction, he was refusing to take the bait.

"Put your seatbelt on," Edison grumbled as Franklin sat beside him. "If the police see you not wearing one I'll be in a load of crap over it. Bloody political correctness."

Franklin shook his head in disbelief as he buckled up. Of

course he wore his seatbelt - he had seen far too many bodies smashed to bits without them. Some days he found it hard to fathom just how the pair of them could be related, and not only be so different, but to know so little about the other that they might as well be strangers.

As they drove, Franklin was quickly made aware of just how many things annoyed his brother when he was behind the wheel. Every traffic light, every speed bump and every pedestrian crossing the road was worthy of contempt or even an aggressive honk of the horn. Franklin found the whole experience inordinately stressful, driving had always seemed to him like a sedate means to traverse two locations; for Edison however, driving was a battle of wits and speed.

Clifton Village was always beautiful in the sunshine. Being one of the more popular draws to what little tourism Bristol experienced, its wide road and quaint backstreets were immaculate, lined with fancy bakeries and quaint boutiques. Little tables where university students basked in the morning sun nursing their hangovers, pouring back mugs of overpriced coffee alongside artfully disheveled mothers with babies in expensive looking buggies. Young drunks, negotiating the cobbled streets in high heels, mascara running down their faces, raised barely a look as they tottered past - Clifton was the home to a unique brand of decadence all of its own.

The street they were heading for, Royal York Crescent, was a grand sweep of towering houses with sunken basement gardens behind railings. The pavement before it was raised high above street level to accommodate underground vaults that served as garages for the residents. From the road the houses could not be seen, so the two brothers parked the car nearby and climbed the steps to the pavement to be level with the ground floor flats. They found a bench at the halfway point of the terrace beside a post box, so old fashioned and handsomely ornate, it looked as if it belonged in a museum. They sat and waited. Just in sight was the house they were looking for; it had a green door with a lion's head knocker and a brass plaque declaring that a Victorian war general once lived there.

"So," Edison began. "This is how the other half live."

"Not sure if it's the *other half* Edison. You seem to be doing pretty well for yourself. Not many people can afford a house in Redland all to themselves."

Edison shrugged his shoulders and unpeeled his banana. "You got three rooms in your place."

"It could have been your place - it *should* have been your place."

"Do you really want to get into this again? I never was built for that kind of thing, it's better that you got the business."

Franklin decided to let the matter drop and made a start on his banana. Once he was finished he switched on his phone and opened up Manhandlr. Immediately the surge of faces flooded the screen. The man who had worn Ben's face last night was nowhere to be found.

"He hasn't switched it on," Franklin said, mostly to himself.

"Let me see that," and Edison snatched the phone from him. Scrolling down the page, Franklin watched his brother's eyes widen. "All these men are looking for a shag?"

"Mostly, I think."

"Dirty buggers," Edison condemned. "It's like ordering a pizza."

"Don't judge. I'm pretty sure if you could meet women so easily for a quickie you'd be signing up in no time."

Edison nodded as he handed the phone back. "So. We just sit here and wait all day do we?"

"I don't know. Maybe. Somebody has to leave at some time, don't they?"

"I can get us a coffee," Edison suggested. "But you're paying."

Franklin was just about to reach for his wallet when the door of the house opened and a man appeared. Dressed in jeans and a polo shirt the grey haired man, with a surprisingly muscular build for one his age, stepped onto the street.

"It's him!" Franklin could barely contain his excitement at this good fortune, the same man he had seen waiting in the car outside Evan and Lucy Farmer's tower block all those weeks ago. Edison said nothing, his face turned away from the man and towards Franklin.

The man reached through the doorframe and pulled a woman through it. The woman was small and slight, and easily a decade younger than the man, who had her by the wrist, her petite stature dwarfed by his stocky build. Franklin could not hear what he was saying but he seemed angry, talking fiercely into the woman's face as an irritated father might talk to his child. The woman just nodded as curls of dark hair drew like curtains across her eyes.

"It's him," Edison said gravely. "I knew it was going to be him. The one person who could cause the most trouble for me."

"The police officer?" Franklin gasped. "The one who wants the case closed?"

"That's the one."

The man let the woman's hand drop and instead wrapped his arm across her shoulders and pulled her in close. The way he held her was not that of an expression of love or affection; it was an act of possession, to tell the world that this woman was his property.

"He looks like a charmer," Franklin commented.

"You don't want to be on the wrong side of Martin Maybridge. He's got a real temper - they say it's why he keeps getting turned down for promotion. People don't like him."

The man was now marching the woman away from them; she was pinned against him so tightly she almost had to walk on tiptoes to reach his height and pace.

"Is that his wife?"

"Yes. She was at the New Year party a few months back. She's pretty but very quiet, doesn't even drink." Once the pair had vanished around the corner, Edison allowed himself a deep exhalation, before lighting up a cigarette and replacing the air in his lungs with smoke. "This could be really bad, Frank."

"I know."

"I don't think you do. On the force... we're supposed to look after each other, you know, watch each other's back and all that. You don't go around accusing your fellow officers of triple murder - not unless you want to end up in serious trouble. All of a sudden there are claims that you tampered with evidence... planted drugs at a crime scene. Before you know it, you're in front of a tribunal and fired without a pension."

Franklin laughed spitefully. "We all know the police get away with anything they want so long as there is someone to shred enough files or fix everything in their favour."

Edison merely shrugged. "I'm sure it happens; more than you may even know. But the thing is, you're untouchable if the police want you to be - or if they want you gone there'll be nobody vouching for you, and suddenly, there are files everywhere about your misconduct."

"That's disgraceful,"

"That's the truth."

Franklin shook his head in disbelief. "Am I supposed to have sympathy for police corruption?"

"You're supposed to have sympathy for me, Frank. Look at me, I live alone, I can barely dress and feed myself. At least you have a cat, I can't even keep a cactus alive. My work is all I have and even that isn't much. I've had three different partners in five years and do you know why? Nobody can stand to work with me; they keep on asking to get transferred. One of them moved out of the city altogether. How do you think that makes me feel?"

Franklin didn't know what to say. Over the years he had run a gamut of emotions with his brother, from anger to disgust, from exasperation to resignation, but never pity. "Three people are dead Edison. We can't just ignore it to make things easy for you."

"I know," he replied grimly. "I hate to say it, but you've been right from the start and I've tried my hardest to disprove everything but I can't anymore. I think you're right this time too - I think Martin Maybridge is a murderer."

"So what are we going to do about it?"

"We're going to keep our mouths shut until the right time comes. If we're going to take this bastard down, we're going to need some proof."

The two men sat in silent agreement. Not since they had become adults had Franklin felt closer to- or more proud of, his brother.

36.

Beneath a sky heavy with clouds, Franklin drove the little Smart car through the winding one-way system between Bedminster and Knowle West as Rowan sat beside him.

"I'm not convinced," she finally said, as the overhead clouds began to break and wash the streets of concrete and stone.

"What hasn't convinced you?"

"That the killer was a policeman... It just doesn't make sense, well, not the whole sense."

Franklin raised an eyebrow to her. "It's fine to have invested your time in a different theory Rowan. That man Art did sound like a very unsavoury type."

Rowan shook her head thoughtfully. "It's not that... it's just that there has to be more to it that we've both missed. It almost feels too clean."

"Well," Franklin conceded. "That's what we're here today for. Keep your ears open for anything I miss, but otherwise, let me do all of the talking."

Knowle West was one of the harder areas of the city to love. It had been built seemingly overnight in a postwar city that was aching to expand its borders. A jungle of stark, concrete tower blocks lurched over brutalist shopping centres that were no more than receptacles for litter caught on the wind. Social decay had led to poverty, which had led to crime and the entire area had become the place where one fell to when there was simply no further to drop.

The tower block they were in search of was a sheer, characterless facade of functional simplicity. The reinforced glass door was shattered within its frame, and the little buttons to buzz you in had mostly fallen from the board on which they had been haphazardly mounted.

Franklin pressed the button to the appropriate flat and a thin, shy voice answered.

"Hello?"

"Hello. Is that Lucy Farmer?"

A brief pause. "Yes."

"Ms. Farmer. My name is Franklin Gallow. I was the

funeral director for your mother-in-law Donna Hawley last month. Would you mind if we came in for a chat - nothing serious at all, just some administrative matters."

The woman sighed. "Very well."

The door began buzzing and vibrating in its frame. Franklin pushed it open and he and Rowan began the ascent of six flights of stairs to the flat Lucy shared with her husband and baby son. She was already waiting on the landing when they reached her floor.

"I'm sorry," she said. "Is this about payment? My husband usually deals with all of that."

"No nothing like that at all. Is your husband in this afternoon?"

She shook her head. "He's staying with his dad." Lucy Farmer looked pale and tired. Her skin was loose and dry; her eyes red and flushed. Her unkempt hair was tied back in a loose ponytail and looked full of grease. Her tee-shirt was smeared with stains of infant food and baby vomit. She looked to Franklin like somebody in desperate need of a good night's sleep.

"Come inside," she beckoned them through the doorway to the darkened flat. Somewhere Franklin could hear a baby crying. The stuffy air smelt of talcum powder and cigarette smoke.

"This is my assistant, Rowan," Franklin said.

Rowan and Lucy nodded politely and one another before Lucy offered tea and coffee, which they both declined.

"Now," Franklin cleared his throat. "At Gallow & Sons we have been going through a series of changes to make our company... more compatible with the modern world, and as such, we have been selecting some of our clients to take a survey so that we can best judge their experiences and learn how to grow into the future."

Lucy nodded slowly as she led Franklin and Rowan to the living room, where a single beam of milky light from a window illuminated pieces of dust that were caught in the air. The pair found a spot on the sofa that was not entirely covered in baby clothes and sat down.

"A survey? Is that all? I was so worried that my husband had messed something up with the payments..." Lucy looked across the two faces of her guests. "I would very much like to take part in your survey. You took great care of Donna and we were most grateful."

Franklin flashed her a soft smile and then reached into his briefcase for a copy of the survey he had hastily written out that morning. As he passed it across the table, he let the photograph slip from his fingers, where it fell face up, just as he had hoped.

The woman's reaction to the face of Ben Tramor was a scream stifled by a shaking hand. "Why do you have a picture of Ben?" she gasped.

Franklin and Rowan swapped the briefest of glances before he asked, "How do you know Mr Tramor?"

Lucy was still staring incredulously at the picture on the table before her. The round faced man with his arms crossed over his chest, a cheeky grin revealing just a hint of a shared joke with the cameraman.

"Is he dead?" Lucy whispered.

"He is. It was a hit and run not that long ago."

Tears began to roll down the woman's cheeks. "I shall be next," she whispered.

"What can you tell us about the car crash?"

Lucy's eyes, frenzied and darting madly about the room came to rest upon Franklin's. "How did you know about the car crash? Are you the police?"

"We're helping the police. You aren't in trouble though, I promise you that. But it does sound as if you might be in danger."

Lucy fell back into a threadbare armchair and reached for a packet of cigarettes. In her trembling fingers she pulled one from the pack and lit it. Hungrily she sucked upon it.

"I'm the only one left... It was all my fault."

"This is nobody's fault but the killer, Lucy. Please just tell us what you know and we can help you."

The woman stared into her own thoughts, her eyes drooping into some distant yet vivid memory.

"It was in April... April 3rd I think. The baby was at nine months then and, all he was doing was crying, and my mother in-law used to come round to help when things got too much. She was a drunk but she wasn't a terrible person.

She was fun and funny to be around and I'd never known that before. Once a week, on Fridays we had taken to going for drinks together, just so I could have a few hours out of the house and I could enjoy myself. She drank so much, but I never judged her, and I think both of us enjoyed the company.

"It was that night though... the third. It was early in the morning and we had stayed out drinking for hours and Donna was driving me home. She was drunk - of course she was, she was always drunk and always in trouble for it too. We were just coming up to Cabot Circus, you know that strange footbridge that goes over the road, when Donna plowed into the side of a car that was waiting at the traffic lights.

"Before we even knew what was happening there was this huge crash as a car piled into the back of us. We were sandwiched between cars and my head had hit the dashboard. Neither of us were seriously injured but we were shaken. Perhaps that's why we weren't thinking straight - and why we did what we did..."

"What did you do?" Franklin pressed softly.

"We got out of the cars and met each other. In the car that had crashed into us were Henrik and Ben. They were having a late night tryst of some sort... did you know they were together?"

Franklin nodded.

"In the car we had crashed into was a man. He didn't seem annoyed with any of us even though Donna and I were at fault for crashing into him; he just wanted to be out of there as soon as possible. He told us to get our cars fixed as soon as we could and gave us all money right there - five hundred *each*." Lucy looked sadly around her gloomy living room. "Five hundred pounds goes a long way if you're someone like me."

"Was there anyone else at the scene?" Franklin asked.

Gradually Lucy began to nod. "His wife was there... in the car." Her eyes welled and overflowed with tears. "Oh Mr Gallow, I'm so ashamed!"

"Where was she?"

Lucy swallowed hard and looked pleadingly at the funeral

director. "She was lying on the back seat of the car. Her hands were tied behind her back and there was tape across her mouth. I saw her through the window; she was trying to scream and to kick for help. She must have known that I saw her because our eyes met and she was just *begging* for my help but I did nothing. The man said that we saw nothing and it was none of our business; that he was teaching his wife a lesson for disobeying him. He said that he was a policeman and if we tried to do anything, he would make sure we all regretted it. He said he could trace us if he wanted to and that we'd all do better to just go home and forget everything we thought we saw."

"A policeman?" Franklin ventured.

"A policeman," she confirmed. "I've lived with the shame ever since; that none of us stepped in to help her when she was so desperately in need. We wanted the money though and Donna would have lost her license again if she had been caught drinking and driving. Henrik and Ben... they had their own reasons not to have anyone find out that they were together... so we all just agreed that... we would do nothing?"

"You *left* her?" Rowan gasped. She had kept quiet throughout this admission but seemingly could take no more.

"I know it was a wicked thing to do, but you don't understand. Things had been desperate for me, and the money helped so much... None of it seems worth it now, not now that people have died."

"What did this man look like? The policeman?"

"He was in his mid forties I'd guess. He had grey hair and was kind of big - but big in the way that it was more muscle than fat - he looked like the kind of man who could flatten me with a single punch." said Lucy.

"Or his wife," Rowan added to which Franklin glared a warning glance at her.

"Mrs Farmer. I shall take your story to the police - and they no doubt will want to question you at some time, maybe even make a formal identification of a likely suspect - a man who fits your description. His wife is still alive."

Lucy erupted into tears at this point. "Oh thank god!"

"If he managed to track Donna and Ben via their number plates, then he may not know who you are, but nevertheless, you must take every precaution until this man is arrested. Don't go out alone and don't answer the door to any strangers - and I include the police when I say that. If a policeman is by himself don't answer. Answer only to police officers who come in pairs."

"I can't believe this is my life..." Lucy was shaking her head.

Franklin and Rowan, both shaken and disturbed by the tale Lucy had recounted, left sometime later. The sky had broken into a thunderstorm as the pair made their way across the city in the car.

"So you were right," Rowan said. "It was a policeman."

"Perhaps," Franklin added. "But there's more to this story, I am sure of that, and as for Lucy... I don't think she's even close to telling us the whole truth."

Rowan let this sink in fully. "How do you mean?"

"I don't think she killed anyone," Franklin went on. "But she's responsible for every death that's happened so far."

A roll of thunder split the sky in two.

37.

"Your brother is a coward," Rowan intoned darkly as she moved around the diminutive body on the stretcher. "He's just as bad as the rest of them. Donna, Henrik, Ben. Especially Lucy; she didn't even have the grace to get herself killed."

The pair were measuring the body of an old man, as they spoke dispassionately of the crimes. "I don't know," said Franklin. "Poverty makes people do things out of desperation - pretty much everyone we've met along the way has been poor."

"Except for Henrik," Rowan was quick to point to out. "His family is rich."

"Yes, but he had something he wanted to keep hidden. That can be more than enough of a motivation to stay silent."

"Well, it's certainly no excuse for Edison. I thought cops were supposed to be brave."

Franklin had no answer for this one. He had rung his brother as soon as they got back to the funeral home and Edison had reacted to news of the crash with something close to hostility. "It's still not *proof*," he all but hissed down the line. "We saw his wife; she's alive and well. Perhaps it was just a kinky game or something."

"I'm growing exhausted with him," Franklin confided. "I really thought I'd won him over yesterday. I am a little sympathetic though. He's in a dreadful position and doesn't know how to react."

"He's a coward," Rowan echoed. "If anything happens to Lucy Farmer, there will be blood on his hands."

"I think there's more than enough on hers," Franklin added.

Franklin added the measurements of the corpse of Mr Dover to a blank diagram of a human form on a sheet of paper that had been designed for the purpose. The empty line drawing of an androgynous body shape was soon decorated with measurements from every angle. "The casket must be at least half a foot shorter in length," he informed Rowan who was flicking through a catalogue of designs.

"Here we go," she said as she stopped on a page of glossy photographs. "Oak exterior, silk lined. Christ, have you seen the prices?"

Franklin nodded. "Had he been a few inches shorter I could have squeezed him into a child's casket, that would have saved them a bit of money."

"It's such a terrible waste. I want one of those cardboard ones, or even better, why can't people share their coffins? There's no need to incinerate it. Why not just whip him out of it, send him down to the furnace without it then rent it out to the next corpse that comes along?"

Franklin was not sure if Rowan was joking or not, so he offered no more than a wry smile as he picked up his phone and called the company that would be constructing Mr Dover's casket.

While Franklin was waiting for his call to be answered, Rowan slipped out of her blue boiler suit and went to check her own phone, which was in the office. Refusing to even acknowledge Peterman's existence as she passed him in the hall, Rowan stepped into the office and fumbled through the pockets of her coat which was hanging on the back of the door still dripping with rain.

Just as she had expected, there was a missed call and a text message. The text message read:

"Rowan. Thank you for your CV. I was very impressed. If you are still interested please come for an interview at 9am tomorrow morning. Thanks. Mandy."

Rowan slipped the phone back into her coat pocket and returned to the death chamber where Franklin was finishing his call. She tried her best not to look as suspicious or guilty as she felt in that moment, but the pressure of having to lie would likely make it harder. Lying came easily to Rowan, but only when it was on the fly - the fast creation of a fabricated story out of nothing more than imagination, embroidered just enough to be feasible. It was these calculated lies that never quite seemed to ring true.

"Franklin..." she began. "I just heard from my parents, they have something planned for tomorrow. I'm not sure what it is but I think it might be something to do with them separating. Would it be OK if I have the day off?"

Franklin did not need to think about it for long. "That's fine. I hope it isn't anything too serious?"

Rowan shrugged her shoulders and that seemed to be all the reassurance Franklin required.

"In fact," Franklin said. "I think we're pretty much done for the day. Not much more we can do for poor Mr Dover; you might as well get going before the rain starts again."

"Thank you," Rowan replied. Her voice wavered only slightly with guilt in the face of his generosity and kindness. Franklin would surely never forgive her for looking for work elsewhere if he found out, even if it *was* for a greater good - or at least a hunch that could lead to a greater good.

That evening, long after Rowan had left, Franklin sat himself on the sofa with a mug of tomato soup while Felicity purred beside him drifting in and out of a shallow sleep. The TV was suitably trashy, his bottle of cider enjoyably strong. He was fully prepared to have a night where sleep gripped him so completely that he would awake eight hours later with Felicity curled up on his chest and the cheerful chirp of breakfast television in the background.

He checked Manhandlr again - a habit that had become almost hourly since the night he had seen Ben Tramor there. Obsessively inspecting the faces of strangers, or near strangers, as so many faces had become familiar with time, searching for the dead man he had cremated, hiding somewhere in the city.

Downstairs there was a rat-a-tat at the door and Franklin was snapped out of his nightly inspection of the gallery of rogues. Consulting his watch, he was surprised to learn it had only just after 8pm and nowhere near as late as his tiredness had suggested to him. He jogged down the staircase and into the reception. Outlined in the glass was a tall, thin figure that Franklin was startled to recognise so quickly.

"Alf!" Franklin smiled as he opened the door. "What are you doing here?" Franklin was surprised not just by the genuine warmth he heard in his own voice, but his curious instinct to hug his son; an instinct he only just managed to cast aside.

Alf stepped in from the dark and the gentle rain. He was wearing a wax jacket and the kind of flat cap Franklin had once associated with farmers but was now more likely seen on fashionable young men about the city.

"This is a surprise," Franklin beamed, to which Alf simply nodded before the two went upstairs to the living room.

"Can I get you anything? Tea? Coffee?"

Alf simply shook his head. "I don't drink caffeine after 6pm," he informed his father.

"Oh, well. How about a cider? You're old enough now," for some reason Franklin thought that Alf would be impressed with him remembering his age.

"I'm going to the pub later. I don't want to have too much alcohol in one night." Alf glanced over at the open bottle on the coffee table. "I see you've started though - drinking at home. Alone."

Franklin wasn't sure where the words came from but he found himself saying them nonetheless. "Don't knock it. You owe your life to your mother and me staying in drinking." It was an incredibly risky joke to make and Franklin was just about to apologise when to his surprise, Alf broke into a roar of laughter.

"I suppose that's true," he giggled and Franklin felt his heart soar with pride at making his son laugh.

"So why are you in Bristol?"

"It's a friend of mine's 18th. She wanted to go out for a few drinks in the city. It's not long on the train and some friends have a sofa I can crash on."

"Sounds like fun," said Franklin. "Whereabouts are you going?"

"Nowhere you'd know," Alf shrugged.

Franklin chose not to push the matter because Alf was almost certainly right. It had been a long time since he'd been out for a night on the town. "So what brought you here?"

"It was nothing really... just a favour. When I go to Uni in October, we're all supposed to submit something we've been working on over the summer, for the art college. They put on a big display every year at Bower Ashton campus of the fresher's work. I'd been thinking of something to display there and I was wondering if I could get a photograph... of you."

Franklin could barely stifle his gasp quickly enough.

"You're making a piece of art about *me*?"

Alf nodded. "Don't get too emotional, you haven't seen it yet."

"But... I'm just a bit surprised that's all."

"If you're going to get all weird about it, I won't stick around; I'll just do something else instead."

"No, no, please don't. I would be honoured to see what you come up with."

"OK. I was hoping you could wear your full funeral attire and stand somewhere that looked... morbid."

Franklin nodded obligingly. He all but skipped into his bedroom and dressed as quickly as he could in his full suit, cufflinks, shoes and top hat - the hat was rarely used but if it was for art, he would have to look the part. When he returned to the living room, Alf was attempting an awkward stroke of Felicity who stared at this strange invader as if he were about to consume her whole.

"How about the parlour downstairs? That's where we put bodies on display when families come round to view them before the service."

"There isn't anyone in there *now* is there?"

Franklin shook his head and led the way downstairs to the wood lined visiting room. Alf produced an expensive looking camera from his pocket and asked him to pose in front of a huge vase of plastic lilies in a funereal shade of purple.

Franklin had never posed for anything before and did not at first know how to stand comfortably. After the whir and click of the camera, he adjusted himself slightly and waited for the next photograph to be taken, but instead Alf simply closed the shutter and replaced the camera in his pocket.

"You're just taking one picture?" he asked.

"Yes," Alf replied. "You're an undertaker, not Kate Moss."

"Funeral director," Franklin corrected.

Alf simply stared at his father cynically. "Well, I think I'm pretty much done."

"Excellent," Franklin said as he walked Alf through to the reception. "When do you think I'll be able to see the artwork?"

Alf simply shrugged. "I'm not sure if you're going to like

it. You might prefer to give it a miss."

"Nonsense, I'll want to see it. Not because it's about me but because it's *by* you." Franklin's head was heavy with words and he felt almost incapable of silencing them. "I know I wasn't a father to you. I missed out on everything because I didn't know you existed... but I'll tell you one thing, no matter how hard you try to keep me at arms length, I'm going to get to know you - and I'll win you over one day. I don't think you can go on resenting me forever."

"I can try," Alf warned, his eyes narrowing, but with just the faintest trace of a smile spreading across his face. Without another word, the young man stepped out into the night and was gone.

In less than ten minutes, Franklin was in his pyjamas and watching the contents of his TV hard drive. Idly he played with his phone, that annoying habit he had developed of being unable to focus on only one thing if other distractions were present, until he came once again to Manhandlr.

The usual lineup was there. The naked torso who lived on his street, the alarmingly young boy who claimed to be eighteen, the wizened old man who was looking for men under 25. But there was a new face, a not unfamiliar one, but one new to this sordid little app that occupied so much of Franklin's time.

Alf's smiling face beamed up at him from the gallery of men, his red hair glistening in the sunlight of a park somewhere. "*GingerNuts,*" he had called himself. His profile simply read "*Up 4 anything 2night.*"

Franklin immediately turned off the app and let the phone slip from his hand, disgusted and ashamed by this unwanted glimpse into his son's life, every bit as intrusive as if he had peeped through his bedroom keyhole.

38.

Rowan woke up to the smell of coffee brewing downstairs. Wearily remembering the day she had planned for herself, she pulled on her dressing gown and left her room.

In the kitchen, her father was boiling an egg and humming along to the radio. "Morning Ro'" he smiled to her. Rowan was instantly suspicious.

"Where's mum?"

Her father fished the egg out from the water and simply warned her, "She asleep on the sofa. She has a headache."

"A headache? Don't you mean hangover?"

The man's head drooped. "Perhaps. But you can't blame her, can you?"

"I think I can. It's been two years; when is she going to start being a mother again? And you're not helping either. Since you came back, she's been worse than ever. You know that nobody would blame you for bailing on us. I'm not going to be around here forever anyway."

Oscar placed his egg into an eggcup shaped like William Shakespeare's head and cracked the top open with a teaspoon. "Do you think I'm still here because I want to be? I think you're forgetting that we were once... happy." His voice trailed away.

"We were once a lot of things but we're barely even a family anymore."

"Don't be unkind, Ro'. We're all trying our best - and anyway, how am I supposed to keep an eye on you if I'm not here?"

"I'm almost twenty. Most girls my age are at uni and looking after themselves."

Oscar dipped a toasted soldier into his egg. "Did you give any more thought to applying for university again this year? It's not too late."

Rowan's father was a pharmacist and had, for as long as she could remember, imparted to her and Ruby the importance of education. With the death of her sister, Rowan's education had fallen into a tailspin from which she had felt no need to recover. "I have a job, Dad. I'm happy with it."

"How's it going at the supermarket?"

Rowan helped herself to a slice of toast and left the kitchen without responding to her father. After a shower and a coffee, she was hurtling across the city on her bike, allowing herself plenty of time for the job interview but determined to get there with plenty to spare.

The bike, along with her iPad and much of her wardrobe, had been gifts from members of her extended family in the weeks and months following Ruby's murder. People she had neither heard from in years, nor could recall by name, lavished expensive goods on her as if in attempt to assuage their own guilt. She had accepted them all with a deep sense of suspicion; for each one seemed to say, "have this, so that we might never have to see you again, and let us pray that nothing so terrible could ever befall our home as it has yours."

The charity shop was on North Street, at the slightly less salubrious end away from the trendy bars and artisanal bakeries. A scruffy place with a disorganised interior of coats piled upon each other in mounds and books stacked up on the floor, alongside diseased looking cuddly toys and boxes of jigsaws held together with Sellotape.

She was a full fifteen minutes early, so after folding up her bike she went for a walk along a residential street leading towards the flat of the drug addict, Manto Makeba - the corpse who had somehow attended the murder scene of Henrik Nielssen. She had a missed call on her phone; it was from Franklin.

"Rowan," he spoke softly on the phone. "I know it's your day off, I'm sorry for calling you... I didn't know who else to phone."

"What's wrong? You sound out of sorts."

"I suppose I am rather. I had a weird night. Alf came over to see me and I saw him on Manhandlr... did you know he was gay?"

"I've never met him Franklin. How would I know that?" she replied flatly.

"Yes, yes, that's true."

"Is that a problem for you? You never struck me as a

bigot."

"I'm not!" Franklin was quick to inform her. "It's just that, you know when it's late at night and all sorts of things are going through your head and it just occurred to me in the small hours that... Maybe it's my fault."

"Your fault?" Rowan tried halfheartedly to suppress a laugh. "Don't tell me that you're yet another one of those god-awful liberals who turn conservative at the first sign of the real world."

"I'm not, I promise. It's just, I know how absurd it sounds, but if I'd been there for him when he was growing up - a strong male role model - a dad, then maybe he wouldn't be like this."

"I want you to think back over what you've said to me after I hang up and imagine hearing someone else say it. Then you might understand just how ludicrous and offensive you sound. Alf is the way he is without your help. Now pull yourself together."

She heard him sigh on the phone. "Am I making a fool of myself?"

"You've gone beyond that, but you can stop yourself before you become a full on homophobe."

"I just think... maybe I feel a lot more guilt over being an absent father than I thought I did. Whatever the circumstances, he still knows nothing about me at all."

"It isn't good that he's on Manhandlr though, is it? I can at least be concerned that he's too young to be..."

"...Sleeping around?"

"If you want to put it like that, then yes."

"This is the bit that really isn't any of your business, Franklin," Rowan informed him. "He's an adult and can do whatever he wants with whoever he wants – you don't know him well enough to be dishing out fatherly advice and I really don't think he'd appreciate it much if you did."

"Yes," Franklin replied thoughtfully. "You're right, I just... feel like I'm always going to be kept at arms length and never allowed to be his dad."

Rowan felt a sudden surge of sympathy for her boss that unexpectedly washed away any sense of ire she had felt towards him. "Well, there's some good news to come out of all of this. I think it proves that there's some hope for the future..."

"Oh?"

"If Alf really didn't care what you thought of him, he probably would have told you he was gay straight away. That he kept it back might mean that he wants approval from you.

There was brief silence on the line. "That *is* good news. Thank you."

"No problem. Are we done?"

Franklin's voice sounded less wearied now when he spoke. "I think we are."

Rowan was not quite done with reassuring her boss. Over the course of the two months she had worked for him, Franklin had become the closest thing she had to a reliable friend at that moment. "D' you know what, I think Alf was unlucky and it was unfair of his mother to keep him from you. I think you would've been a good dad - and it's not too late for you now. Trust me, I know crappy parents, and you are too kind to be one."

"Oh Rowan. That's the nicest thing anyone has ever said to me." his voice sounded astonished.

"Don't get too used to it. I hide my feelings well."

After saying their goodbyes, Rowan paused briefly outside the small terraced house that Manto had once occupied a floor of. A breezeblock building with a flat roof and a wonky gutter. She checked her phone. It was a five-minute walk from his flat to North Street. She hurried back there for her interview.

The woman behind the counter had a large moon face and was draped in costume jewellery. Her hair was dyed red and cut into jagged, boyish points that belied her middle-aged face. She looked up from the erotic paperback she was brazenly reading and laid it on the counter before her. "Rowan, is it?" she smiled. "I'm Mandy."

The two women shook hands and Mandy chatted merrily about the weather as she led Rowan through a door to a small kitchen with a microwave, kettle and laptop charging by the sink. They sat on two plastic chairs, the likes of which Rowan hadn't seen since she was at school and the light conversation suddenly slipped into a job interview.

"So, what made you interested in volunteering in our shop?"

Rowan had prepared herself for this. "I believe that the issue of homelessness is the greatest problem facing people in the developed world. I wanted, even in a small way, to help out."

Mandy nodded approvingly. "Most young people just say that they want some voluntary work on their CV. Not that I blame them, there's no shame in trying your best in this economy."

"I suppose so," Rowan concurred.

Mandy inspected a printout of the CV. "It says here that you work four days a week in a supermarket. So I suppose you're just looking for a day or two?"

"If that's possible, yes."

"I'm sure we can fit you in. Are you able to start right away? I can show you the ropes this morning if you'd like."

"That would be wonderful. Thank you."

The woman offered Rowan a warm, wide smile and nodded approvingly. "Eager to get started, that's what I like to hear!"

Within her first hour Rowan had already mastered the till and had begun sorting the shop floor into something less haphazard and chaotic. First the books were grouped by author, then coats were placed on hangers and huge bin liners full of clothes were sifted and sorted. Most of what arrived in donations was either too old, too threadbare or too worthless to be sold. Rowan found herself as disgusted as she was astounded by what people thought worthy of charity - old knickers with loose elastic, disposable nappies that were mercifully unused, even an elaborate vibrator complete with attachable accessories. Among the junk though, she was soon to find treasures. Leather handbags a mere season out of date; expensive shoes still in their original boxes, coats and dresses that when new, would have cost her a month's wages. And gloves, what she had been looking for, that were kept in a shoebox on the floor by the door.

It did not take Rowan long to establish where the two security cameras inside the shop were. One focused on the counter while the other watched the floor of the shop through a fisheye lens. If she was right and the glove belonging to Manto had been donated here, then surely whoever had bought it would appear on CCTV and that person was almost certainly the killer.

The idea had struck her one night. How else would the glove containing the DNA of a dead man appear at a murder scene unless it had been donated to a charity shop and then sold to someone who no doubt wanted to keep his purchases as discreet as possible.

It wasn't just that this charity shop was closest to where Manto Makeba had lived, but she knew that the vast majority of drug addicts go through periods of homelessness. Maybe his family would have chosen such a charity to donate whatever meager possessions he had.

At lunchtime Rowan left briefly to buy herself a Pot Noodle and returned to the kitchen to eat it. On the little laptop that sat by the sink, Rowan could see Mandy through the two cameras that constantly filmed the shop; sitting at the counter and working her way through her book.

She searched through files on the computer until she came across one that seemed most likely to be the recordings of the previous two months footage. Hundreds of hours were stored in individual folders that cluttered up the screen. She was in a hurry so opted to collect every one she could. She would sort them by date when she got home.

Dropping them onto the icon that represented her memory stick in the USB drive, she watched Mandy anxiously on the screen as the files fluttered into their new home. Once completed, she snatched the stick from the computer and dropped it into her pocket.

At the end of the day Rowan said goodbye to Mandy and ached with guilt as she left the shop, knowing that she would never return. This was for the greater good she reminded herself and certainly if Mandy knew what she'd been doing, and why, she would be forgiven for wasting her time.

As she was about to cycle home a tall blonde woman in a long purple dress and faux fur coat approached her. She was brandishing a stack of leaflets.

"Good evening, miss," she smiled. "Have you heard the good news?"

"Sorry?"

"Jesus is returning - and we have proof. Did you know that death is life everlasting and our loved ones are eager for us to hear from them?"

Rowan's shoulders dropped. Religion had never worked for her but she nodded silently at the woman and politely took a pamphlet from her. One of Rowan's first jobs had been handing out leaflets for a pizzeria and she knew how soul crushing it could be.

Once the woman had moved far enough away Rowan walked her bike over to a bin and was about to dispose of the pamphlet when the words on the cover caught her eye.

"What do YOUR loved ones want to say to you? Come to our meeting and hear directly from the departed!"

Whether through intrigue or soft heartedness, Rowan folded the pamphlet and slipped it into her pocket.

39.

From her bed in the Stokes Croft area of the city Rowan sat propped up against pillows as she scrolled through each video file in turn.

It was impossible to know where to begin but it struck her as reasonable that the killer would have bought the gloves in the handful of days preceding the night that Henrik and Donna were murdered - May 5th.

She had borrowed her father's laptop in order to view each of the files from her memory stick and as soon as she started became almost overwhelmed by the enormity of the task. The CCTV camera recorded hour upon hour of the comings and goings of customers, while Mandy, and whoever was volunteering in the shop, either sat motionlessly behind the counter, or shuffled about in a futile attempt to make sense of the garbled chaos that abounded.

Scrolling through and jumping across minutes, Rowan watched patiently as grey and pixilated figures whizzed about the shop, her eyes focused on the little shoe box on the floor, watching and waiting for somebody to pause, to crouch down and then search through for a pair of freshly donated leather gloves.

It would be quite a search, of that she was certain, but she would not give up until she had found him.

Miles away on the other side of the city Franklin was fast asleep in his bed and snoring contentedly as Felicity wheezed and purred on the pillow beside him. When the call came to break him from his slumber Franklin was neither dismayed nor alarmed. He was on duty for 24 hours that day and as such could be asked to remove a body at anytime, day or night.

For all the places that a person could die in a city of half a million residents, there were only a handful he heard from in the dead of night. Mortuaries, hospitals and hospices, retirement homes, occasionally even a prison, but the number that flashed on the screen of his phone was not one he recognised.

Already out of bed and rubbing his sleepy eyes, Franklin

reached through the darkness to the cold, white glove of his buzzing phone as it danced across the bedside table. The alarm clock informed him that it was half past three in the morning.

"Good morning, Gallow & Sons. How may I be of assistance?" Franklin began in the best telephone voice he could muster at this hour.

"Is that Franklin?" a woman's voice asked, with more than a hint of urgency.

"Yes it is. Who may I ask is calling?"

"I'm sorry to wake you. I didn't know who else to ring, but you said the other day that I should call if anything happened..."

"Lucy? Is that you?"

"Yes it is," her voice cracked slightly. "I'm so frightened. My husband is away fishing with his dad... they go every year so it's just me and the little one here. I came home this evening and there was a car parked outside the flat. I was certain I recognised it - not because of the crash, this was a different one, but I'd seen it about, parked in the same place but never paid much attention, but then I saw him sitting there, the policeman, in plain clothes, and he saw *me*. I was so frightened but I tried not to be so that he wouldn't know, and then I took my baby and ran up the stairs and waited by the window. He was parked there for two hours or more and then he just left. I got up in the night to feed Jacob and looked out the window and he was back again. He's still there now and I am just so scared. Please come here at once!"

"I'll be there straight away," Franklin assured her and hastily pulled clothes on over his underwear and in no time at all was out the door and on his way. He elected not to take the Smart car, in case Lucy and her baby needed to make a hasty escape for whatever reason. He decided instead on a mirror-black Mercedes that was used for processions in only the most elaborate – and costly, services.

The streets of Bristol were mercifully quiet, with only the occasional mistimed traffic light to delay his journey as he sped across the city as quickly as the law would allow him. It was only once the empty roads of Bedminster gave way to the harsher facades of Knowle West, that it suddenly struck

Franklin how much danger he could be putting himself in.

The skinny man had never been a fighter and was certainly not one now. The policeman in Clifton had been thick set and built like a barrel. A heavy punch from a man liked that could send Franklin's narrow frame flying, never to wake again.

To his horror, as he approached the block of flats, he saw that a car was still parked in a little bay beside a newsagent that stood in the shadow of the enormous tower. Franklin checked his phone and redialed Lucy on the number she had called him on.

"Franklin?" Lucy seemed to gasp with relief.

"I'm here," Franklin reassured her as he stepped out onto the street. The car ahead was an old looking red Ford. The kind of vehicle he could imagine being parked among these streets, or indeed over much of the impoverished south of Bristol, but that would have looked as alien as a spaceship in the streets of opulent Clifton Village. Shrugging off his concerns, Franklin slowly approached.

"Hello?" he called out nervously to the vehicle, adrenaline deafening him to the danger he could be in. The car suddenly sprang to life, lights glared and the engine roared. It backed up slightly and for a minute Franklin thought it was not going to stop, but instead it lurched forwards and swerved around, briefly revealing a slight dent in the bumper that made Franklin think of Ben Tramor's death. With a screech the car pulled out of sight, though not before Franklin had time to enter its number plate into his phone.

"Lucy. Are you still there?"

"Yes I am. Was that him leaving?"

"It was. Do you want me to come up?"

Without answering, the door to the block of flats began buzzing and Franklin pushed his way into the lobby. He darted up the stairs to find Lucy, her hair bedraggled and down at either side, standing anxiously on the landing bouncing her baby boy up and down in her arms.

"I can't do this anymore!' she wept. "He's doing it just to frighten me, I know it!"

Instinctively Franklin wanted to reach out and touch her, to comfort her somehow, but knew that she was too distraught for such affection from a stranger. Tears streamed down her cheeks as she sobbed over the sound of her crying baby.

"You must tell me what happened. I can't help you otherwise."

"I killed them!" she almost screamed, her voice echoing shrilly up the stairwell.

Franklin took a step away from her. It suddenly struck him what a perfect trap she could have set for him. Lulled here out of a sense of responsibility in the middle of the night, an accomplice waiting downstairs to finish him off if he tried to flee.

"You killed them? But how?"

She was shaking her head. "Come inside and I'll tell you."

Franklin read the situation as best as he could. A woman alone with a screaming baby could only pose so much danger to him, especially in a block of flats that was full of neighbours who were already aware of the commotion happening within their tower. He nodded and followed her inside, but made sure that the door to the flat was left ajar.

"It's so much worse than I let you think," she cried as she lay her baby down on the sofa and fell into it beside him. "I used to work a couple of shifts with Donna at the supermarket. She got me a job there so that I could have a couple of quid more a week and just... get out of the house. I used to work the tills because I wanted to be able to sit down for a few hours and one day *he* came back. It was probably less than a week after the accident and I don't think Donna recognised him but *I* did. There was no woman with him and I thought the worst, but I said nothing to anyone - not even her, but I served him and acted as cool as possible. I don't know if he knew who I was, but if he did, he didn't let on. He paid with one of those cards, you know, those loyalty cards where you save a bit of money on your next purchase?"

"I know what they are," Franklin was finding himself frustrated by her roundabout way of storytelling, coupled by the insatiable screams from the baby.

"So I looked him up on the computer and *everything* was there. His name, his address, his phone number. Even a list of the last hundred items he bought... and his email too. I don't know what I was thinking, but I wrote it down on a receipt and then one of those nights when I got back from a drink with Donna I decided to contact him, anonymously. I demanded two thousand pounds - the same amount he had split between the four of us on the night of the accident. I said I'd go the police otherwise and tell them what we saw... the woman in the back of the car."

"Did he pay you?"

She shook her head. "I never heard from him again. I suppose he knew that even if he did pay, I'd be back for more - and I would have been. He can't have known it was me who sent it, but he would have known it was one of us who was going to expose what he had done to his wife, so he must have... he must have..."

"...Come after all four of you?"

She nodded as tears fell from her eyes.

"He lived in Clifton, right?"

Again she nodded.

"What was his name?"

Lucy blinked but did not seem to have to think to retrieve his name, as if it were etched upon the inside of her eyelids. "Martin Maybridge."

Without another word, Franklin was calling his brother. When he woke his voice was more of a croak. "Frank. Do you know what time it is?"

"I have the proof you need. Martin Maybridge killed three people and may be looking to kill a fourth."

His brother's voice was suddenly alert. "Please say you're joking, Frank. It can't be Martin - please don't let it be a cop."

"Have you been drinking?"

"Yeah, a bit. I'm not in tomorrow."

"Then we'll come and meet you there. We can't leave her here by herself."

"What are you talking about? Who is *her*?"

"I'll explain everything when we get there. Just... try to sober up a bit, you're going to be looking after a baby."

"What?"

Franklin hung up on his startled brother and switched his phone off; he did not want Edison calling him back to dispute his plan. He and Lucy began collecting items for an overnight bag for her and baby Jacob. With a collapsible cot in his arms, Franklin led the way downstairs while Lucy hurried behind him. Once Jacob's car seat was securely fastened in the backseat of the car, they drove away into the inky gloom of the early morning.

In Stokes Croft, Rowan was finding her head heavy and her eyes dry as sleep seemed to be surrounding her but she would not yield to it. The video she watched was from the morning before the murders and finally a blurry figure, in such low resolution as to barely even register as human, was captured kneeling down to the shoebox on the floor rifling through for something.

Rowan made a note of the time and date before switching to the camera recording the counter where Mandy was putting down her book and straightening herself up as a customer approached. The second he stepped into frame she knew who the man was.

It was the man with the long plaited hair and creepy moustache that had made Rowan's flesh crawl when he had known her name. The man who lived in the flat about Donna Hawley's Southville home, a brief stroll from where the charity shop stood. The man was named Art Branwell, and he was a killer.

40.

It was five in the morning and Rowan was too agitated to sleep. She had attempted to call Franklin six times but was continuously met by the infuriating sound of his voicemail recording.

"Franklin, as soon as you get this call me back. I know who the killer is."

Already she could imagine him plotting his next move, planning his escape to God only knew where, with the same intricacy he had pieced together his horrific crimes, whilst Franklin chased after the wrong lead, an innocent man whom he had become convinced was responsible. She couldn't let him go free, he wouldn't be like Ruby's killer, skulking off into a sea of strangers, completely invisible until he chose to strike again.

If there was no one there to help her, and nobody there to stop her, she would have to find him herself.

Downstairs she could hear her mother sobbing as she crept past the slightly ajar living room door. She let herself out into the cold of a spring morning and cycled away beneath the glossy sky.

In Redland, Franklin sat across the kitchen table from his brother who sipped on a too hot and too strong cup of black coffee as he nursed away the worst of his hangover. He had just returned from the funeral home after swapping the Mercedes for his Smart car in case the former were needed that day – Peterman had a habit of keeping his schedule a mystery.

"Thank you for doing this," Franklin said.

Edison just shrugged his shoulders. "You should have told me before you went to find her. That was too much danger to put yourself in."

"She's safe now though, that's all that matters."

Lucy was asleep in the spare bedroom of Edison's house, with Jacob beside her. She had barely spoken since they had made it past his front door and had slept ever since she'd got into bed - a deep, silent sleep that only the truly exhausted can appreciate.

Over a breakfast of cornflakes and toast, Edison fondled his phone nervously until electing that now was as good a time as any to make the call. Getting up from his chair, he walked into the hallway so that Franklin might hear only fractions of the conversation, which was no doubt causing Edison a tremendous amount of fear.

"I wouldn't be saying this unless... Yes I am certain... Can't we do any better? Yes, I will take full responsibility..."

Franklin had so little appetite that all he could manage to do was push his cereal through the milk until it was completely sodden. A cup of coffee helped him feel more like himself but with it came a dawning sense of just how high the stakes were - the crushing weight of responsibility that he'd put on his brother and that nagging worry that he could be completely wrong.

When Edison reappeared in the kitchen, he looked pale and shaken. He gnawed nervously on his bottom lip before he spoke. "This is really happening. There's no going back now," he said somberly.

"You made the right decision," Franklin comforted. "What's the next step?"

"I need to go up to Clifton. The police are going to take him in for questioning. They can't charge him yet because there hasn't been a murder investigation into the first two deaths, but we might be able to get him on the hit and run. There must be enough evidence there to form a case against him." Edison wiped his face with his hand. "I can't believe that I'm talking like this about one of our own. Do you think you could drive me up to Clifton? They're going to want to talk to me and I don't think I'm quite sober enough to make it there myself."

Franklin just nodded. After writing a note for Lucy, the pair headed off to Clifton Village in his Smart car, Edison nervously drumming his fingers on the dashboard.

Rowan looked up at the house on Beauley Road. Lights were beginning to switch on down the street as its residents woke for the last day of work before the weekend, but this house - the house in which Donna Hawley had rented the ground floor flat whilst Art had the one above, remained cloaked in darkness behind drawn curtains.

Rowan folded up her bike and hid it as best as she could behind an unconvincing plastic topiary bush - the front garden's only attempt at decoration, and rang the doorbell to the first floor flat. She waited agonizing seconds that turned into minutes, before she tried again. There was no response.

The sky was turning light and bright and the first of the street lamps along Beauley Road had begun dimming. Tucked between the plastic plant pot and the brick wall of the house she spied what she had noticed the last time she was here. She knew what it was then but its significance had not struck her at the time.

The smooth little rock that was impossibly light to the touch of her boot could only be one thing. She upturned it with her hand and a little set of keys on a loop fell out onto the paving slab beneath. Steadying her breath and listening to the panicked beat of her heart in her ears, she pushed it into the lock and turned it. The lock clicked open.

It was seven in the morning when Franklin and Edison arrived at Royal York Crescent in Clifton Village - the grand sweep of impossibly vast houses that curved into the distance as far as the eye could see.

Franklin did not need to be told that his presence would not be wanted on the doorstep of Martin Maybridge's opulent home, so he waited in silence as his brother got out and met two police officers in the car parked ahead of his.

Edison's face was grim as he spoke to the two men who looked no more pleased to be doing this than he did. Franklin watched as they took the steps up to the elevated pavement and shuffled in no great hurry towards the door of the wanted man.

Franklin removed his phone from his pocket and noticed that he had not switched it back on since he had been at Lucy's flat. He held down the button until the screen flashed into light and a gentle buzz informed him of a message. Above him, he watched as Edison rang the doorbell to Martin Maybridge's house and breathlessly waited until the door opened and the tiny frame of his wife was revealed in pyjamas and slippers, her face one of confusion and fear. Unable to watch this morbid scene play out, he held his phone to his ear and called his voicemail. Rowan's tone was clear but frustrated on the line: "I know who the killer is." The words were almost reassuring to him - somehow Rowan had come to the same conclusion about Martin Maybridge as he had. He hung up the phone just as his brother sloped down the steps towards him.

"He's not in," Edison said in a wavering voice as he opened the door. "The other officers are checking the house, but according to her, he's been away at a meeting in Oxfordshire these past few days. He goes there a lot apparently; doesn't make any sense, we do all of our stuff in the city."

"Where in the world is he then?"

"Beats me, but I think I need to head to the station, do you think you could give me another lift?"

"Of course, just let me make a call. I need to check on Rowan."

The door swung open and Rowan was met by a curious stench of nothingness. Donna's flat had been stripped of everything. All furniture and decorations, anything functional or valuable was gone and all that remained was a film of dust that thickened the air. She and Art had shared a bare, unfurnished hallway with the entrance to her flat on Rowan's right. The door had been left open, for there was nothing left to hide inside. She peeked around the corner into the abandoned living room that was obscured in the dark behind drawn curtains; the silence beyond met her like a wall.

She crept quietly upstairs, knowing that the house was almost certainly abandoned yet not wanting to risk being proven wrong; she made it up onto a landing where another door opened to the flat above. Rowan rapped upon it and waited for a response. When there was none, she tried the handle and when it would not budge, she tried the second of the keys she had found inside the fake pebble. It opened and she slipped inside.

If Donna's flat had been stripped of its possessions, this one felt bare by design. The living room seemed to consist of an unmade foldaway bed, a single chair by the window draped with a few clothes and an old fashioned boxy television on a small chest of drawers. The room was eerily abandoned, as if this was not a space he had intended to stay in longer than he needed to. If it was evidence she was looking for, and she was not entirely sure that it was, then this room was unlikely to hold many secrets. If she had instead been hoping to find the man himself, Rowan had suddenly come to the stark realization of just how foolish that was. She was alone in his home, completely defenseless.

A narrow MDF wardrobe occupied a corner of the room and Rowan found herself taking a step closer to it when suddenly her phone began chirping in her jacket pocket. She answered it to Franklin.

"Rowan. Are you ok?"

"I'm fine, just a little shaken."

"Do you know where Martin Maybridge is?"

"The policeman? No idea, why?"

"You said you know who the killer is. It's Martin..."

"...No it isn't." Rowan cut Franklin's voice short as she opened the wardrobe door and peered inside.

Then to her complete horror she heard a voice from the bottom of the staircase. "Who's there?" It was a man. Her blood ran hold.

"He's here," Rowan whispered. "Art, he's here and he knows I am too."

"What? Where are you?"

"In the flat above Donna Hawley's," Rowan breathed as she stepped inside the wardrobe and closed the door behind her.

Heavy steps marked each footfall on the staircase as the man drew closer.

"What the hell are you doing? Get out of there!" Franklin hissed on the phone.

"I can't. I'm trapped."

"Don't make a sound. I'm coming to get you," but he did not hang up.

"Rowan Kaplan!" a huge voice filled the room. "I know you're here, I saw your bike."

Rowan slid down to the floor of the wardrobe. A few

jumpers and a pair of trousers were all that hung above her. Not near enough to cover her with.

"Is that him?" Franklin whispered, but Rowan could not answer for fear of making a sound.

It was then that her hand touched something dry and furry, a rat's tail of hair that brushed against her. In her fingers she felt the wig, with its long, wiry plait, and, in a little plastic bag beside it, a fake moustache. Everything fell into place and her mouth dried in panic as the awful truth dawned with a sickening weight. Art and Martin were the same man.

The door of the wardrobe was thrown open in an explosion of frenzy that shook the whole unit around her.

The grey haired man towered over her and stared directly into her face.

"Franklin," Rowan bellowed into the phone with huge gusts of sound. "Help me!"

Franklin heard a scream so fierce that it seemed almost inhuman. It was followed by an almighty crash and then a thud as the phone dropped to the floor.

"Rowan!" Franklin cried as he started the engine. "We're on our way. I'm coming to get you."

The line went dead.

41.

The first thing to strike Rowan as she stirred into consciousness was her utter amazement that she was still alive. The second was the tremendous pain in the back of her head - a thundering agony that seemed to fill up her very thoughts, a sickening drumming sound over which she could barely hear her own mind.

She was blanketed by a thick darkness that robbed her wounded head of its ability to comprehend her circumstances. Where was she? She was laying on something soft, while a hard plastic object dug into the small of her back. There was a smell; a familiar smell that tumbled through her mind as she groggily tried to retrieve the memory it was attached to.

A car. She found herself mouthing the words. She was on the backseat of a car and the plastic thing in her back was a seatbelt fastener. She listened intently to hear if she was alone and when she heard nothing, she tried to move. It was then the panic set in. Her feet were bound together with rope around the ankles, her arms, bound at the wrists, were behind her back. She tried to scream but discovered that her face was wedged into the seat and any sound she made was muffled and lost to the darkness.

Something suddenly changed. As Rowan rocked her body from side to side until her face was freed, she blinked into daylight as the black space was flooded with light. Between the seats in the front of the car she could see the silhouette of a man standing against a dreamy aura of white. It was a garage door that he had opened and outside was freedom.

She screamed again, and this time there was no doubt that it had travelled as the man immediately marched towards the car, opened the door, and dropped inside.

"Quiet now Rowan Kaplan," he warned her. "You don't want me to cover your mouth do you?"

He slammed the car door shut and started the engine. The car accelerated and the pair sped out of the garage without stopping to close the door.

"Where are you taking me?" Rowan whimpered

The man checked his phone nonchalantly before dropping it into the cup holder next to his seat. "You don't want me to ruin the surprise do you?' he responded dryly before turning back to face her and offering her a sickly wink.

Martin Maybridge was thick set with wide arms and huge hands. Rowan had an age advantage, as she was at least two decades younger than this mountain of a man, but had not a hope of defending herself in a direct fight. If she was to survive she knew that she would have to use her wits.

Through the windows Rowan could spy glimpses of blue sky over the tops of trees. They were heading south into the country but where else, she had no idea. She fought with the rope that bound her wrists and wriggled her hands until she felt just the slightest indication of the knots pulling free.

"Did you kill my sister?" Rowan asked feebly. She needed to distract him if she was to crawl free, but the question had been one she had needed answering for weeks.

"Ruby? Was that her name?" Martin replied. "That one wasn't me - I never do it for pleasure, just for necessity."

Rowan believed him. If nothing else he had no need to lie to her now.

"Why did you kill the others?"

"Necessity." he responded as he caught her eye in the rear view mirror.

"What did they do to you?"

"One of them was blackmailing me. I had to do away with all four of them - and I will do, trust me. You were just a little collateral damage along the way. Sorry about that, but I did tell you to keep your nose out of places it didn't belong. I was *trying* to save you…"

"They were blackmailing you because you tied your wife up and put her in the backseat of your car?"

Martin laughed to himself. "My, my, you really have been thorough - I probably should have given you a bit more credit, even though you were stupid enough to break into my house today."

"But you didn't kill your wife, did you?"

"I didn't. She is alive and well."

"Does that mean that you aren't going to kill me then?"

Martin turned to look back at Rowan. "I'm sorry Rowan

Kaplan. I can't let you go free, but I promise you that I'm not a monster, I'll make sure that you're dead before I bury you."

Whether it was because she was running on nothing but adrenaline, or because her head was not allowing her to fully appreciate the terrible danger she was in, Rowan did not feel scared; nor did she feel resigned to her fate. She would not let herself believe that this was the end. There would be a solution and she would survive. She would not die at the hands of another like her sister; there had to be a way out.

Her hand slipped free from the binding. At once it felt as if the tables were turning.

"How did you know who they were?" Rowan asked as she fumbled with the knots around her other wrist. "The four people involved in the car accident in April. How did you track them down?"

She saw Martin smile to himself in the rearview mirror. "There are two things you can always rely on if you're a policeman," he replied. "Your memory and the fallibility of others. You can never quite know exactly how people will behave but experience will give you a pretty good idea. Nobody could have predicted that after that crash the four of them would become friends, united by secrets and a shared experience. Donna used to invite the others over and they would all drink and cause a racket..."

"And you relied on your memory to recall the number plates. That how you tracked them down when they tried to blackmail you?"

"You *are* a clever girl, Rowan Kaplan. There's nobody better suited than a police officer to track someone down and as soon I received that email, I knew I was going to have to set up my base nearby. I could never have imagined that the flat above Donna's would be available but is it any wonder that nobody wanted to live near that obnoxious, loud drunk singing at all hours of the night? It was one of those fortunate occurrences that I took full advantage of. I studied them, I followed them to their houses after their little meetings; I watched them from afar, worked out their schedules and then planned on how to do away with each in turn in a way that would look like an accident or suicide."

"Except for Ben Tramor," Rowan corrected.

"He was a mistake. I was getting sloppy," he quickly responded.

"And me," she added.

"Indeed," the car took a sharp left and Rowan got the sense that they had left the main road and were heading down a much bumpier country lane.

"Is this where you took your wife when you tied her up?" she asked.

"Oh no, we always went to Leigh Woods."

"So you did it lots of times?"

"Yes," he replied coolly. "You see, I am not one of these modern men, the castrated types who think women should be running the country instead of a home. I keep my household in the proper way, and as such, there are strict rules as to how my wife must behave. The rot sets in and things fall apart so quickly; so I came up with the rules, nothing too terrible but orders for when my food must be made; how I like the house to be kept and more straightforward stuff on how I expect to be treated. I didn't marry Germaine Greer so I don't expect my wife answering me back like her. I make sure I approve of all of her friends as I don't want her getting silly ideas from them, I make sure she's reading the right books and will only let her watch TV with me." Martin looked at Rowan and smiled. "I know you with your modern ways must think of me as a beast, but I'm not. I just believe there to be a proper way of doing things and a proper distinction between a man and his wife."

"So you tie her up and take her to Leigh Woods?" Rowan asked as a second hand slipped from the binding.

"Just to frighten her. I don't hit her unless I really lose my temper. I find a psychological approach much more useful. I leave her tied up in the woods for a few hours; she's terrified of the dark you see. She can scream all she wants but nobody can hear her and when I return she is always placid and ready to behave. It works every time."

"Well, I suppose that makes sense," Rowan tried.

He laughed. "There's no need to agree Rowan Kaplan, I know you don't think I should be treating my wife that way, but that's the problem with people today. We've let things slide to such an extent that all the old ways are forgotten..."

As Martin grumbled to himself about the ills of modern society, Rowan was reaching for the phone that rattled around in the cup holder beside his seat. Snatching it away in her hand, Rowan quickly swiped at the screen once a picture of Martin and his wife flashed upon it.

She knew she couldn't call anyone, and a text message was useless, as she didn't know where she was, so instead she scrolled past a selection of apps until she found the one she was looking for.

"...People talk about the glass ceiling but they forget that there are some things that men just do better than women. Where would the world be without men? There would be no bridges or trains. We'd never have made it to the moon. Don't you think it's undignified for a lady to work? And to drink pints and to talk to her husband as if it were she who were in control of him. You see, ultimately that's why I know I'm not a monster and it's why I can look at myself in the mirror every morning. I'm taking back control of my life from those who've wanted to rob me of it."

Rowan was not far from asking him to kill her now to prevent her having to listen to anymore of this nonsense, but instead tried to focus on the screen as she flicked through the phone. It had to be here somewhere.

Rowan found Manhandlr and turned it on. Immediately the app asked permission for location tracking to be used. She allowed it and then turned the screen black before slipping it back into the cup holder.

The trees outside had given way to clear open skies and the early swallows to huge, glossy herring gulls. She was near the coast. She closed her eyes and listened to the breakwater as it drew nearer. All the while Martin's phone relayed to a satellite precisely where they were; now if only Franklin could find her signal.

42.

As soon as he spied her Brompton bike folded away and hidden uselessly behind a plant pot in the front garden of the house on Beauley Road, Franklin felt his panic, raw as it had been since the phone call, overflow into a guttural roar that he released into the hallway as he dashed through the open door.

"Rowan! We're here!"

Nothing. He bounded up the staircase with Edison fast behind him before bursting into the upstairs flat.

"Rowan!" he called again into the emptiness of the abandoned room. "Where are you?"

Edison was panting but was already at work, pulling bed sheets up and upturning the mattress. It was then Franklin saw the phone on the floor, shattered beyond any semblance of use as if crushed angrily underfoot.

"I've led her to her death..." Franklin said softly to himself.

"There's no time for that kind of talk," Edison urged as he stomped across the room to the wardrobe. "Here," he called to his brother as he opened the door and pointed inside.

The back of the narrow space had been broken into splinters as if something had been driven through it with an incredible force. Through the gap beyond cracks in the plasterwork of the wall marked the spot where a splatter of blood had begun to congeal into a crimson flower. Like a sickening vision, Franklin imagined Martin grabbing Rowan by her hair and smashing her head into the wall behind until the young woman lost consciousness. He felt vomit rise as beads of sweat began to pour down his face.

There was no time to protect the sanctity of a crime scene, so Franklin helped his brother upturn the wardrobe where it landed face down with a terrific crash, breaking apart into sheets of flimsy wood. The two brothers began searching desperately through the splintered mess that lay before them.

The wig and false moustache looked like dead animals in the ruins. The wig was long and disgustingly lifelike, while the moustache was elaborate and theatrical. As Franklin turned them over in his hands the terrible mistake Rowan had made became horrifyingly obvious.

"Martin was living here," he told his brother. "He had a disguise and was pretending to be someone else. That's why she was so convinced that Art Branwell was the killer."

"That stupid girl," Edison sighed. "What was she thinking?"

Franklin couldn't bring himself to answer, for in many ways, the truth was too unbearable to face. Rowan lived her life not just in a way that someone who was preoccupied with death might; but in a manner of somebody who no longer cared if they lived or died. No wonder she'd come here - sacrificing her own life was a worthy price to pay for catching a culprit who would not run free like the killer of her sister.

Edison was already calling the police. "Hello," he began. "This is Edison Gallow, I would like to call for backup at a residence on Beauley Road in Southville."

As his brother spoke, urgently yet with the clarity and precision years of training and experience had taught him, Franklin stared dumbly at the chaos of the room and wondered how their fun little game of sleuthing had come to this. Perhaps Edison was right and Rowan was just a silly girl who had paid the ultimate price for her snooping.

No, Franklin reminded himself. The Rowan he knew was not stupid - far from it, as time and time again her sharp intellect and intuitive instinct had dazzled him. She was one of the smartest people he'd ever met and, even if life had dealt her such a bad hand that death held no fear, she would still not go down without a fight.

If she could get to Martin's phone, perhaps she would send a message to him to say where he was. If she was alive then she almost certainly could not speak in his presence however... and then it fell into place. If she could do that, then his clever, brilliant friend would know how to be traced.

Franklin turned on his phone and immediately opened Manhandlr. Queasy neon green filled the screen and the same old gallery of faces and torsos replaced it. There amongst them was Ben Tramor. He tapped on the page for destination information and to his incredulous joy; there was the little marker, heading southeast on the main road towards the coast.

"Where are you going?" Edison called to him as Franklin tore down the stairs.

"I know where she is," he shouted back.

Picking up her bike from the front garden, Franklin hurled it into the boot of his Smart car and in no time at all, the two brothers were speeding through the city streets at the kind of clip that only Edison with his police mandated advanced driving skills could match.

Edison was still on the phone, only this time he was making demands. "We know which direction he's headed in and we won't lose track of him. A young woman's life is at stake here and the man who has kidnapped her is one of us. We need to throw everything we have at this; absolutely everything."

Once the call was finished Edison dropped the phone into his pocket and turned to look his brother straight in his face. "We're going to save her, Frank. I promise you."

Franklin touched his brother's shoulder and his eyes welled with tears. Turning back to the phone he watched the symbol draw clear away from the city - the gap between them closing with every minute.

Rowan shifted her weight onto her shoulder and found that she was able to haul herself up just high enough to steal glimpses through the window as the car hurtled down the quiet coastal road.

She did not recognise precisely where they were but the silty, grey expanse of water far below was unmistakably the Severn Channel - the vast stretch of river that opened onto the sea, separating Bristol from Wales on the other side.

She knew that Martin would not try to make the crossing, as that would require him to stop to pay a toll. At the very least, Rowan told herself; if she was going to have to die it would be in England. There was a strange solace in knowing that her own nation would have her bones - wherever they were, even if they were never found.

How strange it seemed to her that her imminent demise could seem possible. That her body could be so frail as to be broken apart, for her heart to stop beating and her brain to stop thinking. Everything she had ever been and everything that she would become, stolen from her without even her memories to keep on that long journey through forever. What would her parents think? Could they ever recover from the murder of both of their daughters?

Martin turned on the radio and began merrily singing along to a tune that was released decades before her birth, completely unfazed by the task ahead. Rowan with her hands now free but held discretely against her back, began gently undoing the laces of her Doctor Marten boots, slipping each one off in turn and squirreling them away behind her. Once they were gone, the binds around her ankles did not seem as impossible. She needed to free only one foot, and as the rope slid against her sock, she twisted her foot to a near impossible and agonizing angle, it suddenly it went - her leg kicked out and hit the back of the passenger seat.

"Stop wriggling back there!" Martin called to her over the music.

A new song began on the radio, this time it was one she knew all too well. It was Petula Clark singing "Down Town" - the mesmeric ode to the dizzying delights of a city by night; it was a song that had come to mean everything to Rowan after a video of her sister singing it in a bluesy, sexy voice was recorded on the night she was murdered.

Rowan had never been sure if she believed in fate. Like so many mysteries of life, she'd tried her best to find answers but had never found them forthcoming, yet in that moment, it seems too perfect to be a random fluke. She could feel Ruby reaching out to her, telling her to stay strong and if she had to die, she would die fighting.

The car breached a steep hill and in that moment Rowan understood why Martin had chosen to take her here. Below them she could see mile upon mile of sweeping sand dunes covered in spiky grasses that rippled in the wind. There was nobody around to help her - a body here could lay undiscovered for years until the sea came to reclaim it. She grasped at her boots by the laces as the car began to slow and Martin pulled into a small lay- by at the edge of the road that backed onto the first of the sand dunes.

The moment he unfastened his seatbelt, Rowan struck. With a scream that filled the car with terror and rage, she swung her boots by their laces at the man's head, just as he turned in fright at the sound. The heel of one of them smashed into the man's temple and he cried with shock and blinding pain before slumping forward onto the wheel.

"You crazy bitch!" he wailed as blood began to flow from the side of his head. "What did you do that for?"

Rowan followed up her strike with another, this time to the back of his skull and with the same ferocious strength. His nose hit the horn in the centre of the wheel and for a moment it screamed across the sand dunes. Rowan threw open the side door before launching herself through it.

Scrambling to her feet just as Martin kicked the driver's side door asunder, Rowan tore towards him and slammed it shut on his leg as he attempted to get out. He shrieked in pain so Rowan did it again - and again.

Martin's face was a blood-drenched mask of rage. His once shockingly pale teeth, bared like fangs, had turned pink, his eyes were crazed as he drove the door open with an inhuman strength which sent Rowan toppling backwards as she tripped over the rope that was still tied around one of her ankles.

Martin was on her at once, almost falling on her like a cat seizing its prey. Rowan met his body with a knee to the groin, which caused the man to cough blood upon her shirt. Imprisoned beneath his bulk and pinned to the ground beneath his huge hands, Rowan met his eyes and the two stared at one another. At first all she could hear was the sound of their panting, but then came something else; a mysterious, whirring that drew closer and closer until even Martin seemed to hear it through his blood filled ears.

Over the ridge of the road by which they had come, a police helicopter rose and flew over them at an incredible speed. A fleet of police cars followed it, sirens blaring, and within a moment they had surrounded Martin and Rowan.

His expression was completely blank – that of a man who has suddenly understood that there was no escape, that his careful plans had amounted to nothing and he would be caught, sentenced and imprisoned like any other criminal. It was the face of a man who had learned in that moment that he wasn't as clever as he'd always thought himself to be.

The appearance of Franklin's little Smart car was met by the victorious trumpets at the end of "Down Town" and as it drew closer, Rowan felt the weight of the man rise from her as policemen seized him by the shoulders and locked him into handcuffs.

Franklin leapt from the passenger side of his car whilst Edison was still slowing to halt. He ran towards her and the two met with open arms. Franklin pulled her in close to his chest and kissed her on the forehead.

"You clever, clever girl!" he sobbed then breaking the hug for a moment he found the stain on her shirt. "There's blood on you..."

"It's his, not mine."

"Look at the state of him." Franklin gasped in amazement as Martin was being led, limping and shamed, into a police car while his nose rained blood onto his shirt. "You beat the bastard up pretty good. You probably didn't even need us."

"You sent a bloody helicopter!" Rowan found herself crying as she let herself sink into her boss's embrace. Over his shoulder she locked eyes with Edison who was smiling as he stood solidly beside the car. "Thank you," she mouthed at him. He nodded in reply.

43.

As the police car pulled away Rowan watched as Martin, his head slumped against the window and with a ball of cotton wool pressed to his broken nose, was led away and driven out of sight. His face was one of utter surrender; a man lost in dark thought and deep regret. Regret not for the crimes - of that Rowan was certain, but regret for getting caught, for underestimating a teenage girl and her will to live.

"What happens now?" she asked Edison as more police cars began to depart. "Will I have to give a statement?"

He nodded. "I can ask one of the officers to give you a lift back to the station now if you want to get it over and done with."

Rowan stared out towards the Severn Estuary and shook her head. "I think it's going to be a lovely day. I'd quite like to go for a little walk."

Edison turned to his brother who gave him a reassuring tip of the head. He knew he was no longer needed. As he turned to walk away, Franklin said, "I'm proud of you Ed. You did the right thing."

Edison smiled gently. "I did eventually. I should have listened from the start."

As his brother walked away and stepped into a waiting police car, Franklin could not recall ever having seen him look so weary.

"Do you think he's ashamed that he didn't believe us?" Rowan asked after witnessing the same crumpled gait.

"A bit, but I think we forget that the police in the city are a pretty tight bunch. I don't think anyone on the force wanted to believe it could be one of them."

Once the convoy of cars had breached the hill and the cloud of sand they had churned up dissipated, Rowan and Franklin walked side by side along the edge of the dunes.

"That was a stupid thing to do, Rowan. Going to that man's flat."

"I know,"

"Do you have any idea how frightening it was to hear that happening over the phone?"

"I know."

Rowan sat on a bank of sand and Franklin joined her. The pair gazed out across the pigeon grey beach towards the far away water, in silence for some time.

"How does it feel to survive something like that?" he eventually asked.

Rowan shrugged her shoulders. "I don't know. Is it a bad sign that I don't feel anything right now? I don't feel as if anything of significance has happened to me. Does that mean I'm suppressing something or going to get PTSD or something?"

"I have no idea," he replied honesty. "But if it does, then we can get you help."

"Do you believe in God?" she asked bluntly. Franklin had been surprised that she had never asked him this question before as it was often the first anyone asked when they discovered he worked with the dead, but it's timing here seemed troubling.

"No," he said simply.

"I felt she was with me there in the car. Like she was trying to help and look after me - it felt so real, I could almost hear her voice telling me that I had to survive; it felt *so real*."

Franklin sighed pensively and patted Rowan on the back. "I'm no expert on these matters, trust me, but if you can still find your sister in your head when you need her, and in your heart are still all the things you remember her for... then in a way, she hasn't really died."

Rowan smiled at Franklin as she wiped away a tear.

"It's been a long time since I had a friend," Franklin went on. "I didn't even really know I had one until you were in trouble. I like it - but you can't ever do that again."

Once she had finished laughing, a sincere and kind laugh, she confessed, "I don't really have any friends either. After Ruby died everyone left. I see them about sometimes in the uni holidays and they're always having fun, going out drinking and looking all grown up. I'm just left here, like nothing has moved on, as if it's still the night when it happened and all I need to do is wake up so my life can start again."

"Maybe that's what today is. You're going to have a tomorrow and a long... long life after that."

"God we're pathetic," Rowan chuckled.

"That may be so, but at least we're not pathetic alone."

"My only friend is a forty year old man..."

"I'm 39!"

"Not for much longer."

"Don't remind me; that I could be that age is just... impossible. *It's pathetic.* I still live in my parents' home..."

"Believe me, I find it bad enough that I do too. That's something that's going to have to change. Crap! My parents, they're going to have to find out about everything. They think I've been working in a supermarket all this time!"

"Why did you tell them that?"

"They think I'm obsessed with death."

"Oh," Franklin replied; he was far from surprised. "Are you?"

"Wouldn't you be if you were me? I'm not obsessed with it; I just want to understand it. It happens to all of us but we pretend it never will, I just want to be ready for it when it comes for me."

Franklin nodded, only slightly troubled by her candour. "I suppose that makes some sense."

As Rowan stood up from the sandbank she said, "You know I'm not going to stop looking for him, don't you?"

Franklin just nodded. "There's no way I can stop you. But I can ask you to please be careful."

"I'll try; but danger isn't going to stop me. I can't let my sister's killer go free."

"Of course, and I'll be there to help you. I promise."

As the pair drove back to the city in Franklin's Smart car, Rowan opened the window and let the cool breeze from the estuary fall upon her face. Sand dunes gave way to hedgerows and grassy embankments, where lines of the last of that spring's daffodils bowed their heads and died.

44. Three Weeks Later.

Franklin had permitted himself a day off work for his fortieth birthday but had spent it doing very little of much worth.

The 3rd of July came and went each year without celebration but this time he had hoped that something might happen. Turning forty had filled him with no sense of joy and he did not feel compelled to mark the passing of what could easily be half of his lifespan with forced jubilance. He had spoken to his parents on the phone and encountered his father's annual complaint that he had been born a day too soon to share a birthday with America, but otherwise it was a day like any other.

He had expected that he would somehow feel different that day, as if this landmark would make itself known and he would feel older and frailer. That morning as he inspected himself in the bathroom mirror he saw the lines; they had been there for a long time and weren't going to go any time soon. He saw the dusting of grey that was creeping among the ginger meadow of his hair, and yes, he knew there were times when he realised that he was holding a book too close to his face as his eyes were struggling to focus, but otherwise he felt good - fine even.

That evening, after taking a stroll along the harbour side, Franklin settled in with a bottle of cider (premium this time, rather than standard) and a microwave pasta bake (from Waitrose instead of his usual Asda) and searched through his TV box for something to watch. Skipping over the rapidly piling Danish mystery series that *The Guardian* was insisting he watched he discovered that he had three episodes of *Neighbours* to catch up on which filled him with contented joy. He was about to press play on the remote when there was a knock at the reception door downstairs.

Franklin's first instinct was to yell, "bugger off!" down the staircase but thought better of it when he realised it could be a grief stricken relative here to visit a body. Most likely it was just Edison trying to force him out to the Tobacco Factory, in which case he could tell him to bugger off to his face.

It was Edison, smiling at him through the glass door.

Wearily, Franklin unlocked it and was about to say his piece when he was met by a jubilant "surprise!" from the garden as figures skipped onto the footpath to let their presence be known. Aside from Edison, Franklin's parents were there, brandishing food in Tupperware boxes, including what looked like a birthday cake. Alongside them Rowan was beaming cheerily at him with Meredy; Peterman skulked and smoked beside her and looked generally as if he would rather be somewhere else. A few paces behind him, to Franklin's amazement, stood Alf, looking nonplussed and with his hands in his pockets, and next to him was the one person who meant there was no way of slamming the door.

"Verity!" he exclaimed before he could even stop himself from doing so. "What in the world are you doing here?" He had found himself stepping from the doorway and all but cantering to greet her. She looked radiant in a clover green cocktail dress with her mousey blonde hair piled messily upon her head.

"How else was I going to get this one to come along?" she replied, gesturing to Alf.

"She made me do it," he huffed.

"Good to see you again, Alf." Franklin replied, choosing to ignore the snark.

Without another word, Alf shuffled gloomily inside the funeral home, followed by a train of guests, all seemingly aware that this reunion did not need a witness. The pair shared an awkward hug that went on just a little too long for either of them to feel comfortable with. Afterwards Franklin smiled at her and said, "You look..."

"...Old? I feel it!"

"I was going to say sensational!" he laughed.

"Has it been almost twenty years? How has this happened to us? We're in our forties now. We're bloody grownups!"

Franklin turned back to the reception where he noticed Alf being ambushed by his parents who were chatting incessantly at him. He stood, nodding politely, in a manner that suggested to Franklin his animosity was reserved only for him.

"He's a good kid," she assured Franklin. "He just takes a while to trust people, especially you, but he'll come around.

He hides it well but he's kind and thoughtful; he cares about things. He reminds me a lot of you when you were his age and we'd just met."

"D'you know I'm starting to warm to him?"

"That's nice to know as you'll be seeing a lot more of him when he moves to Bristol this October." Verity sighed mournfully to herself. "How am I going to cope without him? It's been the two of us for so long that it's going to feel so empty. I'd give anything just to have him be a kid again, so I could have all those years ahead."

"Hey, it's not over!" Franklin quickly intercepted the maudlin conversation as Verity's eyes began to fill with tears. That emotional honesty he'd always admired seemed not to have withered with the years. "You'll always be his mum."

She nodded. "I know that, I just don't want to let him go just yet." In that moment she laughed but the laughter exploded into tears and she fell into his arms. In an instant the pair had gone from awkward conversation to those two friends on the sofa again, getting drunk and telling stories. No time had passed between them.

"Thank you," Verity said.

"Not a problem, any time you need a hug!"

"No, not that. Thank you for *him*."

Franklin smiled. "Thank you for telling him about me."

"Has he told you anything about himself yet? How much do you know?"

Franklin sucked on his teeth and decided to just risk it. "I know he's gay, if that's what you mean."

Verity's face did not move. Franklin was instantly relieved that this did not appear to be news to her. "He told you?"

Franklin shook his head. "I worked it out."

"Were you shocked?"

"Not one bit," Franklin lied. "Having a gay son is the closest I've ever come to being interesting, but you mustn't tell him that I know, it would really mean a lot to me if he told me when he was ready. Then I'd know he trusted me."

"You're a kind man, Franklin Gallow," she said and she kissed him on the cheek. In that instant his stomach filled with tickling fingers. All the love that had once run through his body for this woman had never gone away. It had simply been hiding for all these years.

With that, Verity led the way inside, with Franklin trailing behind her.

The visitation room began to fill with people and Franklin's parents started laying out finger food on foldaway tables. Corks popped and champagne was passed around the room. His father suggested a toast, which was followed by his mother's request for a speech, which he politely declined. Franklin was a terrible public speaker and was all too aware that this evening he was going to have to impress Verity into visiting more often, and a clumsy speech, that no doubt would end up taking him to the edge of tears, was not the way to do that.

As the room filled with chatter he was approached by Edison, who invited him outside. "I need a smoke. Can we go round the front so Mum and Dad don't see us."

"Of course," Franklin replied, still astonished that his brother believed that the family's most open secret - that of Edison's smoking habit was somehow still hidden from their parents.

Edison led the way out through the reception and around the garden until they were at the front of the house, beside the garage that housed the array of various vehicles.

"What's wrong?" Franklin asked, the moment Edison lit up.

"Nothing, I just don't really know anyone except for Mum and Dad."

"You know Rowan."

"I don't think she likes me very much,"

"She does. You saved her life," Franklin reassured him.

"Perhaps, but did you see the mess she made of Martin? If anything, I think we arrived just in time to save him."

Franklin nodded in agreement. "So what happens next? Are we going to have to be witnesses?"

"Probably not. The courts don't look too kindly on amateur detectives like the you, so we'd like to keep your names out of it as far as possible. Rowan can be an unnamed victim, so all we need is her statement."

"I bet the police will be happy with that; it makes it look as if you knew what you were doing."

Edison exhaled a huge puff of smoke. "There's that too."

"It might be a bit late any way, people have asked me about it. They seem to know that I was involved. My barber wanted to talk all about it last week. These things have a habit of getting out."

"Well, we can protect Rowan at least. It's about time somebody did."

Franklin studied his brother's face closely. "What do you mean?"

"I mean that I know why she doesn't like me. I know you think I'm a crap policeman who doesn't know his arse from his elbow, but I recognised her the moment I saw her. She's the sister of that girl who was murdered a couple of years ago. I was there when she gave her statement that time too,"

Franklin gasped. "Why didn't you say anything?"

"What am I supposed to say? The case has gone cold. We *know* who did it though; we've known since her body was found, we just don't have the evidence to prove it."

"Edison... Please don't say that it was..."

"...It was her father. There's no doubt about it but we can't get anything to stick."

Franklin felt his blood run cold. "You can't be serious."

"Do you think I'd joke about something like that? The man has a terrible alibi and his whereabouts are shaky. You should see the interview tape, he just wears his guilt all over his face."

"Jesus..." Franklin sighed. "Do you think Rowan's in danger? Should I say anything?"

"Get her out of that house."

"She's saving up, she wants to find somewhere soon."

"Then perhaps it's time you gave the girl a pay rise, don't you think? She's certainly earned one."

Franklin could not agree more. Heading back inside, he found Rowan and Meredy laughing together on the sofa in the reception, glasses of white wine in their hands and tears streaming down their cheeks.

"Did I miss something?" he asked.

"No, no," Meredy giggled. "Just a private joke."

"At my expense?"

The two women looked at each and immediately burst out

laughing once more.

"So I suppose this party was your idea?" Franklin aimed this question at Rowan.

"Perhaps," she said with a sly smile.

"Can you give us a moment please?" he asked Meredy, who didn't need to be asked twice. In an instant she was gone and Franklin was sitting beside Rowan in her place.

"Thank you for this. How did you know how to track everyone down?"

Rowan shrugged. "It's easy; Facebook. I just sent messages out a couple of weeks ago and everyone said yes."

"I know it sounds silly, but I really do appreciate it. Do you know that everyone I love in the world is here right now? It's a very special feeling."

Rowan's face hardened slightly. "You know they won't be around forever, don't you?"

"I know. But right now, at forty years old, everyone I love is alive and well and under my roof. I know I won't have them forever, but I just want to live in the moment and remember that if that's what forty is, then I really have nothing to complain about."

Rowan nudged her shoulder into his. "You old softie."

"I was thinking that on Monday, perhaps you and I could talk money. I think it's fair to say your trial period is over and it was a huge success, it's probably time you got a rise."

"Wow. I should organise parties more often... or almost get murdered."

"It's about time you moved out of your parents house anyway."

"You got that right."

Franklin wanted to tell her to be safe, to be wary and to get out of her house as soon as possible, but there was simply no way without letting on what he knew. He made his excuses and went upstairs to fetch his cider from the fridge.

The moment he opened the door, he was aware that he was not alone in his flat. Seated on the sofa, with Felicity curled into a tight ball beside him purring heavily, was Alf.

"Hi," said Franklin. Alf nodded in return.

"It was a bit noisy downstairs. Just wanted to cool off for a bit up here, I hope you don't mind."

It was then that Franklin noticed something that pricked his eyes with tears. Open on the coffee table in front of his son was the laptop he had bought him.

"So you decided not to sell it then?"

Alf gave him a look that Franklin decided to take as a smile. "I sold the other one instead, this one's much lighter."

That was all it took for Franklin to be filled with an almost overwhelming sense of joy. There was hope for the future; one day he could be his dad.

"I'm pleased to hear that," he told him. "Could I get you a cider?"

Alf seemed to think about the question for quite some time before he said, "Yes."

Franklin removed two bottles from the fridge and opened them. On handing one to Alf, his reply was "I didn't know you watched *Neighbours*." He felt himself blush with embarrassment on seeing that he had left his television on the hard drive screen with the name of his favourite soap opera highlighted. "I haven't seen it in years," Alf continued.

"We could always watch it now," Franklin ventured, knowing full well how stupid a remark it was to make.

"Sure." Alf replied to his complete bewilderment.

The two men clinked their bottles together and Franklin moved to the sofa where they both sat and chatted freely about the nonsense they enjoyed. Words came easily and the company was welcome. Just a father and a son, enjoying a drink together.

Printed in Great Britain
by Amazon